Mary Sheldon, da⋯
Sheldon and actres⋯
New York and Lo⋯
Clare's Hall, Oxford, before going to Yale and
Wellesley. She now lives in Los Angeles, with
her daughter, Elizabeth.

MARY SHELDON

Under the Influence

FONTANA/Collins

First published in Fontana Paperbacks 1990

Printed and bound in Great Britain by
William Collins Sons & Co. Ltd, Glasgow
Phototypeset by Input Typesetting Ltd, London

This book is dedicated to my friend and teacher,
Christopher Stone – the man who is magic.

Acknowledgements

So many thanks to the usual suspects: my Mama – first, last, and always – my father, Judy Clark, Tiela Garnett, Dorris Halsey, Rohanna Anderson Trott, Michael and Deborah Viner, and my precious Elizabeth. And so much appreciation to the following people for their friendship and love: Scott Donnelly, Mimi Henry, Joyce Howard, Marc Mantell, Nancy Spector, Jean Sanders Torrey. Special love to Alexandra Sheldon and Kimberly Kingsbury – the Butterfly Connection. My gratitude to Richard Bach, Shakti Gawain, and Jane Roberts for their books, to Dan Fogelberg for his songs, and to Dr Dominic Polifrone and Barbara Hardcastle of the Hollywood Church of Religious Science for their wisdom. And, of course, thank you, Shelly – my D-Flawless Diamond.

Prologue – 1972

PLEASE JOIN US FOR
A GALA CHAMPAGNE RECEPTION
IN HONOR OF
BLAKE ALDEN'S NEW POSITION
AS VICE-PRESIDENT OF M.T.A. STUDIOS

On: Friday, March 23, 1972 7:00 p.m.
Place: 2015 Beverly Drive
Beverly Hills, California 90210
Dress: Black Tie

Ten year old Laura Alden stood at the top of the stairs in her Christian Dior nightgown and watched the party going on below. She had tried to separate herself from it, but it was no use. The dance music from the hired band thrummed in the floorboards underneath her bed, and the clinkings of all that rented silverware and glassware made it impossible to do her weekend homework.

She liked being at the top of the stairs. Unseen, she could watch everything that went on below. She saw Elliot Cohen, the President of M.T.A., wander over to her mother's collection of limoges boxes, delicately examine the heart-shaped one, and then put it into the pocket of his tuxedo. She also saw Adrien Tendu, the black singer, go into the women's powder room, which, Laura thought, was pretty funny, considering he was a man.

Then a tall, thin woman with short black hair and

eyes as dark and pungent as olives came into the hall-way. Laura shrank back against the bannister with annoyance. Desiree Kaufman was her mother's long-time best friend, but Laura couldn't stand her. Laura liked soft people, and Desiree was overwhelmingly sharp. Besides, Laura suspected that the dislike was mutual.

Desiree looked up and spotted Laura. 'Julia wants you to come downstairs,' she told her.

'But I can't,' Laura said. 'I'm in my nightgown.'

'She said to put on your robe.'

Laura knew there was no excuse; no escape from Desiree. Quickly, she put on her matching Dior robe and ballet shoes. She felt mocked, embarrassed. *Why do I have to come down?* she wondered.

She hoped she could sneak, unheralded, into the party. That no one would even notice her. That maybe she would look like a short, junior guest, who just happened to be wearing a robe and nightgown.

She reached the drawing room. The sounds, the smiles, the clothes, were fantastically intense. Laura caught sight of her father over at the bar, laughing with some friends. She thought he looked absolutely wonder-ful – like an advertisement for wine, or a tuxedo shop, or a vacation hotel.

Blake turned and saw Laura. She put her finger to her lips, but it was too late. He was grinning, hurrying over.

'Ladies and gentlemen,' he announced loudly, 'we have a new and unexpected guest of honor – Miss Laura Alden!'

Amused, the guests applauded. Laura thought she would wither away from shame. And yet her heart beat with excitement.

'Enjoy yourself, baby,' her father told her, going back to his friends. 'This is a very special night.'

Now an official member of the evening, Laura looked around. The drawing room was kinetic with energy, stuffed with guests. Some were old friends of the family. Some were the new crowd, harvested since Blake had made those last two successful movies.

A blond lady, very drunk, came up to Laura.

'Tell me,' she said. 'Tell me a little secret, dear. What kind of hair dye does dear Julia use?'

Laura fled from her.

Shortly after, she was approached by a famous, ancient director. 'What a beautiful nightgown,' he told her heavily. 'Do you know how lucky you are? Do you have any idea how much that nightgown must have cost?'

Laura had heard that many years ago, the director's whole family had perished in the Holocaust. She felt terribly guilty about her nightgown, and turned away.

Next, a handsome blond man came up to her. He wore a tag that said 'Press' and he carried a tape recorder.

'Hi,' he said. 'So you're Laura. What are you going to be when you grow up? An actress like your mom or a producer like your dad?' She felt he was making fun of her, and she said she didn't know. He ordered a double Scotch from the bartender and asked her if she'd like one, too. Laura told him that she didn't drink. He seemed surprised.

'I thought all Beverly Hills kids drank.'

'Canapé, Miss Laura?'

Laura looked up. There was her nurse Elsie – who for years, had bossed and bullied her in daily life – now dressed up in a uniform and politely offering her hors d'oeuvres on a tray, as if she were a grown-up. And calling her 'Miss Laura.' It was all a little bewildering.

Then, close behind her, Laura heard a laugh. She turned, and there was Julia.

Julia – slender, radiant, wearing a filmy red and gold caftan – looking like a monarch butterfly. She came up to Laura and hugged her. Laura felt ridiculous standing beside her mother; a complete caterpillar. And yet she couldn't get close enough to Julia's perfume; to the deep, mysterious glitter of Julia's rings. Couldn't get close enough to Julia.

'Toast! Toast!' someone cried.

And then, all at once, there were five, ten, a hundred spoons knocking on champagne glasses.

Smiling, protesting, proud, Blake and Julia drew together. Laura was tightly between them, their arms around her.

'To our Hollywood Royalty!' Richard Michaelson said. 'To the Aldens!'

Laura woke early the next morning. The silence felt strange after the intensity of the night before. She went quickly into Julia's room.

It was always scary to see her mother vulnerable in sleep.

'Mama!' Laura said.

Julia woke immediately. 'Hello, baby,' she said. 'Where's my tea?'

By the time Laura brought the tea in from the upstairs kitchen, Julia was sitting up in bed, tousled, naked, with her cigarette in her mouth and her game of solitaire laid out.

'Well,' she said to Laura, 'did you have a good time last night?'

Laura found it hard to say. 'I don't know,' she told Julia at last. 'Did you?'

Julia also thought about it.

10

'I like it better when it's just us,' she said. 'But don't tell your father. These parties are so important to him.'

'I won't tell,' Laura promised. Then she sighed. 'Will we have to have a lot of parties now that Daddy's Vice-President of the Studio?'

Julia smiled a little grimly.

'I'm afraid so,' she said. 'But it's sure better than the days when no one wanted us.'

That was true.

'Well, I'm never going to have any parties when I grow up,' Laura told her mother.

'You'll have to,' Julia said. 'You'll be very famous and important and a lot of people will want to know you.'

'I won't be famous and important,' Laura told her, flushing. She resolved to stop getting such good grades in school.

'Well, then, you'll marry someone who's famous and important,' Julia said evenly, slapping down more cards.

'No, I won't. I'm too ugly to get married.'

Julia put down the cards at this, as Laura had known she would.

'Oh, baby!' Julia protested. 'Don't say that. You're going to be an absolute beauty when you grow up. Why, just wait till you start your periods, and you get a waistline . . . You'll be able to get any man you want. Except an actor, of course,' she added hastily. 'You must promise me you'll never marry an actor.'

Laura nodded. From the time she was five years old, she had had to make this promise. And she still wasn't sure what was so bad about actors.

'Now come and keep your old Maw company while she has a bath,' Julia told her.

She rose and Laura followed her into the bathroom. Laura loved this room, all done in pink marble, and filled with marvellous little bottles of foreign scents.

11

Julia drew a bath and got in the tub. Her body looked like pink marble itself. Laura looked ruefully down at her own bruised and blackened knees. Then she heard her mother sigh and looked up, anxious.

'What's the matter, Mama?'

'Just a bit of gas,' Julia told her. 'I guess I ate too much of that Brie last night. Could you hand me a Tums, baby?'

Laura reached into the medicine cabinet and shook two Tums from the huge bottle. She was surprised to see that it was already half-empty. She and Julia had bought it only the week before.

Julia got out of the tub and dried herself off.

'What are you going to do today, Mama?'

Laura asked the question with some apprehension. Since Blake's new job, Julia was constantly busy with all kinds of new boring-sounding commitments – charity lunches with Hollywood wives, endless fashion shows.

Julia smiled at her. 'I thought you and I'd escape this madness and go off to the Brentwood Mart.'

Laura hollered with joy.

They dressed in jeans and t-shirts, and they sneaked out of the house, ignoring the post-party ringing phones.

They rode to the Mart in Julia's beloved 1965 dark blue Mercedes. The day was yellow and hot. They rolled down the windows and sang songs, laughed. And Laura got her mother talking about the old days – when Julia had gone to New York at nineteen to be an actress, when she had worked at a drugstore to make a living, and when she had first met Blake. Laura loved those stories. They felt as much a part of her own body as her blood.

They reached the Brentwood Mart and went inside. For as long as Laura could remember, she and her mother had been coming to this tiny outdoor market of shops and food stands and rides. In fact, it was probably Laura's favorite place in the whole world.

She looked up at Julia.

'I don't ever want to grow up,' she told her mother suddenly.

Julia laughed.

'No,' Laura said sharply, knowing how stupid it must sound. 'I mean it. I never want to grow up.'

And then, as she stood looking around the Mart, a moment of great clarity came to Laura.

She understood that her wish was going to be granted. She suddenly saw that all the bewildering upheavals that had been happening in her life – the new house, the new school and jobs, the new friends, even her own relentless progress towards physical adulthood – didn't really mean a thing. That, in the end, nothing important would ever really change.

And the Mart would always be here.

Laura was filled with an overwhelming power. The power of possessing life itself. Recklessly, she grabbed Julia around the waist. 'Oh, Mama,' she said, inarticulate with joy. 'Oh, Mama.'

Julia looked down at her. Her eyes filled with tears.

'Oh, baby,' she whispered.

It was a moment Laura would never forget.

THE PRESENT

Chapter One

It was a few days before the New Year, and all of Los Angeles seemed to be suffering from post-Christmas letdown. Laura drove down Sunset Boulevard, and counted the endless glittering carcasses of trees out by the garbage pails.

She shivered as she made the turn into Bel Air. The top of her red Mustang convertible was down, largely because she had been too lazy to put it up. So she did her best to pretend she was enjoying the fresh air.

There was a strangely brittle quality in the wind this afternoon. As Laura drove, she watched countless flower gardens being watered by countless sprinklers, and she half-expected the roses to shatter into pieces at the touch of the hoses.

She reached Bellagio Road, and turned into the first driveway on the left. The intricately-ornamented gate moved discreetly aside at her approach. She drove up the wide brick driveway and pulled up in front of the huge Tudor house.

No one was around. That was odd. Usually, at her parents' house, there were at least three gardeners in front, trimming the bushes or mowing the lawn.

Laura got out of the car and let herself into the house with her key. The hall was in darkness, the house was mystifyingly silent.

But of course, Laura thought suddenly. *It's Monday*. All the help was off, her father had that big meeting with the stockholders – and her mother – hadn't she said something about going out to tea with Desiree Kaufman today? Laura felt foolish. She should have called first, before dropping in like this.

Still, now that she was here, she didn't want to go back home just yet. She put her purse down on the commode and stood still in the hallway.

In their June issue, *Architectural Digest* had said that the Alden hallway was probably the most perfect in Southern California. The huge space trumpeted white and gold. The stairs splashed down in a fountain of Aubusson. A small Monet floral hung on a padded silk wall. An elegant gilt commode held a bouquet of fresh-picked roses.

Laura smiled, looking at it. That commode had originally been a piece of twenty-five dollar junkstore furniture, but Julia had antiqued it with a toothbrush so successfully that everyone assumed it was an eighteenth century original. Even the man from *Architectural Digest* had been fooled, and had written of it with special admiration.

How Julia had laughed.

Laura walked throughout the downstairs, through the enormous, elegant rooms. Everyone agreed that of all the houses Julia had ever done, this was the best. It was not Laura's favorite – she preferred some of the smaller homes of her childhood – but then she had never really lived here. Her parents had moved in once she had started Stanford. But of course Julia had still decorated a little blue bedroom with Laura specifically in mind, in which she and Jeff sometimes stayed. 'The honeymoon suite,' Julia called it, with a delicate smile.

And it was filled with the furniture that had always been Laura's – in house after house after house.

People who weren't from Hollywood always found it

hard to understand why the Aldens had moved so many times. But to Laura, it had always seemed only natural. The year Blake did *Manifesto*, they had had a Tudor home in Beverly Hills. The year Blake did *Occupied Territory*, they had only been able to afford a bungalow at the Chateau Marmont. The year Blake made *Crucifix*, they were in Rome. The year he had won the Oscar, they were in Malibu. And so on. And all the years he hadn't been able to work in Hollywood at all, they had wound up in New York, in a tenth-story apartment with cockroaches.

This house on Bellagio was the twenty-fourth home that the Alden family had lived in.

Laura and Julia had always talked about what it would be like, being a normal family – living in one house, Laura going to one school, Julia going to one grocery store, Blake going to an office. And then they would just look at each other and laugh helplessly. Because Alden life was just not like that.

But even with all the moving, there were certain special treasures that could be counted on to be there always. Like the commode in the hallway, or Laura's bedroom furniture, or that urn over there on the bookshelf.

Laura went over and touched it gently.

It had been her first trip to Europe. They were on a cruise of the Greek islands, and her mother had fallen in love with the ruined island of Delos. When they got back to the boat, Julia had opened her purse, and nonchalantly taken out a three thousand year old relic she had stolen.

'That vase was just rotting out there,' she told her horrified husband. 'No one cared about it. With me it will be respected. And loved. And I don't care if I have

17

to go to jail.' So Laura had smuggled it through Customs for her.

In the drawing room was another treasure. The small painted fan that Desiree Kaufman had given to Julia at the end of the run of *Promenade*. Laura looked at this less sentimentally, but it still represented a good story.

Twenty-five years ago, Desiree Kaufman, a young playwright from New York, had met Julia Foster, a young actress from Virginia, and had been so taken with her that she had decided to write her a play. The play had turned out to be the Pulitzer-Prize-winning *Promenade*, and it had made them both celebrities. And all these years later, even though Desiree was a celebrity still, and Julia had long ago given up the stage for Blake and Laura, the two women had remained the closest of friends.

With a slightly tightened lip, Laura put down the fan. She had still never got over her dislike of Desiree Kaufman.

A cloud came over the sun. The room grew a shade darker. Laura frowned. How melancholy everything seemed today. *I'm being ridiculous*, she thought. *Just because it's a misty afternoon, and Mama's not here.* But the feeling remained. Invisible eyes seemed to search for awful sights. Invisible ears seemed to wait breathlessly for terrible news.

A sharp memory came to Laura. She had been five years old, and her parents had gone out for the evening. She had missed Julia so much that she had gone into her mother's bedroom, rescued a pair of Julia's used hosiery from the wastebasket and sobbed hysterically on the bed, hugging the nylons to her, until the maid, scandalized, had led her away.

Laura shivered. She decided to go upstairs and take a peek into her mother's room. That ought to reassure her. *Who knows?* she thought wryly, *I might even find another old pair of stockings.*

She pushed open the door.

And there, sitting up naked in bed, drinking tea, smoking a cigarette, and playing a game of solitaire, was Julia.

Sunshine returned with a cosmic bang. Laura laughed a little hysterically. 'Mama! I didn't know you were home!'

'Hi, baby,' said Julia. 'Wait just a minute.' She moved a few more cards. 'Got 'em all!' She laughed in victory.

She rose from the bed. 'Come keep your old Maw company while she has a bath,' she told Laura.

They went into the bathroom. Julia had decorated this one in green and gold, and the taps were solid onyx. But the antique perfume bottles on the sink were still the same ones Laura had loved since childhood.

'I thought you were going to tea with Desiree today,' Laura said, as Julia drew the bath.

'I was a little too tired to go,' Julia told her.

Laura looked at her mother anxiously. 'Are you feeling all right?'

'Merely fantastic,' Julia assured her. 'But your father's planned a big dinner at Scandia with some investors from New York, and I've got to be in good shape to charm them.'

That made sense.

Julia got into the tub and soaped her back in silence. She looked, Laura thought, a little pale. 'You're sure you're okay?' Laura asked again, a trifle sharply. 'You want some Tums?'

Julia shook her head. 'No,' she said. 'Now tell me what's new with you.'

'Well,' Laura said, 'the big news is that Jeff is up for

19

this commercial. We'll know tonight if he gets it. It could be really big.'

'I'm sure he'll get it,' Julia said. 'But what I asked was, what's new with *you*?'

Laura shrugged. 'I've started a new children's book. About a little French hippo called Philippe. I hope it'll be good. I'm afraid Jeff thinks the plot's a bit silly.'

'I wouldn't worry too much about that,' Julia told her tartly. 'After all, you have had four books published. And Jeff's only an actor, not a critic. Besides,' she added, 'you know what *I* think of your work, baby.'

It was an old joke that the reason Laura was able to write such good children's books was because she'd never quite given up being a child herself.

Laura smiled. 'Yes, but,' she reminded her mother, 'why should I believe you? *You're* only an actor, too.'

Julia laughed. 'True,' she said. 'I sometimes forget.'

She sprang out of the tub.

'Now help your old Maw get dressed.'

Julia was drying herself when suddenly she put down her towel and turned to Laura.

'I just want to tell you something,' she said in an odd, abrupt voice. 'That I know how important to the world you're going to be someday – and that I don't have to be around to see it.'

Laura jerked back. 'What are you talking about?' she said sharply. 'Of course you're going to be around to see it.'

'Yes, of course,' Julia told her quickly.

They looked at each other, then looked away.

'There's going to be a big sale on crystal tomorrow at Geary's,' Laura said loudly, wanting to change the subject. 'I got the flier in the mail. Want to come with me?'

20

Julia smiled. 'I'd love to.'

Laura tasted the vision. She and Julia going into the lovely Beverly Hills china shop – a favorite since childhood – buying beautiful, solid, lasting things, and then having lunch afterwards, maybe at the Bistro Garden. And the vision dispelled some of the afternoon's anxiety.

'Great!' she said, relieved. Then she caught sight of the time on Julia's onyx clock. 'I'd better be on my way,' she told her mother. 'I promised I'd run a few errands for Jeff. He said he'd be home early.' She went over to Julia, kissed her goodbye. 'Have a good time at Scandia, Mama. Knock those investors dead.'

'I will,' Julia smiled at her. 'I love you, baby,' she said.

When Laura left the room, Julia sat down in front of her marble pullman and began to put on make-up. At first, her motions were listless and mechanical. Then suddenly she sat upright, smiled at herself in the mirror, and did the job to perfection.

'Looking good, old girl,' she said aloud. 'You're looking mighty good.'

It was seven in the evening. Laura sat by the window and waited for Jeff to come home. She knew she would be able to tell in an instant if he had gotten the commercial or not.

'Of course it doesn't matter either way,' she had said to him airily that morning when he left the apartment. 'If you don't get this one, you'll get the next one. Or the one after that. Talent will out, Jeff. Just remember that.'

But of course it did matter. It mattered terribly. Those nights when Jeff came home without the job were awful. He would go into the bedroom, and shut the door, and nothing Laura said or did made any difference. That

21

frightened her – not being able to make a difference when Jeff was unhappy.

There was a thud as Birdie, the huge black cat, jumped onto her lap. Laura began to stroke her, ignoring the damage the fur was doing to her new silk pantsuit.

'You are such a brat,' Laura murmured. Birdie purred in smug agreement. *My baby*, Laura thought adoringly. *She's my baby. At least until the real thing comes along.*

Then she stiffened with irritation at herself. She wished she hadn't thought that, about the baby. Not tonight – when she was feeling so nervous about the commercial. For it started her on the usual course – a whole run of other thoughts she would also have rather not had.

Stop it, she told herself angrily. *You're only twenty-three; you have all the time in the world for marriage and babies. And the last thing in the world you want to do is rush Jeff. And yet . . .*

Then she reminded herself about the commercial. If Jeff got the commercial, it could mean a big career boost. Maybe a cameo – maybe a series. And then maybe, if that happened, he would feel a little less funny about asking her to marry him.

Laura sighed. 'But I don't understand why all that should even matter,' she had told Jeff time and time again.

'Because it does,' he would answer her tightly. 'Your father owns the goddam studio. If I don't make it on my own first, people will say I married you just to get ahead.'

Would they? Laura didn't know. She didn't really care, either. But she couldn't say so to Jeff.

Was that the real reason anyway? she found herself wondering suddenly. *Or could it be something else?*

22

Stop it, she told herself angrily. *Just stop it. Of course Jeff loves you. And he'll ask you to marry him when he's good and ready. Besides, these days, what does marriage matter, anyway?*

'Jeff and I don't need a written commitment,' she had told her parents coolly a hundred times. 'The feeling between us is the only thing that counts. And we think it would be smarter to wait until our careers are set. I mean, if I'm ever going to win the Newberry Award for my children's books, I can't worry about things like ironing Jeff's handkerchiefs. So we're just letting whatever happens happen.'

But sometimes, when 'what happened' were things like women on the beach or sales girls in stores looking at Jeff in a way that left no doubt as to their desires, Laura would get scared. Plain panicky scared.

And she also sometimes got scared when she looked at herself in the mirror.

No, I won't, she thought. *It's total masochism.* But, dropping Birdie from her lap, she did it anyway.

Well, she had to admit it. She looked all right tonight. Laura smiled at herself with relief. A tall thin mirror-girl smiled back. She had pale skin, with pale red freckles, and pale green eyes. And topping it was a frenzied cascade of auburn hair. Laura was all red and green. Jeff had once said jokingly that she reminded him of a dried-out Christmas tree.

But tonight, Laura decided, there was nothing dried-out about her at all. She thought she looked rather intense and interesting; and the new black silk pantsuit, bought on sale at Neiman Marcus, was a definite success.

I'm a real product of my environment, Laura thought, smiling. *It was Daddy who taught me to shop at*

23

Neiman Marcus, and Mama who taught me to shop on sale.

The words 'Mama' and 'sale' clinked pleasantly together in Laura's mind. Oh, yes, that's right, they had a date to go to Geary's tomorrow at ten. They would buy the place out, then go to the Bistro Garden for lunch. It would be terrific.

I just wish she hadn't looked so tired tonight.

Then Laura turned around, and began to put the final festive touches to the apartment before Jeff's arrival. Other than taking away a few dead flowers and tidying a few magazines, there was not much to be done. The apartment was already pretty clean. Jeff liked it that way. And Laura, who didn't, had learned to be tidier for his sake.

She sat down in the over-stuffed blue armchair, her glance soothed by all the little loved objects around. She simply adored this apartment. The tiny entrance hall, the crazy octagonal closet, the stained glass window panel. Ghosts of lovely future possibilities – antique furniture, dinner parties, Christmas mornings, children – seemed to haunt the place endlessly.

Her father had hated the apartment on sight, of course.

'Why Culver City?' he had grumbled. 'Couldn't you have found something in Westwood? And why isn't there a doorman?'

And Julia had been beautifully tactful, even about the stained glass window, and had given them money for a sofa. But the big surprise was Jeff.

Laura had been sure that he would want an ultramodern place, and she had been ready to do a lot of lobbying and pleading for this one; but Jeff had taken one look around and had grinned at the real-estate lady.

'Wrap it up!'

Laura smiled, remembering. These constant surprises

in Jeff — they were such a part of his magic. She could spend a lifetime, she decided, turning the kaleidoscope that was Jeff Kennerly. And get a glorious new image every moment . . .

It had been a rainy Monday morning, the first time she had ever seen him, and she had had a cold. She hadn't wanted to go to the swim meet at all, but Sally, her room-mate at Stanford, was in the breast stroke competition, and she wanted Laura there for moral support. So Laura had come, grumpy and dosed with Dristan. She sat in the first row of the bleachers. *Pneumonia, for sure*, she thought dourly, every time she got sprayed by the enthusiastic swimmers.

Half-way through the competition there was a diving exhibition. Laura closed her eyes to sneeze, and when she opened them again and looked up, there was Jeff Kennerly on the diving board. She thought at first that he was a hallucination, brought on by too much Dristan. He looked like a figure on a trophy — perfect, and frozen in an eternal golden moment.

He got ten out of ten for his dive.

Laura never asked Sally what his name was, nor did she go to any other swim meets. But she didn't forget him, that perfect golden figure.

The September of Laura's Sophomore year, he was in her English class. He sat to Laura's right, and she started taking notes on him instead of the sonnet form the class was studying. The notes were for the Fitzgeraldian novel she planned to write someday. The one about doomed golden youth.

But even Laura had to admit that there wasn't too much that was doomed about Jeff Kennerly. He was adored, brilliant, charmed, and his father owned half the

Rocky Mountains. *Well, good for him*, Laura thought. *He needs to have it easy. He's shallow. He's light-weight. He's soft.*

And then in October, she saw Jeff in a production of *Death of a Salesman*. After the play, she went back to her dorm, sat on the edge of her bed and stayed awake all night. She struggled to organize her thoughts, and finally realized three things:

That Jeff was not shallow, lightweight and soft.

That Jeff was a very gifted actor.

And that she was hopelessly in love with him.

The next day in English class, she wanted to tell him how good he was in the play, but she couldn't. Every girl around was coming up to congratulate him, and with each gushing morsel of praise, Laura was drawn deeper into a depressed silence. She didn't have a chance with Jeff Kennerly. Didn't have a chance. Better face it now. And she waited out the class in misery.

When the bell rang, she started to rise. But a very strong brown arm was preventing her. She looked up and saw Jeff grinning.

'Wait a minute, young lady,' he said. 'Don't deny you were at the play. I saw you sitting there in the fourth row. Didn't you think I was any good at all?'

And Laura burst into tears.

He took her out to dinner that night, to Houlihans in San Francisco. They sat by the window, facing each other. Nervousness buttered away at Laura so hard that soon she was clammy. Here she was – actually out on a date with Jeff Kennerly. And all she could do was stare at her bread plate.

Then he looked at her and smiled. 'You know, Laura,'

he said, 'I first read about you when I was fifteen years old.'

'What?' she asked, astonished.

'That spread they did on your father in *People* magazine. There was a picture of you in the article – you were standing by a swimming pool. I thought, "Who is this girl?" I cut the picture out,' he added simply, 'and kept it on my bulletin board for years.'

It stopped her heart.

The drive back to Stanford seemed very long. It was dark and Jeff was suddenly so quiet. With every mile that passed, Laura grew more and more anxious. They had discussed everything imaginable over dinner – school, childhood, politics, ambitions – but there was one thing they had not discussed. Jeff had not mentioned ever wanting to see her again. *It's my own damn fault*, Laura wailed inside. *I screwed it all up. I never should have been so intense. I never should have asked all those questions. I never should have told him the story about stealing the bracelet.*

He realized the truth now, she thought miserably. Realized that the real Laura Alden was nothing like he had imagined – nothing like that girl in the magazine photograph.

They arrived at the campus and Jeff walked Laura up to her dorm room. There was a murmur about what a pleasant evening it had been, a friendly shake of her hand – no attempt to kiss her goodnight. Laura pretended she didn't even notice.

'Well, goodbye,' she told Jeff blithely, and reached into her purse. With a thud of horror, she realized that she had forgotten her key. Tears of self-anger came into her eyes. This was disaster. It was midnight. Sally was spending the weekend away. It was too late to wake any of the other girls on her floor. She'd somehow have to track down the bursar. That, or sleep in the hall.

'Anything wrong?' Jeff asked.

'Oh, no,' Laura told him quickly.

She didn't want his last impression of the evening to be seeing her sprawling for keys.

But he was still looking concerned. 'What's wrong? Don't you have your key?'

'Oh, I'm sure it's here somewhere,' she told him lightly. 'And even if it's not, I'll just wake Sally.'

'I thought you told me she had gone to Sacramento.'

Laura nodded and looked wretchedly away.

Jeff put his hand under her chin and raised her head. 'Maybe you'd better come to my room,' he said.

She looked down at his hand. It was so close to her that the fingers blurred. Then she looked up at his face. It was a long time before she could get the words out.

'All right,' she said.

At six the next morning, Laura woke up. In shock, disbelief, in joy and in shame.

It was the first time she had ever slept with a man.

She looked over at Jeff's golden body on the small bed. Oh, God, what must he think of her? Going to bed with him on a first date. He would think she was a tramp, that was what he would think. *He's probably sure I planned the whole thing*, she thought hysterically. *Left the key on purpose, told Sally to go to Sacramento*. She wanted to bawl.

At that moment, Jeff woke up. He turned over, with a lazy contented sound.

'Hi,' he said. 'How are you feeling?'

She blushed. 'Fine,' she said, trying to sound in control. 'Thanks for taking me in. But I'd better go now. I've got to see the bursar about my key.'

28

And Jeff smiled. That half-tremulous, half-teasing smile. 'Don't bother,' he told her. 'It's back in your purse.'

She stared at him. 'Back in – you mean, you took it?'

He nodded. 'In the restaurant. While you were in the Powder Room.' Then he grinned anxiously, 'Couldn't think of any other way. Please don't be mad.'

She sat on the bed, dazed. He reached up quickly and took both her hands. '*Are* you mad?' he asked teasingly.

'Yes,' she said.

But she wasn't. Rather, she felt a strange, languid peace; the peace of someone who has at last abandoned himself to the flow of the river.

'Don't be,' Jeff said. 'I promise I'll make it up to you.' And he took her in his arms and kissed her.

At first Laura tried to hide the fact that she was staying in Jeff's room every night. She would leave at five in the morning, before any of the other boys on his floor woke up. The thought of being caught by one of them made her want to die of shame. And though she was never caught, she still felt a little gritty, hurrying down the staircase. It was easier once she was outside again. She would rush across the quad to her own dorm, trying to look to any passer-by, like an innocent early-morning jogger. She would then let herself quietly into her room, get undressed, and come yawning ostentatiously out of her bedroom, when Sally came out of hers.

At first, Jeff laughed at these machinations. 'Why do you even bother?' he would ask Laura. 'You should just hear some of the things the guys have to say about Sally. Believe me, you're the Virgin Mary by comparison.'

And then, as time went on, he grew impatient with her scruples.

'If you really loved me, you wouldn't care what

29

anyone else thought,' he would tell her. 'What's more important – other people's opinion of you, or mine? Grow up a little, why don't you?'

Laura tried to grow up. She got to the point where she no longer pretended to Sally that she had slept in her own bed. She got to the point where she could nod coolly to the boys on Jeff's floor when she emerged from his room in the morning. But she could not get to the point where she could tell her parents that she was living with a man. And not only a man, an actor.

In March of Laura's Sophomore year, Julia called to say that she was coming up for the weekend to visit – and Laura knew that her mother must finally be told about Jeff.

She planned her strategy. Before Julia's arrival, she took down all Jeff's pictures from her wall, and tried to make her long-abandoned bedroom look lived in. Julia arrived on Saturday morning, and Laura spent the whole day entertaining her.

And then on Sunday, the trap was laid.

'My, my,' Laura said idly, looking at the school paper, 'I see there's a diving meet at the indoor pool today. That might be fun to go to.'

'Offhand, I couldn't think of anything in the world that would bore me more,' Julia told her briskly. 'You go. I'll just sit here on your unmade bed and do my crossword puzzle till you get back.'

Laura stared at her. 'But, Mama, you *have* to go.'

Julia put down the crossword. 'What's his name?' she asked.

Laura's heart was going frantically when she and her mother reached the poolside. It seemed incredible to think that Julia and Jeff, the two halves of her life, were about to be united at last.

The competition began. Julia, originally disinterested, was soon the biggest groupie there. There was one boy in particular she was championing. He was a freshman, skinny, panicky, and not terribly athletic.

'Bravo!' Julia screamed when his less-than-perfect dive was done.

Just wait till she sees Jeff, Laura thought with a little catch at her heart. *She'll fall out of her seat.*

'Jeff Kennerly,' the announcer said, and Jeff stepped onto the board.

His dive was perfect. Julia applauded it dutifully. Laura turned to her, so shocked and hurt that tears came to her eyes.

'Why didn't you shout Bravo the way you did for that other boy?' she asked her mother.

Julia's answer was a long time in coming, but when it came, Laura was never to forget it. 'Because,' she said, 'it was so obvious from the beginning that this boy was going to succeed.'

That Christmas, Julia gave Jeff a wonderful green velvet jacket, 'to set off those divine eyes.' For his birthday, she bought him a Minolta. She took him to the Ivy for lunch, and introduced him around everywhere as 'her son.' And when Laura finally broke the news that, after graduation, she and Jeff were setting up house together, Julia only nodded and didn't say a word against it. It was obvious, Laura told herself all the time, that Julia adored Jeff.

It was ten to eight now. He'd be here any second. Laura looked over at the photograph of Jeff on the television set. It was her favorite in his new batch of stills. She

31

loved that vulnerable expression on his face. In fact, she loved it so intensely and so personally that she almost wished he hadn't showed it to the photographer.

This was one of seventeen photos of Jeff in the apartment. Laura knew that Julia was secretly a little scandalized by all those pictures – but then Julia didn't understand. Those pictures of Jeff at every turn meant a lot to Laura. They were like little golden boosters, lifting her through every step of her day. And Julia had never felt the need of little golden boosters.

I just wish she hadn't looked so tired tonight, Laura thought again. Then she remembered with relief that her parents were going to Scandia that evening. *Mama always has a good time there*, Laura told herself. *She can relax, have some wine. She'll probably order the schnitzel, and I hope there's some dessert that'll just knock her socks off!* Laura imagined Julia smiling, exclaiming like a child over the wonderful dessert – and that made her feel better.

Then suddenly there was the sound of a key in the lock, and after that there was Jeff.

Laura's heart squeezed inside out. She could instantly tell two things. One was that he had gotten the commercial. And two, that the possibilities for the evening were endless.

Making love with Jeff, Laura thought again of a kaleidoscope, shifting from moment to moment; now tender, now passionate. There was everything contained in that experience. Did other women feel like this, she would wonder sometimes, looking at a faded lady before her in the market, or a girl with the yellow punk streak standing at the corner waiting for the light to change? Was there this unutterable bliss in their lives, this perfect moment? No, of course there wasn't. There couldn't be. There was only one Jeff Kennerly.

Jeff's arms were around her now, his body like a genie dragging out of her own body a new Laura. Not the everyday one, full of fears and excuses and double counter-thoughts, but a free one, a flying single-minded one, a Laura who could do no wrong. Together she and Jeff could do no wrong. Each touch, each caress added quivering perfection to quivering perfection.

And at first she didn't even hear the phone.

'Damn,' Jeff said on the third ring. He paused, then moved to unplug the cord. But Laura stopped him. The feelings, the joy were frozen as suddenly solid within her as goldfish in a winter stream.

She knew what the call was. 'Pick it up,' she whispered.

They were at Cedar Sinai Hospital in fifteen minutes.

The elevator was shriekingly, hideously, slow. When it finally got to the fifth floor, Laura staggered out. Her legs felt as if they were gripped by steel polio braces. A nurse came by. In the elevator, Laura had rehearsed, over and over, the question she was going to ask. She asked it now. But the nurse didn't answer. The nurse just stared at her. Laura asked again, this time louder. The nurse kept staring. It was then that Laura started screaming. High, shrill screaming because they wouldn't let her see her mother.

Jeff came up behind her. His arms were around her. He told her that they weren't keeping her mother from her – it was just that Laura was talking in gibberish, and that the nurse couldn't understand what she was saying.

A tall freckled man with hair like red straw came out of the waiting room. His Armani suit was rumpled. Laura had never seen her father in a rumpled suit before.

33

She wondered if this meant that the world was coming to an end. When he saw his daughter, Blake tried to smile. But when she came near him, the smile exploded into shrill, terrified sobs. She held him, and felt him try to wring reassurance out of her arms. *And this means*, Laura thought slowly, *this means that the world is coming to an end*.

He was babbling; how sudden it had been. Just as they were sitting down to dinner, Julia had said her chest hurt; how she had given a little cry and then had fallen. He thought for a moment she was bending over to retrieve a napkin. But she had not come back up.

Laura closed her eyes. Julia saying her chest hurt. Julia falling under the table. The scene was in her mind, forever.

Laura felt she was filled with an overwhelming power. The power of possessing life itself.

Recklessly, she grabbed Julia around the waist.

'Oh, Mama,' she said, inarticulate with joy. 'Oh, Mama.'

Julia looked down at her. Her eyes filled with tears.

'Oh, baby,' she whispered . . .

They took Laura down a long hall. Each room was filled with death and terror and stupid little flowers. They led her to the Coronary Intensive Care Unit, where an intern stood guard. And there, in a screened-off cubicle, was Julia. Every line, every freckle of Julia. But over her was a nightmare octopus of glass and wire and machinery. Laura whimpered when she saw it. She started pulling at the doctor's arm.

'Please – let me take it off her,' she whispered desperately. 'You don't know how she hates hospitals. You don't know how this must be frightening her. Please! Please take it off!'

But he would not do it.

Julia's eyes opened. They jerked and spun. Laura could not tell if her mother recognized, or even saw her. But her hands knew Laura's. She held them. Her mother's hands were warm and soft and hard-worked. Laura kissed them, and those hands patted hers with all the loving calmness in the world.

Laura wanted to say everything and could say nothing. She was so afraid of exciting her mother, of making alarms go off, that she could only look down and try to smile. But Julia said everything. She lifted up one warm hand, encircled Laura's wrist with her fingers and gave it a little squeeze. And then the surgeon said it was time for Laura to leave.

Laura was four years old. She and her mother were in Palm Springs. They were climbing a mountain. Laura had felt a sudden stinging in her feet and, looking down, she saw that ants were climbing over her toes. Roaring with fear, she refused to take another step. So Julia hoisted Laura up on her back and carried her piggyback down the mountain. And as she carried her, she made up a little song in honor of the occasion. 'The ants are coming to bite us, to bite us, today!' she sang in a deep sepulchral voice. Laura started laughing as hard as she could, and soon they were safely back down the mountain.

She had always been safe with Mama. Always.

The surgeon came out and told the assembled group that he was deeply sorry. That everything possible had been done. But that Julia had died.

35

Blake came slowly into the screened-off cubicle. The demeaning tangle of tubes was off Julia now. He looked down at her face. Gently, he touched the little nose, the violet-shadowed eyes. And he saved the baby-fine hair for last.

It had been on that trip to Europe when Laura was seven; that magical trip. Magical because Blake thought he would never see Europe again. It had been such a bad three years at the studio, and after the failure of David and Goliath, *most people thought he would never produce a film again. But then had come* Calliope. *And the first thing Blake had done after its success was get tickets for Europe on the Q.E. II.*

He would never forget how beautiful Julia had looked as the ship pulled away from the New York dock with the wind wild in that hair. She had said all along that he would be back on top again; she had said all along that they would return to Europe. He had not believed it, but she had. She was linking fingers with him now by the ship's rail, and he had felt her strength flowing golden into him and had known it would always be there.

From her chair in the little waiting room, Laura could hear her father sobbing. Sobs that sounded like he was pulling the skin off the world.

Jeff sat hunched beside Laura in the green metal chair. His every sense shrank from all sensation – the sound of footsteps, the smell of ether and flowers, the linoleum floor, the fluorescent lights. There was death in everything, and he did not want to catch it. He looked longingly out the window. There was the big grey Beverly Center across the street. Only last week he had bought a plaid shirt there. It seemed incredible to think of that

36

now. And there on the ground floor he could see The Hard Rock Cafe. Jeff fixed his eyes on it, suddenly starved for a hamburger. Then he felt guilty for having such a desire when Laura's mother lay dead two doors away.

They went into the parking lot and found the car. Julia's beloved '65 dark blue Mercedes. Laura got in. The car smelled exactly the same as always. It did not know that Julia had died.

'Do you want the car now, Laura?' her father was asking her.

'But it's Mama's!' she said, shocked.

There was a silence.

'Sure, Daddy,' Laura said quickly. 'I'd love to have the car.'

Jeff was happy she had agreed. He had always liked that car.

'Your mother would have wanted you to have it,' he told Laura.

They followed Blake back to the house on Bellagio. It looked very welcoming and gay – all the lights were on.

Blake turned to Jeff and Laura.

'Would you like a drink?' he asked.

'No,' Laura told him.

'Sure,' Jeff said.

They went into the bar. Blake found a glass, ice, then looked helplessly around. He had never fixed a drink in his life. It had always been Julia who had done that.

'What would you like?' he asked.

'Just a Coke,' Jeff said quickly.

He watched Laura's father's hands as he poured the Coke. The cola fell in an uncertain, undisciplined stream. The hands were white, piteous. Jeff was embar-

37

rassed. He remembered Laura's mother's hands. Her hands were so strong and so full of life. And she could do anything.

Laura looked down at the table in front of her. Julia's reading glasses were poised at the edge. And yet Julia was dead. *Mama is dead*, Laura told herself slowly. But the words were insane and wouldn't compute.

The three of them stood by the front door, like awkward guests at a party.

'Well,' Blake Alden said. 'You two get along home now.'

He looked very small, standing in the huge lighted hallway. Laura couldn't bear it.

'Come back to the apartment with us, Daddy,' she told him. 'You can have our bed. Jeff and I can sleep in the living room.'

'No,' Blake said. 'You kids run along. Honestly. I'll be fine.'

'Do you want me to spend the night here with you?' Laura persisted.

'No,' Blake told her, and deep down she was relieved.

Standing there, a strange image came to her mind. The image of herself and her father as two characters in a play – two footmen, perhaps, chattering onstage before the main character made her entrance. Everything they had to say to each other was purely incidental and supporting, just filler until the star arrived. And Julia had been the star. To both of them. But now that she was gone, Laura thought, the two footmen would have to improvise without her. Endless badly-written scenes – forever and ever.

Laura leaned over and kissed her father hard in the emptiness.

Blake Alden got ready for bed. It was the first night in

twenty-five years that Julia had not been there to put out his pajamas and robe for him. He went through all the drawers in his bathroom, but could find no pajamas. Finally, in a bottom drawer, he came upon an old flannel robe and put it on. Then he sat down on the bed and waited for the rest of his life to go by.

As she was getting into bed that night, Laura saw the flier about the sale the next morning at Geary's. *I can't wait!* she thought happily. *Mama and I'll have such a wonderful time. And lunch at the Bistro Garden afterwards!*

It had been her hands he had first noticed, twenty-five years ago, the night Desiree Kaufman gave the dinner party. Her hands at the table. Then he had noticed the face. It was nothing like the faces of the other starlets there that night; it was fine, clear-cut and earnest as a Victorian silhouette.

'What beautiful rings,' he had said to her.

'They belonged to my mother,' she had answered proudly, in the softest of Southern accents. 'She was a great lady.'

And an hour later, he had turned to Desiree. 'I've just met the girl I'm going to marry,' he told her.

At four in the morning, Laura awoke from a dream in which her mother had died. She awoke to find that the dream wasn't a dream.

This time it computed.

She woke up half the apartment building with her screams.

39

Chapter Two

Julia was cremated at noon, the following Tuesday. Blake had invited Laura and Jeff to lunch at Laserre in the Valley. The two men talked about Hollywood. Laura did not listen. She kept watching the big wooden clock. At precisely twelve, she excused herself. She went into the Ladies' room and stood by the sink.

'Goodbye, Mama,' she whispered. 'Goodbye.' And she closed her eyes.

A fat lady in polyester came out from one of the booths. Laura could feel her staring. She stared so hard that Laura finally opened her eyes.

'Cute shoes,' the woman said.

The memorial service was the following day, and afterwards there was a party at the house. All the people from Laura's childhood were there; friends and associates from all those Hollywood parties, Thanksgiving parties, birthday parties. It was hard to believe that this wasn't just one more party. Hard to believe that it wasn't just a coincidence that everyone was wearing black.

Laura felt very strange, almost euphoric, filled with a fierce, alien aliveness. She wondered if it was because she hadn't eaten in three days.

Then, looking around the room, she saw Desiree Kaufman watching her. The glow faded abruptly away.

I hope she doesn't come near me, Laura thought.

She's on the verge of a collapse, Desiree thought, looking at Laura. *Poor stupid little girl. How could Julia have left her in such shape?*

From across the room, Jeff saw Desiree and smiled. He had never understood why Laura disliked her so. He considered her one of the most attractive women he knew. And she had a curious kind of wit that was like a whip – while in one way it warned you off, it also had the power to draw you in. So he went over to her now.

But today Desiree had no wit for Jeff. 'Take care of Laura,' was all she said. He resented for a moment being lumped inevitably with Laura in Desiree's mind, and then the content of her words sank in and made him angry.

'I don't need to be told that,' he said icily. 'I love Laura.'

'Good,' Desiree only said, and turned away.

She moved quickly toward a less congested part of the room. She felt very irritated by Jeff. She had always known, of course, of his attraction to her, and while she had made it clear that she wasn't interested, she had always been a little flattered. In fact, she had taken his side, lazily and amusedly, several times against Julia.

'That boy's ruining my daughter,' Julia had huffed and puffed. 'This is not the man I want for Laura.'

'Whom did you have in mind?' Desiree had asked wryly. 'Someone with a hump on his back and glasses two feet thick? Someone without brains or talent or ambition?' She had always refrained from adding, 'In fact, it's a miracle Laura managed to get him,' but this was how she felt about it. Jeff was undeniably a lion, and Laura was nothing more than a little white rabbit. A little white rabbit with pale green eyes. And yet today she found herself angry at Jeff for coming to talk to her when he should have been by Laura. Strange. And even stranger, Desiree found herself anxiously seeking out the little white rabbit again. *I hope she doesn't faint*, she thought irritably.

She caught sight of Laura. Laura felt Desiree's glance, flushed, and looked away. Desiree smiled grimly. *She hates me*, she thought. *Let her faint or not, as she chooses.*

Blake Alden came up to Desiree.

'You have everything you need?' he asked.

It was what he always asked every guest, at every party. A catechism of responses lay poised under Desiree's tongue, but she only nodded and watched him walk away to the next guest. His eyes were bright and unfocussed, his walk tremulous.

Desiree saw that he was wearing the wrong shoes for his Givenchy suit. Julia had dressed him impeccably for twenty-five years, and now all that was over. Desiree felt suddenly very bitter and very old.

She raised her glass of champagne. 'To Julia,' she said shortly, and drank.

The pain was unbearable. The waves of misery came a thousand times a day, swelled by the most ridiculous, the most trivial things. Watching a beautiful performance on television and thinking that Julia would never see it. Buying a lovely blouse and knowing that Julia would never borrow it. Laughing at a funny movie, then crying because Julia would never go to it.

But despair made Laura canny. To make up for all the things that Julia would now never do, she relived in her head all the things that Julia *had* done. She spent hours every day with the memories, brooding over them, hoarding them.

She drove around every morning on little pilgrimages. Here, on Weyburn, was the bookstore where Julia had bought her adored Jean Plaidy novels. Here, on Beverly, was the shop of the hairdresser who had managed to dye Julia's hair bright green. Here was Julia's secret little shortcut through Overland.

She was everywhere, everywhere. All of Los Angeles had become her graveyard.

Some vacation film came back from the developers. Blake and Laura tore the package open with excitement. But there were no pictures of Julia on it. They remembered, too late, that she had always been the one who held the camera.

In the weeks after Julia's death, Jeff was very busy. So Laura fell into the habit of going over to her father's. It was probably the most time she had ever spent with him in her life.

She would go over to Blake's house immediately after breakfast. He would be waiting for her. He would leave the ringing phone, the unanswered condolence cards, and he and Laura would sneak out and go to the movies. They would hold hands like they were on a date, and talk and laugh. They saw film after film – three, four a day. Until the afternoon came when they looked in the newspaper and realized that there were no movies left to see.

They stared at each other.

And Laura stopped going over.

One night, she had a dream. She dreamed that she was sitting under a tree, and that a strange man with strange dark eyes was holding her hand and saying that everything would be all right. She awoke. There was no tree, no young man, and nothing was all right. The wave of pain broke over her head, and she screamed and screamed until Jeff came.

She tried to get her life in order again.

She cleaned the apartment. Soon it was immaculate. But it made no difference.

She kept wandering around. Wishing Jeff were home more often. Wishing she had a baby.

She tried losing herself in her work. But she could not be lost. That joyous impulse to write for children was suspended. Finally she put her book equipment in the closet where she wouldn't have to look at it.

Day leaked after day.

She tried re-contacting old friends. She had not realized how out of touch she had become, or how much Jeff and Julia between them had filled in her hours. But the friends did not seem overjoyed to hear from her.

She tried immersing herself in the real world. She went downtown to a woman's residence hotel one day and served hot soup to the destitute. Those women, swollen-legged, unkempt, all pride whipped out of their faces. It only depressed her more.

She tried concentrating on Jeff. The extra attention that had gone to Julia, Laura now transferred to him. She became obsessed with buying him presents. Clever, unusual things, like hiring a plane which flew special banners. She ordered one for his birthday.

But finally Jeff said she was bankrupting them, and he made her put a stop to all that buying.

And day leaked after day.

'Laura,' Jeff said, holding her late one night. 'It's been a whole month. It's time you started coming back to life again.'

There was an edge to his voice, as though he expected Laura to say, 'But I can't.'

'But I can't,' Laura said.

'Of course you can,' he told her. His voice was hearty. 'You'll see. You'll come to life again like a little flower.'

Laura got a sudden vision of kindergarten children pretending to be little flowers, and coming to life again when the sun touched them. Unwillingly, she smiled. Her face was in the crook of Jeff's elbow, and he felt the smile.

'And I'll tell you what else,' he added encouragingly. 'We're going to start spending more time together, you and I.'

She flushed with pleasure and surprise. Warmer and warmer grew the touch of the sun.

'Really?'

'Yes. We'll start a campaign. You know what we're doing tomorrow? We're going on a picnic. I'll take you to Will Rogers' State Park. And maybe go horseback riding afterwards. What do you say?'

She said yes.

And later, when she woke in the night with the thought that her mother was dead, Laura was able to follow it up with, 'But Jeff and I are going on a picnic.'

She awoke the next morning to an emptiness in the bed beside her. She jerked upright and saw Jeff. He was dressed, and not in horseback riding clothes.

'Where are you going?' Laura asked him.

He grinned. 'With all this drama going on around here, we forgot about my commercial. I've got a shoot today.'

'Oh,' Laura said flatly. She knew she shouldn't add this, but she couldn't help it. 'But our picnic.'

The grin dived out of sight.

'Laura,' he said very patiently, 'we can have our picnic

tomorrow or any other damned day you like. But this is work.'

Laura remembered, unbelieving, how, a scant four weeks before, she had been so completely thrilled by the thought of Jeff's commercial. She huddled back in the bedcovers. Jeff began to comb his hair, to put on after-shave. With every motion he made, he seemed to grow more and more remote from her, until at last he was as unobtainable as a figure high on a billboard. He leaned down and kissed her quickly on the cheek, grateful that there hadn't been more of a scene.

'What time will you be home?' Laura asked.

He shrugged. 'It'll probably take all day.'

She nodded. When he left the apartment, methodically she arranged her bedclothes around her, crouched back amongst them, and waited for him to come home.

Blake was doing his morning exercises, panting as he strode on the treadmill. The machine rolled on with a relentless, metallic clacking. It took several minutes for him to realize what terror there was in the sound. It made him think of old scolds twittering about decay, the whipped speed of time, the hustle to the grave. But he did not turn the machine off. For he knew the silence would only hold the same messages.

In the large mirror of his home gym, Blake could see himself working out. His black shorts were soaked. His skin looked greenish, the freckles damply phosphorescent. He examined his body. Images came to him, nasty, slug-like. He strode faster.

Julia's Red Lion. Her pet name for him, invented on their honeymoon. She had always been so proud of his fine body – had touched it with such joyous ownership. How could it all have disintegrated so quickly?

Blake's shorts started to slide down his hips – he had

46

lost so much weight in the last month. Clumsily, he grasped for them. And God, the face above the sea-slug body.

Drowning, Blake grabbed at the thought of Julia. He found himself remembering something very tiny and very strange. It was a look. A look she had once given him.

It had been years ago, the day he had come home and told her the studio had fired him from *The Springtime Reed*. After that first moment, Julia had returned to herself, had covered him all over with reassurances and Julia-wisdom, Julia-strength. But in that one second, there had been that look. And he had suddenly seen the endlessly-hidden fragility in her, had known exactly how much she depended on him.

And in some strange way, that look had been the thing that had decided him, strengthened him, made success possible again. For, sure enough, a year later, Blake Alden was again producing movies. He remembered there had been a big celebratory party when *Manifesto* was released, and that Julia had looked so beautiful at it.

As he toiled on the treadmill, the image of Julia's look came afresh to Blake. But this time he was empty-handed. He knew that this time he could not soothe it, exorcise it, could not pull off any miracles. This time there would be no rallying, no celebratory party with Julia looking beautiful.

Blake was all too aware of the Hollywood rumors. Now that his wife's dead, Blake Alden's finished.

And so he was.

No! screamed Julia's voice from the treadmill.

You'll be all right, Blake's reflection pleaded to his ashen dripping face.

No, it answered.

Blake switched off the treadmill. The silence was as terrifying as he had known it would be.

Jeff was a little early for his shoot, so he stopped into his favorite cafe on San Vicente for some coffee. Next to the restaurant was the new men's store that had just been written up in *L.A. Weekly*. There was a good-looking Fila shirt featured in the window, and Jeff promised himself that if the commercial went well, he would come back and buy it this afternoon. God knew, he deserved a little treat.

At nine o'clock, Jeff pulled up at the address his agent had given him. It was a small white house in Brentwood – the perfectly typical, perfectly atypical all-American house, where only all-American products were used.

He knocked on the door. A woman in her early thirties opened it.

'Hi,' Jeff said. 'I'm Jeff Kennerly. I'm here to extol the virtues of Angel Soap Powder.'

The woman laughed. She had a nice laugh, a mature laugh. 'You obviously don't do your own laundry,' she said. 'It's the worst powder on the market.'

Outside in the backyard, the cameraman was starting to set up his equipment. Jeff could hear him screaming at the assistant.

Jeff leaned against the door. 'Do a lot of commercials get shot here?' he asked.

The woman nodded. 'It's meant extra income. And I've needed it. Ever since my husband and I were divorced.'

'Ah,' Jeff nodded. She had said it very distinctly indeed.

They smiled at each other for a moment, then glanced away.

The sun went behind a cloud. In the back yard, the cameraman was swearing shrilly.

'They'll be hours setting up at this rate,' Jeff said.

'Hours,' the woman agreed.

There was a pause.

'Would you like to come inside for some coffee?' the woman asked.

'That would be very nice,' he told her.

Jeff felt wonderful, driving back home at the end of the day. It was the most alive he had felt since Laura's mother had died. It was amazing, how a simple thing like those hours spent with the lady in Brentwood could change one's point of view. The last month had been so depressing that he had almost forgotten how wonderful and carefree life could be.

He did feel a little remorseful about Laura, though, so, instead of buying himself the Fila shirt, he pulled into a Conroys and picked out some pink roses for her. He signed the card, 'From your guy.' And that's certainly what he was, he thought. Laura's guy forever. He loved her.

Chapter Three

'Miss Kaufman! This way, please.'

The maître d' of the Moonwalk Cafe led Desiree to her table. She swept, a three-master, through the tiny islet between tables. The maître d' followed behind, like a plumply perspiring tugboat, tooting repeatedly about what a pleasure this was. Trina Feltner, who was hosting the luncheon, watched in amused dismay.

'For heaven's sake, Desiree, this place just opened last week. You *couldn't* have been here before.'

The maître d' bowed, and left.

'I haven't,' Desiree said.

Sometimes her fame was like an antique ring caught in the lining of a jewellery box. Temporarily hidden, but sooner or later bound to be discovered, and brilliant when shined up.

There were four of them waiting for her at the table, all wives of men in the industry, all wearing designer suits and blue-rinsed hair. It was not Desiree's favorite luncheon group, but she had had a difficult night, and when Trina had called and invited her this morning, she had had no better plan.

Greetings, kisses cold and warm, were exchanged. Desiree sat back against the green velvet banquette, already regretting her decision, already feeling the weight of a wasted afternoon.

Over cocktails, the women asked one another what was new. Each answered with varying degrees of sincerity. Desiree's response was, as always, by far the least truthful. And, that over with, the women were now free to get on with the main conversational agenda: how the Aldens were doing since poor Julia had died.

'I saw him at Spago's the other evening,' Trina began. 'Frankly, I was shocked. He looks absolutely haggard.' Then catching at a waiter, she asked for another wine cooler.

'And Roger tells me that the movie's come to a perfect standstill,' Amy Kenyon added eagerly. She was new to the group, still on trial, and married to the least important of the husbands.

'Well, it's no wonder,' Toni Mirman said. 'Just think what he must be going through. Julia was everything to him.' She turned to Desiree. 'But you're the one who would know all about that.'

'Yes, I'm the one who would know all about that,' Desiree agreed evenly.

'Still . . .' Amy said thoughtfully, 'An attractive man like that. I have a cousin – from Denver – who would love to meet him. When the time's right, of course,' she added quickly.

The other women stared at her. The remark lay there.

'If it comes to that, we all have cousins,' Merilee Max said coldly.

'I only meant,' Amy began, then gave it up.

'The one I feel sorry for is the daughter,' Toni said.

'Laura?' Trina gave a little laugh. 'Well, I've always felt sorry for Laura.'

'Why?' Amy asked, eager to re-ingratiate herself.

Trina shrugged. 'Have you ever met her?'

'No,' Amy admitted.

'Well, she's – unprepossessing, to say the least. But then, what would you expect? Being in Julia Alden's

51

shadow from the day you're born? It can't have been much fun.'

Merilee frowned. 'Still,' she said, 'I understand they were very close. She just looked devastated, the day of the service.'

'Well, yes,' Trina allowed. Her own daughter was in Vermont, undergoing treatment at a drug hospital. 'That's certainly true. Laura couldn't make a move without her mother. I don't know what she's going to do without her now.'

'Well, at least she has that boyfriend.'

'Oh, my dear!' Toni interrupted with a laugh. 'The minute that gorgeous man gets a break, he'll be on to someone else.' She flashed an icy smile at Amy. 'Your cousin from Denver, perhaps.'

'Excuse me,' Desiree stood up. 'I'm afraid I must go. I've gotten the most awful headache.'

The day came when Laura finally re-opened the closet where she had stored her book materials, and pulled out the unfinished story of Philippe, the French hippo. Then she got back to work – for the first time since Julia had died.

She felt proud – as if she had taken a big step in a big jungle.

Three hours later, she stopped. She was exhausted. She lay down on the couch and turned on a talk show. By the time the second commercial came on, she had fallen asleep.

And then, in her sleep, she heard her mother laughing. Laura sat up, her heart shrieking. 'Mama!' she screamed. 'Where are you?'

There was no answer. Laura felt foolish, shaken – it had only been a dream.

And then she heard Julia laugh again. Wildly, Laura looked around the room. And there was her mother.

The movie was an old one that Laura had never before seen. Julia played a schoolteacher from the South who had fallen in love with an Indian. She was utterly wonderful, utterly resurrected.

Laura watched the film through, without moving, barely breathing. When the credits came on and the show was over, Julia went back to being dead. Laura turned the set off and stared at the black screen. When it got unbearable, she ran out of the apartment, jumped into her car, and drove off.

'Hi, sweetie!' Blake said with surprise, as she came into his office.

'Daddy!'

The relief of seeing him so alive, so real, was tremendous, inarticulate. He would understand about the movie. He would understand how she had felt, seeing Julia there on television. She hugged him hard.

Blake was wearing a new Armani suit, and his hair had been freshly and meticulously cut. As she drew away from him, Laura realized something with a sudden shock. Her father was looking well. In fact, he was looking wonderful. The weight lost after Julia's death had been regained, the pallor was gone, the white line had left the corners of his mouth. *When had that happened?* she wondered dazedly. *When had he started to be all right again?*

She stared at him.

'Can I get you something to drink?' Blake asked solicitously.

'No,' she said. 'I just came to see you.'

'Glad you did, sweetie. It's been a while.'

'Yes, I know.'

Alison buzzed on the intercom. 'Mike Stanyon on the phone.'

Blake made a face. 'Sorry,' he said. 'I've got to pick up on this one.' He took the phone. 'Mike! How are you? No, I haven't had a chance to look them over. And I'm not going to, either, until I get some kind of – '

He talked on. Laura watched him on the phone; observed his confident ease.

Blake hung up finally and smiled at her. 'You're looking good,' he said.

She knew she looked like hell.

'What's going on?' he asked.

She stared at him. She started to say something about seeing Julia in the movie, but stopped, suddenly unsure. In the face of her father's broad smile, her angst seemed totally inappropriate.

Last time I saw him, he was just like me, she thought bewilderedly. *We were wrecked together.* But all that was gone now. It had only been six weeks. But there was absolutely no trace left of the man who had sobbed in Laura's arms, the day Julia had died.

Alison buzzed again. 'It's Mr Bright on line two,' she said apologetically.

'Sorry, sweetie,' Blake said, reaching for the phone. 'This damned deal. Archie!'

Laura sat back on her chair and waited.

The conversation over, Blake hung up the phone.

'So how's Jeff?' he asked pleasantly.

'He's fine,' Laura said. 'Working a lot.' She despised herself for not being able to get beyond this stupidity.

'Good, good,' Blake said.

The buzzer sounded again. 'So sorry, Mr Alden, but your sister from Atlanta is returning your call.'

'Sorry, sweetie,' Blake said. 'But it's her birthday.' He

reached eagerly for the phone. 'Hey, sis! Having a good one? Fine, fine. Oh, I'm doing great. Just great.'

And he is. He really is, Laura thought with coldness and with awe. She looked behind Blake's desk. The photograph of Julia in the silver frame was gone.

Laura stood up abruptly. 'I've got to go,' she said.

Blake gave a little wave. 'Come on by more often,' he said.

Laura drove home, tears, like painful fingerpaint, all over her face.

Blake hung up the phone, then lay back against the chair and closed his eyes.

The image of Laura wouldn't leave him. He wondered if she had any idea at all what torture it was to see her. How obscene and wrong it felt to see her – alone – without Julia there. For over two decades, he had grown so used to the volley of their voices together – Laura's, light, questioning, Julia's resonant, answering – and now Laura's voice alone was as empty and crazy-making as the sound of a child with no one to play with hitting a tennis ball forlornly against a garage wall.

Why the hell had she come today? he wondered irritably. The morning had gone so well until she had come.

Without her, the constant reminder, he had a chance. Lately, he had even grown optimistic, seeing his face and body gradually regain themselves. Buying the new clothes. Getting back to work. Hearing the various voices on the phone each day, needing his attention, needing his talents. All of it fooling himself into thinking that progress was being made.

But Laura destroyed all that. Almost deliberately, it seemed, she destroyed it. What the hell did she mean, sitting there like the Little Match Girl, looking like a freak, not saying a word, staring pop-eyed at the place where Julia's picture had been? Goddamit, he was trying like a son-of-a-bitch to pull himself out of the pit. Why the hell couldn't she try, too?

Blake found himself suddenly fantasizing about what it would have been like if there had been no Laura at all. If it had been just him and Julia. He began to calculate all the hours that Julia had spent on Laura through the years – as a baby, as a child, as a young woman. If there had been no Laura, they would have been *his* hours. Added up, they would have given him – what? An extra year, an extra two years of Julia? An extra two years that Laura had stolen.

Blake broke away from his thoughts, panicked and horrified. He remembered the morning Laura was born. How he had gone into the hospital room and told Julia, 'This is the happiest moment of my life.' His baby girl.

He began to weep.

I am a monster. I am in trouble. I am in trouble.

When Coco came upstairs the next morning to bring Blake his breakfast tray, he wasn't in his room. She was very surprised.

Laura had a bad night. She awakened, the rage and puzzlement over her father still hot within her. She tried to forget about it by working on her book, but it didn't help.

She was making lunch when the phone rang. It was Alison, her father's secretary.

Damn, Laura thought. *Now he wants to talk to me.*

'Hi, Alison,' she said cautiously, and waited for the secretary to transfer her to her father. But the transfer did not come. Instead, there was a strange pause.

56

'Laura,' Alison asked, 'do you happen to know where your father is?'

Laura stared at the phone. 'What?' she asked.

'He isn't here,' Alison said uneasily. 'No one knows where he's gone. He left before breakfast and he's been gone all morning. The studio just called. They were a little concerned. He was supposed to be at a screening at ten, and he never showed up.'

'Oh, well,' Laura said with a casual little laugh, 'I'm sure he's fine. Something urgent must have come up. If I hear from him, I'll let you know.'

She hung up the phone. She closed her eyes.

He's dead, she thought.

She called Alison back in an hour, trying to sound casual. No, Blake still wasn't home, and there had been no word.

By four o'clock, Laura was calling the house every fifteen minutes. Finally Alison hung up on her.

Jeff was whistling when he got back to the apartment building that afternoon. It had been a good workout at the gym. He stretched, enjoying the taut tiredness of his muscles. *A movie might be fun tonight*, he decided. Maybe he'd take Laura to that French film she'd been wanting to see.

He came into the apartment, ready to make Laura happy. 'Hi, baby,' he said, smiling. But the smile left when he saw her face. 'My God,' he said. 'What's wrong?'

'It's Daddy,' Laura sobbed. 'He's gone.'

Jeff stared at her. 'What do you mean, he's gone?'

'He's disappeared. He left early this morning and no one knows where he is.' Her voice rose and rose like a siren.

'So?' Jeff asked, determined not to be sucked into the hysteria.

'So?' The siren went off again. 'Where could he be?'

'How should I know?' Jeff asked her. 'Maybe he went to a movie!'

'For twelve hours?' Laura demanded.

'Maybe he went to six movies!'

He tried to fight the feeling of impatience, the regret for the ruined evening. 'Look Laura,' he said. 'Stop being so hysterical. Your father can take care of himself.'

She started crying again. 'I know he's dead,' she whispered.

Jeff turned away.

I'm a nice guy, he thought tightly. *I don't deserve this.*

And then the phone rang.

Jeff picked it up. 'It's your father,' he said.

Laura snatched the receiver. 'Daddy!' she sobbed. 'Where are you? I've been worried sick!'

There was a long pause.

'I had an appointment,' Blake told her.

Laura stopped crying. There was something shadowy in her father's voice.

'What sort of appointment?' she asked warily.

There was another pause.

'I went to see a psychic.'

Laura stared at the coffee table. Stared at the potted plant on the coffee table; the ring of keys.

Her father had gone mad.

'A psychic?' she repeated in whispered disbelief. 'You went to see a *psychic*?'

'Yes.' His voice was growing colder.

'But you've been gone all day,' she said foolishly. As if that could make it not true.

'I went to the beach afterwards,' he told her. 'I walked around for a while.'

Laura got a sudden vision of her father in his six-hundred-dollar suit, rolling up the trousers and wading through the water. She shook her head numbly.

'Why did you do it?'

And Blake began to sob. 'Because I miss your mother so much,' he wept. 'I thought the psychic might know where she is.'

Laura closed her eyes in pain. 'Oh, Daddy,' she whispered.

The cold misery beat into her. And she had been angry at him. And she had thought he had changed. She had thought he had forgotten Julia.

For a moment she was still, and then she said gently, 'I understand, Daddy. I understand. But this man can't help you. Mama's dead. She's not anywhere now.'

There was a strange pause.

'I'm not so sure,' Blake told her.

Laura stiffened. 'What do you mean?'

'Maybe we've been wrong about that.'

She started to swallow, choked. 'Please don't talk like that, Daddy,' she said. 'These psychics – they're crazy. You know that.'

'Well, maybe we've been wrong about that, too.'

'Stop it! Just stop it!' she said sharply.

'What did you say to me?' he asked her icily.

'I'm sorry.' She backed off, appalled. 'But – you're frightening me.'

'Don't be silly.' Blake sounded crisp now, in control again. 'There's nothing to be frightened of. It was an interesting experience. That was all.'

'Oh.' The relief was instant. 'Then you won't go back to him?'

But Blake would not answer.

'Daddy,' Laura pleaded shrilly, 'promise me you won't go back to him.'

There was a long pause.

'He kept saying he wanted to meet you,' Blake only told her.

Laura was aghast. 'Never,' she said between clenched teeth.

'You might think about it,' Blake told her. 'He really did keep saying he had a very special feeling about you.'

She made a sound of disgust.

'Look, Laura,' Blake cut in, 'it's been a pretty tough month. This fellow made me feel better today. I should think you'd be happy. Why are you acting like this?'

Laura closed her eyes. *I'm acting like this*, she thought, *because all your life you've laughed at people who go to psychics, and now you're one of them. I'm acting like this because Mama's gone and she can't protect you, and for the first time in my life I see how vulnerable you are.*

She didn't say that. She just told her father that they would talk about it later. That she loved him; and that she was glad the psychic had given him relief. And then she hung up.

She and Jeff stared at each other.

'So the old man's cracking up,' Jeff said.

Laura sat on the edge of the bed late that night. She couldn't sleep.

A memory kept coming.

She was five years old. She came in to the kitchen to get some milk and cookies. Julia was sitting at the breakfast table, playing with a funny board. A little marker flew around it, spelling out sentences.

She barely noticed Laura's presence. Her eyes were

glazed, opaque. Laura felt frightened. She went over and shook her mother's arm.

'What are you doing?' she demanded.

Julia turned on her a blind smile. 'Finding out the future, darling,' she said.

And she went back to the board.

Laura, crying, went in to her father.

'I'm scared, Daddy,' she whimpered, going into his arms. 'I wanted to have my milk and cookies, but I couldn't get to them. There was this horrible board in the way.'

Blake jumped up from the chair and hurried into the kitchen. 'Stay outside,' he told Laura at the door. 'I don't want you to come in.' But Laura heard the shouting. It was the worst fight they had ever had.

Finally they came out of the kitchen. Julia looked very sad and chastened. She said to Laura she was sorry if she had frightened her. She said it wouldn't happen again. Laura went back to the kitchen. The ouija board sat limp and deflated on the table. All of its power was gone now. She had no fear now of reaching across it to get her milk and cookies. She felt smug. She knew that she and her father had conquered.

Laura straightened up on the edge of the bed.

And she was damned well not going to let him be conquered now.

Chapter Four

Jeff had an important interview with *Spotlight Magazine* the next morning, and he left the apartment early. As soon as he was safely gone, Laura got into her car and drove to her father's house.

She was very nervous. She was not even sure what she was going to say to Blake. All the arguments that she had so carefully fixed in her mind last night shredded now into impossibly ill-written dialogue. She trusted that the right words would come when she saw him – the magic phrases that would convince him never to see the psychic again.

She rang the bell.

Pauline, the downstairs maid, opened the door. She explained to Laura in unnecessarily urgent Spanish that her father had gone to the Beverly Hills Hotel for a manicure. Laura was both relieved and disappointed that the conversation had to be deferred.

She went up to her father's office to wait for him.

A half hour passed, but Blake still did not come in. Finally, she went over to the bookcase to find something to read. As she walked by Blake's desk, she saw a piece of paper by the phone, with a name and number written on it.

Laura drew in her breath. She stared at the name with angry, narrow eyes. She picked up the paper to rip it up. But she stopped. What good would that do? Her father could always find him again. And then a surge of excitement came into Laura's face. She straightened, picked up the phone, and dialed.

He answered on the third ring.

'Hello?' His voice was very soft.

'Is this Christopher Garland?' Laura asked quickly.

'Yes.'

'My name is Olivia Richards.' She tried to keep her voice from going too jerkily. 'I'm a writer, and I'm very interested in psychic phenomena. Last night I was at a party, and I met a young woman who said she'd gone to you for a reading – and that you were wonderful.'

He laughed. 'This is true,' he said.

'Some things have come up in my life, and I'd like to have a reading myself,' Laura told him. 'As soon as possible, in fact. Are you free this afternoon? Maybe about three o'clock?'

There was a pause.

'All right,' Christopher told her. And he gave her his address.

Laura dropped the receiver, smiling giddily. By late afternoon, Christopher Garland would be discredited entirely, and her father would never bother with him again. It was a wonderful relief.

Before leaving Blake's office, she straightened a few pictures on the wall. Julia had always liked a room to be tidy.

Jeff arrived at the office of *Spotlight Magazine*, the newest Hollywood journal on the market. It was surprisingly elegant for a fledgling enterprise, and he was glad he had worn the Pierre Cardin jacket. The young receptionist and secretaries were very hospitable – Jeff was offered coffee four times in fifteen minutes.

Finally, Kimberly Wetherly came out of her office.

She was in her late twenties, with a body that implied regular dedication to the gym, and that breezy sense of fashion which Jeff was always trying, in vain, to cultivate in Laura. Jeff smiled at her.

'Hi,' he said.

She matched his 'Hi,' his smile, exactly. Then she led Jeff to the big conference room. There were several club chairs available, but the two chose to sit together on the couch.

Kim switched on the tape recorder.

'When did you first decide to become an actor, Jeff?'

Jeff paused for a moment before answering. 'I was in the eighth grade,' he told her. 'It came down to a choice between drama class or Shop. It was a pretty easy decision to make, really. Anything to keep from having to use a saw. So I joined the Drama Club. They were doing *Inherit the Wind* that semester. I got cast as the court stenographer.' He laughed. 'Quite a challenging part. I didn't have any lines. I just sat on a stool at the back of the stage and took notes.' Kim laughed, too. 'We had four weeks of rehearsal. God, I hated every moment. I even began to wish I'd taken Shop, after all.

'And then came opening night. We went onstage. The curtain rose. The lights came on. I looked out at the audience. And suddenly everything in my head got real clear. I thought, hell, this is it. Why would anybody on earth ever want to do anything else but this?'

'Oh,' Kim said softly. She leaned toward him and he could smell Dior's 'Poison' climbing gently toward him. 'That's beautiful, Jeff. I know our readers are going to love that story.'

'I hope so,' he told her.

Driving home, Jeff thought of some of the things he had

not told Kim Wetherly about that evening of the High School play.

His father coming backstage after the performance. Throwing open the door of the makeshift dressing room, and looking around at the excited, clowning boys in such a way that the room had instantly grown silent. And then he had slowly walked over to a chair beside Jeff, deliberately sat down, and watched him take off his make-up.

'That's right,' he had said. 'Take off the lipstick – just like a woman wears. That's right. Now take off the rouge. And now the eyeshadow. I can't tell you how it made me feel tonight, watching you sit there on your butt for two hours. And I can't tell you how it makes me feel now, seeing you turn into a queer before my very eyes. My God, what a sight. My son, the Actor.'

Jeff waited until his father and the rest of the cast had finally left the dressing room. Then he had lain down on the floor and been sick.

He wondered, driving home, how the readers of *Spotlight Magazine* would have liked that one.

At three o'clock, Laura pulled up to the address Christopher Garland had given her. It was a shadowed, slightly sad apartment building, right by the beach.

Laura felt numb. She had tried, the length of the drive, to figure out exactly what she was going to say to unmask this psychic, but nothing had come to her yet.

It was very difficult to find a parking space, and she drove around and around. But at last she was walking up the path to Christopher's door. She was shaking unpleasantly, and she hated him for making her shake. She found his apartment door, and knocked loudly. The door opened.

Christopher Garland looked like something out of a

fever dream. He was very tall and thin and pale, with intensely black eyes, and his face was caricature-like in its stark angularity.

It's the strangest face I've ever seen, was the first thing Laura thought. *And I've seen it before*, was the second.

One did not forget a face like this.

Christopher smiled down at her, and all at once the madness seemed to go away.

'Come right in,' he said.

Uneasily, Laura followed him inside.

'I'm sorry I'm late,' she said stiffly. 'I had a hard time finding a parking place.'

His eyes grew wide as a doll's.

'But I saved a space for you in the garage. Didn't you see the sign I left?'

Laura did remember seeing a large paper fluttering on the post in the garage, but she had paid no attention to it.

'Well, never mind that,' he said quickly. 'Please have a seat.'

Laura sat down on the couch, and looked suspiciously around at the apartment. It was very neat and modern. No pentangles were in evidence. There were a lot of spy thrillers on the bookshelves, nothing by Edgar Cayce. Christopher sat down in the chair opposite her.

'So, Olivia, tell me again how you heard about me,' he said.

Laura coughed. She found she couldn't look into his eyes, so she stared at the tabletop and began re-inventing the tale of the imaginary friend at the imaginary party. And suddenly, Christopher began to laugh. Laura broke off, stared at him. His eyes were dancing and delighted as he continued to laugh. Then he jumped up from his chair, came over and gave her an enormous hug.

'Oh, Laura,' he said. 'I am so glad to meet you.'

For a moment, it didn't register. And then, when it did, she could only gape with blushing confusion.

'Oh, it's all right,' Christopher said easily. 'People try to pull stunts like this on me all the time. The important thing is, you're here.'

And then the confusion resolved itself into rationality.

'My father showed you my picture,' she told him cuttingly. 'Obviously, that's how you knew me.'

Christopher laughed. 'Oh, obviously,' he mocked her.

Laura felt furious. 'Well,' she went on coldly, 'since you seem to know who I am, I'm sure you also know why I'm here.'

He was looking at her, still smiling. She took a breath, trying to say what she had to say politely, but she was too unnerved and angry.

'Look,' she began. 'I know all about you. The news is full of people just like you.'

'It is?' he asked, with interest.

'Stop it,' she said narrowly. 'I know all about how you so-called psychics operate. You get these people in your power, and you take them for every penny they've got. Like that crazy guru in Montana with his forty Rolls-Royces. And that guy in Idaho who does the channeling.'

'And don't forget that woman in Michigan – the one who was jailed last week,' Christopher added. 'And there's always Manson, when all else fails.'

Laura sat straighter. 'Look here,' she went on with dignity, 'what you do with other people is your business. But when you start getting involved with my father, then it becomes my business, too. I realize that he's in a very vulnerable situation now, with my mother gone, but I want you to understand something. I'm still here to protect him – and I'm nobody's fool. If you behave

67

out of line, I'll do everything in my power to stop you; and that includes going to the police, if necessary.'

Christopher sighed deeply, like a disappointed child.

'Oh, Laura,' he said. 'I had hoped you would be a little more receptive.'

'Receptive?'

'Honestly, Laura,' Christopher went on, with a little laugh. 'Your father's a nice enough guy, but he was only sent to me as a means to an end.'

Her eyes widened as he leaned toward her.

'And you're the end,' he said simply.

She jumped sharply back.

'Laura, don't you really know why you're here?' he asked her gently.

She kept staring. He was changing, he was changing. The whole shape of his face – the planes were shifting – and oh, God, his eyes.

'I'm here because of my father,' she told him in a whisper.

He shook his head, smiling. 'No, Laura. You're here because of your mother.'

She gasped. *I'm in the room with a madman*, she thought with ice-cold clarity. *And I never left a note to Jeff to say where I was going. They won't find my body for weeks.*

Christopher leaned forward. 'She sent you to me, Laura. There are things she wants to tell you.'

'There's nothing she wants to tell me,' Laura said shrilly. 'She's dead.'

Christopher laughed, as if this was the funniest thing he had ever heard.

'Oh, Laura,' he scoffed. 'You don't really believe that, do you? Your mother's no more dead than you are.'

The words racked her with shivers. It was obscene, unthinkable. She kept flashing on the little cement box with her mother's ashes in it. The tension grew and grew until it was unbearable, and then, in an instant, everything changed. Something almost tangible went out of the atmosphere. Christopher, too, looked different. His face had re-settled into normalcy. His eyes were clear again.

He stood up. 'You look awful,' he said. 'Let me get you a cup of tea.'

She was so shaken she did not refuse.

He brought it over in, of all things, an MGM Studio mug.

'Where on earth did you get this?' Laura blurted out.

Christopher shrugged. 'I don't remember. At some Round Table luncheon, probably. I used to go to a lot of them. I was a staff photographer for *The Hollywood Reporter* for fifteen years.' He laughed at her shocked face. 'One can be psychic and still know how to focus a Nikon,' he said.

Aha, Laura thought. So that was why he had looked so naggingly familiar. And that could also have been why he had recognized her.

'I wish you weren't so suspicious, Laura,' Christopher said gently. 'You've no idea how excited I've been about meeting you. We have so much to learn from each other, and it's just going to complicate things if you keep resisting.'

Laura slammed her mug on the table.

'Stop talking like that!' she cried.

He jumped back, quickly, stricken. She looked away, embarrassed.

'Look,' she said. 'I don't mean to be rude. I'm sure there are a lot of people who believe in this sort of thing, but I don't happen to be one of them. I'm not a New Age type. I live in the real world. The only reason I came

69

to see you today was because of my father, and getting back to that, I really would appreciate it if you had nothing more to do with him in the future.'

Christopher paused. 'All right,' he said. 'I've helped him all I can, anyway. There's really no reason for us to see each other again.'

Relief lapped over Laura. 'Good,' she said, and rose. 'Well, I guess I've said what I came to say. So I'll be going. I hope I didn't offend you.'

'Not at all,' he told her.

Christopher stood up also. He walked over to the table by the window, picked up a small vial of anointing oil, and uncapped it.

'Before you go,' he asked, 'would you let me give you a little blessing? It would mean a lot to me.'

The relief froze on Laura's skin.

'I'd rather you didn't,' she said.

'Oh, okay,' Christopher said quickly. He stood there, still holding the little bottle, awkward, unrescued.

Laura felt suddenly ashamed of herself.

'Look, Christopher; please try to understand,' she said. 'I've really nothing against you personally. I'm sure you believe in your philosophies very much. But try to see all this from my point of view. I've got to look after my father, and Daddy's so easily manipulated by the wrong people.'

Christopher raised his eyes to look at her. They were suddenly blazing with black anger.

'Pardon me,' he said courteously. 'But you're quite wrong. Your father's very strong. The one who's easily manipulated by the wrong people is you.'

A moment later, she was outside the door.

As she hurried down the path to her car, Laura noticed a piece of paper fluttering from the post in the garage.

70

The note Christopher had written for her, saying where to park. Laura's eyes narrowed. *Let's see what kind of psychic you are, you bastard.*

She pulled down the piece of paper and looked at it. It was addressed to 'Laura Alden.'

Laura got into her car. She felt very queer, and she had a hard time pulling out of the space.

She was in a restless, hectic mood. She drove badly. She kept thinking of the half hour that had just passed. Unwillingly, she kept re-running the tape over and over. Finally she set fire to it, and watched the film burn to cinders in her mind. The afternoon was gone now. She would never mention it to her father, or to Jeff; she would never even think about it again.

But there was one thing she could not stop thinking about. She could not stop trying to remember where she had seen Christopher Garland before. Although she had told herself that it had been at some Premiere, she knew that it hadn't been. And then, as she was turning onto Sepulveda, Laura remembered that dream she had had after her mother died. That dream of sitting in a meadow, and a man with very dark eyes holding her hands and telling her everything would be all right.

And Laura went cold.

She got home. Jeff was still out. The apartment looked eerie in the twilight. Laura changed into her pajamas, got into bed, and made the pillows into a fort around her. She picked up a thriller and began to read. But after two pages, she threw the book impatiently away.

Christopher Garland.

Laura sat up firmly.

'What you need, old girl,' she said aloud, 'are two packages of Hostess Twinkies.'

She got out of bed. She didn't feel like changing

71

clothes again, so she simply rolled up her pajama bottoms to her knees, and put a coat over them. She then tied one of Jeff's neckties around her neck, and hoped the pajama top looked like a striped shirt. Then she drove to the nearest market, praying she would not run into anyone she knew.

'Hello, Laura,' Desiree Kaufman said.

Laura tried to hide herself behind the fruit juice display. Her whole body twanged with embarrassment. Oh, God, she thought. Of all the people in the world to meet. She knew that it would not escape Desiree that she had gone grocery shopping in her pajamas. But, amazingly, Desiree did not seem to notice either her discomfort or her clothes.

'How are you?' she asked Laura quietly.

'Fine,' Laura stammered.

Desiree nodded.

'I'm glad to hear it,' she said soberly. 'You've been on my mind a great deal.'

Laura did not know what to answer. Desiree was looking at her with such straightness – all the usual irony, the judgment was suddenly not there.

'We've never had much of a relationship, have we?' Desiree asked abruptly. 'That's rather a pity. I loved your mother very much,' she told Laura. 'And now that she's gone, I'd like to know her daughter better.'

Laura stared at her. She knew that this was her shining moment to say, 'Desiree, I never could stand you, and now I don't even have to pretend anymore.' But she didn't. To her own surprise, she heard herself saying slowly, 'Yes. I'd like that, too.'

'Good,' Desiree said briskly. 'Come to tea. What about tomorrow?'

72

Laura would have preferred something vaguer, but she couldn't think of any way to refuse.

'Four o'clock,' Desiree said. 'At my house.' She smiled. 'How odd. It will be the first time you have ever come there.'

Laura ordered in pizza for dinner. Pizza always made her feel safe, cozy, a middle-class American kid.

'Well,' Jeff said as they sat eating. 'Did you have an interesting day?'

She hadn't meant to tell him – had been sure that she would never tell him.

'As a matter of fact, yes,' she said, trying to sound casual. 'You know that psychic Daddy went to see? Well,' she added with a little embarrassed laugh, 'I went to see him, too.'

For a moment, there was no response; and then suddenly Jeff was gasping, gaping at her.

'You did what?' he asked dangerously. 'Did you just say you went to see a goddam *psychic*?'

Laura flushed.

'Well, yes,' she said. 'But not in the way you mean. I didn't go there to *see* him. I went there to unmask him.'

He stared at her.

'What the hell are you talking about?'

There were warning stingers of perspiration under her arms. 'I went there to prove to Daddy what a fraud he is.'

'And how exactly did you do that?' he asked, too quietly.

'I didn't have to. He promised me he wouldn't bother Daddy again.'

'He promised you he wouldn't bother Daddy again,' Jeff repeated flatly. 'Oh, my God, Laura. You're a jewel. What did you expect him to say?' She started to answer, but he glared her into silence. 'Why the hell did you even go? Why didn't you consult me first? Don't you know better than to do anything so stupid?'

'You're not listening to me!' Laura told him, hating herself for sounding so shrill, so babyish.

But Jeff only shook his head.

'I'm really starting to worry about you,' he told her. 'Ever since your mother died, you've been getting weirder and weirder. Staying in bed all day. Not seeing anybody. Not doing anything. And now you've started going to psychics.' He gave a low whistle.

She took a deep breath, trying to sound super-rational, super-sane.

'I told you,' she said. 'It had nothing to do with me. I just went there to protect Daddy.'

Jeff slammed down his knife.

'Oh, God!' he said. 'You really do have a screw loose. "To protect Daddy!" Laura, your goddam father runs the whole goddam studio. Believe me, he doesn't need your protection. It's *sick*, the way you worry about him. You hover around him like he's five years old. If he's ten minutes late coming home, you're hysterical. Right away you think he's dead. Now you're following him to goddam psychics. My God! What will it be next?' He turned away and added in a hurt voice, 'I thought *I* was supposed to be the man in your life. Why don't you show a little concern about *me* once in a while?'

'Oh, Jeff,' Laura said. She reached across the table and tried to take his hand, but he pulled irritably away.

She stared miserably at the cozy, all-American pizza.

'Maybe I have been spending too much time worrying about Daddy,' she admitted finally, 'but it's like – well, it's like kidneys.' Seeing Jeff's expression, she laughed nervously. 'When you've got two of them, you don't really worry. But when one's gone, you find you start getting real anxious about the other.'

'Well, you're wasting your time,' Jeff told her coldly. 'Your father has no need for you or your concern.'

'Oh, but you're wrong,' she cried. 'I'm all he's got now.'

Harshly, Jeff laughed. 'Boy, are you ever naive.'

Laura stared at him. 'What do you mean?' she asked quietly.

'Nothing,' Jeff said, quickly, sullenly.

'What do you mean?'

She had gone very pale.

'I don't think you want to know,' he said.

'There *is* nothing to know!' she told him tensely. 'You're just pretending there is. Just because you want to hurt me!' she added in a cry.

He stiffened. 'Is that what you think of me?' he asked her. 'All right then, you asked for it.'

Laura drove through Bel Air, along the endlessly winding mountain streets. It was a clear night and the lights of the city glittered beneath her. They were not warm lights; they burned with a multi-faceted coldness.

Thoughts were skidding, scattering through Laura's head. She reminded herself of a person on a hot beach, leaping insanely from spot to spot, unable to find a space that was cool enough to settle down. But every thought she touched upon sent her fleeing to another.

Tears ran unchecked along her cheeks.

How long had it been going on, her father and other women? Her mother had been dead less than two months.

Laura's hands jerked on the steering wheel, and the car swerved near the cliff. Laura forced herself to be calm. She told herself that she could understand his loneliness. She could understand all that. Of course she could. She didn't blame him. Of course she didn't. It was only natural. But another woman following Julia – following her mother – following Mama.

'Mark my words, he'll be re-married in six months and dead within the year,' Julia had laughed.

'Oh, no!' Laura had protested, shocked. 'Why, Mama, if anything ever happened to you, Daddy would be devastated. He'd never marry again.'

'Sure he would,' Julia shrugged. 'Some little girl from the third row of the chorus. She'll take him for every penny he's got, and throw out all my furniture.'

'What do you want with all these ugly antiques?' she'll say. 'Let's re-do the whole thing in Chinese Modern.'

Then Julia and Laura had laughed at the absurdity of it – the absurdity of the thought that Julia was ever going to die at all.

Laura's driving was getting unsteady again. Her hands kept fumbling off the steering wheel, and the car kept jerking from side to side as if it were suspended from a noose. All around her were dark streets, nameless. Even though, rationally, she knew that people lived in those houses who could direct her, she felt too scared to test it out. Scared that there was in fact, nobody home in any of the houses, scared that nobody would ever be home, and that she would wander forever in the darkness.

She tried to see her life clearly – the way it would look if she were a character in a movie. For Laura could always solve the lives of characters in movies. And here was the movie: It was about a child who had once had everything – and had then grown up. Grown up to be weak, terrified, not terribly pretty. She had a boyfriend, but she loved him more than he loved her. She had a career, but it meant less than it used to. She had a father, but he was growing more distant by the day. And her life-long guiding star had just gone – super-nova – into oblivion.

There was no ending to the movie.

Laura slowed the car and stopped. She put her head down on the steering wheel, and stayed by the side of the road.

I am lost, she thought. *Totally lost. I am completely without direction and I have no idea which way to go.*

Chapter Five

She had the dream again. Once more he was sitting with her underneath the tree. This time he was angry. She was defending herself; and woke up.

The morning sun was bitter in Laura's eyes. She felt cramped and cold. For a moment, there was stillness. Then it came back to her. Her father dating women. The fight with Jeff. The drive through Bel Air. And she felt like the sunlight had punched her in the stomach.

Jeff stirred beside her. Laura could not bear facing him yet, after what had happened, so she went into the bathroom and got into the shower. She stayed there nearly half an hour, telling herself that the water was warming her.

The bathroom door opened. Jeff came in. Laura watched him anxiously through the frosted glass, wondering what he was going to say. He said nothing. Calmly, he brushed his hair, his teeth. Evenly, he shaved. Laura stood hunched in the running shower, like an ostrich seeking cover, but Jeff did not once look in her direction. And soon afterwards he left.

Fine, Laura thought with numb anger. *If he wants to be that way, fine.* She stood under the shower a few minutes more. Then she knew with sudden clarity that it wasn't fine at all, that she couldn't under any circumstances have Jeff angry with her. She hurried out of the shower, throwing a towel around herself.

'Jeff?' she called, running into the bedroom, but he had already gone.

She looked around. On her pillow was a piece of paper. She went over to it, her heart fluttering with warm relief. An apology note. But when she shook out the paper, she saw that it was no such thing. It was a picture from the *Inquirer*, a photo of her father, holding hands at Nicky Blair's with a blond starlet of the soaps. Laura looked at the picture for a long, cold moment. Then she crumpled it up and threw it in the wastebasket.

She sat for several minutes, stupidly. The phone rang.

'Hi, sweetie,' her father said.

He sounded uneasy.

'Hope I didn't call too early – there's something I've been meaning to discuss with you.'

She braced herself for it. He was going to tell her about the women himself.

'It's about your mother's car.'

'Oh,' she said.

'Are you still interested in it?' Blake asked crisply. 'Because if you're not, I've had an offer from someone who is.'

Laura sensed that he did not want her to be still interested – that he would be happy if he never saw Julia's car again. And that filled her with fury.

'Of course I'm still interested,' she snapped.

'I don't think you can drive it.'

'Oh, yes, I can,' Laura told him tightly. 'I'll be over in fifteen minutes.'

Blake hung up the phone, did a few minutes' work. Then he buzzed Alison on the intercom.

'Could you please come in here?'

In a second, she was there, unctuously with memo pad.

'I want to go over the week's schedule,' he said. 'Make an appointment with my barber for Tuesday at twelve;

79

Wednesday, I have a lunch with Buzz Talbot...' He went through the list; she wrote down the appointments. Then finally he coughed and added casually, 'And make a reservation at the Escoffier Room for Saturday night at eight – dinner for two.'

Blake looked down at his desk as he said it, but he could feel Alison's instantly sharp interest.

'And what shall I write on your personal schedule?' she asked. 'Whom shall I write is your guest?'

'Just write "Dinner for two," ' he informed her coldly.

'Very well,' she said delicately.

Blake flushed. It was ridiculous to feel so uncomfortable, he told himself angrily. Julia was dead. He couldn't live in the past forever. Still, that tone in Alison's voice. Ever since the dating had begun, he had made the dinner reservations himself – called the restaurants in a furtive tone, made sure that the ladies never came to the house. And that the servants, especially Alison, saw nothing. But that was foolishness. He had a right to go out. To be happy. He had nothing to be ashamed of. And why shouldn't he feel as comfortable about telling Alison to make the dinner reservations as he did about having her book his next dentist's appointment? Yet it shook him, her secretive, smug smile.

What do you know about it? he wanted to cry. *What do you know about the way I feel?* The eeriness, the unnaturalness of it all. Dating again. Taking women's phone numbers at parties. Being fixed up by friends like a High School kid. Hearing strange voices on answering machines. Meeting women who were not Julia. Smelling perfumes that were not Julia's. Holding hands that were not Julia's.

He glared at Alison.

And then his thoughts veered suddenly, upwardly,

onto the woman he was taking to the Escoffier Room on Saturday night. And magically, things lightened.

Yes, he thought. *Yes*. There was no doubt about it. Starting to date again was the best possible thing. And Julia, above anyone else, would want him to do it.

As if the changed energy in his mood had released something, Alison rose suddenly. 'Will there be anything else?' she asked.

'No, thanks, that's all,' Blake told her pleasantly.

'I'll call the Escoffier Room right away. Saturday night, eight o'clock. Dinner for two.'

'Hi, Daddy,' Laura said quietly.

She had entered unnoticed from the secretary's office.

Blake turned sharply. Had she heard the date being discussed? He could not tell from her face. But the guilt and irritation swarmed back over him in an instant.

Damn her.

'You came about the car?' he snapped. 'Well, let's get to the garage.'

Laura and her father entered the garage. Julia's blue Mercedes stood there quiet, immaculate.

'I have Alison start the motor every few days,' Blake told Laura.

Laura thought about Julia, imaged inseparably with this car; driving it every day for all those years, and now Alison having to start its engine every week to keep the battery from dying.

Her mouth tightened.

'I'm ready to try it,' she said.

She got into the driver's seat.

'It's yours,' Blake said.

'Oh, honey!'

Julia threw her arms around his neck and kissed him

*over and over with desperate joy. It kept hitting her,
the glory – that the television show had sold, that the
days of the rusty, wheezing Buick were over. Tears
came. Blake giggled feebly at the smiling car salesman,
and added, 'And when I say it's yours, Julia, I mean
yours. I'm never going near this contraption – it's harder
to drive than a Mack truck! Why couldn't you have
gotten a Cadillac, like a normal human being?'*

*'I love it!' Julia flashed, laughing, still not letting go
of him. 'I love it, and I'm never going to own another
car as long as I live.'*

At the corner of Cove and Lexington, Laura put on the
brake. Tears were running down her cheeks. Her perspiring hands slipped finally off the steering wheel and she
rolled the car to a stop. She put her head in her hands,
defeated.

She had been able to drive Julia's car exactly a block
and a half.

'I knew this would happen,' her father kept saying.
He could not keep the glee out of his voice. 'Your
mother was the only one who could manage it.'

On the way home from her father's, Laura stopped at
the Brentwood Country Mart. She ordered an apple
juice, but felt sick when she tried to drink it. She wandered around, feeling numb, watching all the people. She
walked automatically over to the cast-iron toys and saw
a little boy sitting disconsolately on the motionless
green frog.

'Do you have a quarter?' he asked with sudden hope
as Laura walked by.

She had to laugh.

'Sure.'

She produced a quarter and put it into the meter. The

82

frog began to buck and bounce, the little boy began to giggle and glow, and Laura, for three minutes, was absolutely safe in the enjoyment of watching him. Her mother wasn't dead, her father wasn't seeing other women, Jeff wasn't angry at her, and she hadn't failed to drive the Mercedes.

But then the time ran out. The frog and child were lifeless again. Slowly, the little boy looked up at Laura. She put another quarter into the meter.

In the end, she put in enough money for six rides, and for eighteen minutes there was total reprieve of all worry and all wrong.

Then the little boy's mother came out of the grocery store and took him away.

Jeff was on his way to the gym. Driving down Wilshire, he came to the big brown cube that was Robinson's department store. On an impulse, he stopped, and went inside.

Jeff liked department stores. He liked the bustle, the soothing reassurance that something was always going on.

There was a 'Half price Sale' sign over the jewellery counter. Jeff walked over and looked down at the display. He saw a pair of gold hoop earrings, exactly the kind Laura had been looking for. He decided to get them for her as a surprise.

He felt much happier, having made that decision. He had been feeling a little guilty about the way he had treated Laura last night, yelling at her, telling her about her father, putting that picture on her pillow. True, he had been justified in everything. Still . . .

He looked up, smiling.

'Hi,' he said to the sales girl. She had been staring at him while he had been staring at the jewellery.

'Hi,' she said back.

He pointed to the hoop earrings. 'I'd like to get those.'

She took them out of the case, cleaned them adeptly, and pinned them in a velvet box. Then she punched the numbers into the cash register.

'Will this be cash or charge?'

'Charge,' he told her.

'That will be one hundred and seventy-eight dollars,' she said pleasantly.

Jeff flushed slightly. He pointed to the sign.

'It says all gold jewellery is fifty per cent off,' he reminded her.

'That's right,' she said. 'These earrings were over three hundred dollars. They're a real good buy.'

Jeff's hands tightened on the glass.

The sales girl was looking at him.

'Is there a problem?' she asked.

'No, no,' Jeff said smoothly. 'No problem at all.'

There was nothing else he could do. He had to take the damn earrings.

He left the store and stalked to the parking lot.

Fury stalked with him. Fury with himself for not having asked the price, and for not being able to easily afford the earrings at any cost. And fury with Laura for making him want to buy the present in the first place. *What does she want with hoop earrings, anyway? Who does she think she is – a fucking gypsy?* Then he started to get furious at his parents. They had all the money in the goddamned world. Why did he have to live like this? Why didn't they help him out? Why did he have to be humiliated at a department store? And he grew furious at Blake for not ever lifting a finger to get him a job. One phone call would do it. One fucking phone call.

And finally, most bitterly, Jeff grew furious at the sales girl at the Robinson's jewellery counter. Because

84

he had clearly seen, in that moment when she thought he couldn't afford the earrings, all the admiration die out of her eyes.

He hurled the earrings in the back of the car. Then he slumped over the steering wheel and put his head in his hands.

Jeff felt too beaten to go on to the gym. He drove back home. The anger was gone now. He felt vulnerable and alone. He wanted Laura to be there, waiting. He needed Laura, needed to talk to her, to make love with her, needed to have everything be all right between them again.

When he got to the apartment, she was not there. Jeff sat down on the unmade bed. He saw the photo from the *Inquirer* crumpled in the wastebasket.

What is happening to us? he wondered, chilled.

The phone ran. Hoping it was Laura, he picked it up quickly.

'Hello?'

'Hello, Jeff.'

It was the last person in the world he wanted to talk to now.

'Hi, Mom.'

There was a pause.

'What's the matter, dear? You sound tired.'

'Yes,' he said. 'I guess I am a little tired. I've been working a lot lately.'

'Really?'

He coughed. 'Doing a lot of commercials.'

There was another pause. Jeff knew exactly what his mother was thinking. That doing commercials was not working. He started to perspire.

'Everything all right with you?' he asked, trying to keep what he was feeling out of his voice.

'Oh, yes,' she said. Everything was always all right

85

with her. 'We've also been very busy.' And she told him about the three new mergers, and the acquisition. 'But the reason I'm calling – we're flying into L.A. tonight. We have a meeting tomorrow at City National, and the bank is flying us down. Can we have dinner? Laura, too, of course,' she added.

'Sure,' Jeff said, numb. 'That'd be great.'

'We'll pick you up at seven,' she said, and added gaily, 'Look gorgeous.'

Slowly, Jeff replaced the receiver.

Goddam it. Why did this have to happen today – today, when he couldn't take it? He jumped up and strode around the apartment. How did she manage it, always, by saying nothing, to make him feel so sure he was a failure; that he would always be a failure.

'I've been working a lot lately.'

'Really?'

'Doing a lot of commercials.'

And then that pause.

He straightened up. He looked around the apartment at the photographs of himself – Jeff Kennerly, looking so calm, so seductive, so confident. Taken right after he had graduated from Stanford, when the world was wonderful. Goddam putz.

He lit a cigarette, but he was too shaken to smoke. Damn. Damn. Time was moving on. Face it. He looked a little haggard in those last stills. And there had been three new blond guys at the gym last week. Jeff killed the cigarette in the ashtray. Oh, God, when would it be more than fucking commercials?

He picked up one of the framed pictures, and began to weep.

He was glad that she answered on the second ring. It seemed a good omen.

'Hello?'

'Hi, Desiree,' he said smoothly. 'This is Jeff.'

There was a pointed silence.

'Laura's Jeff?'

Damn, Jeff thought angrily.

'I just called to congratulate you,' he went on. 'I see in the trades this morning that they're doing one of your old plays at a little theatre in Antioch.'

'Thank you for calling my attention to it,' Desiree said drily. She had not needed to have her attention called.

'So what's going on with my favorite playwright these days?' Jeff asked.

'Nothing much,' Desiree told him lightly. 'Other than the morning decision: Will it or will it not be euthanasia today?'

He laughed.

'We ought to have lunch together sometime, Desiree, and talk about these things. Maybe I can help.'

There was a long pause.

'Aren't you very busy?' she asked him.

'Not too busy to have lunch with you.'

'Well, then, you ought to be.' And although she added, 'A talented actor like you,' he knew what she had meant, and his face flushed.

'I hope you'll excuse me now,' Desiree went on. 'Your Laura is coming to tea, and I have to get things ready.'

Jeff hung up the phone. Though he called Desiree a bitch and laughed the incident off, all afternoon it left him feeling sore. Failed and sore. He had thought that calling her would make him feel better. He had been so sure she would agree to lunch, and she had not.

There was no doubt about it.

'You're slipping,' he whispered. *Slipping. Slipping.*

When Laura came home from the Brentwood Mart, Jeff was not there. She felt exhausted. She lay in bed for half an hour and then something started to prick at her. *Damn*, she thought wearily. *I promised to go to tea at Desiree Kaufman's today.*

It was the last thing on earth she felt like doing. She considered the alternative – telephoning, lying, re-scheduling, but in the end, she decided just to get it over with.

With a sigh, she rose and dressed.

Desiree's condominium was on 3rd Street, near Doheny. Laura, afraid she wouldn't be able to find a space, ended up parking several blocks too early, and having to walk. Uncomfortably, she hurried toward Desiree's address. It was an eerie area, with many dark, tangled vacant lots and seedy buildings. Laura felt sure she had the wrong street – this was not the environment she envisioned Desiree Kaufman to be living in. And then she came to Desiree's building, and smiled grudgingly. The building was perfection – a little Regency jewel, its front yard airy and well-kept, its paint flawless. Even the sign in front was made of hand-painted Italian tile. While next door, a sad-looking black man sat on his broken porch chair and drank something from a paper bag.

Shyly, Laura rang the bell. Desiree let her in without a fuss, without saying she was glad to see her.

The house seemed very odd to Laura. She was used to her mother's homes, which were open-hearted museums to the Alden past, the Alden way of life. But Desiree's home was completely, purposefully imper-sonal, as if it were daring an onlooker to draw any con-clusions about its owner. The furniture was modern, functional, in unexceptional colors. There were no plants, no pictures on the walls, no plaques or awards pointing up Desiree's career, no tidbits in the bookcase. No questions were invited.

And then, little by little, Laura did find clues. The humidifier in the living room. The massage table in a corner of the bathroom. The huge gym bag half hidden beneath the sofa. The yogurt maker in the kitchen. The bathroom scale weighing to the half ounce. The collection of Jean Sanders' fitness books in the bookcase. *Why, Desiree's afraid of getting old*, Laura suddenly realized. She felt an odd shock of something almost like pity.

Desiree was watching her. She saw Laura looking around, trying hard to find something to praise, and she smiled wryly. *She's comparing it to Julia's house*, Desiree thought. *And she's finding it empty*. She felt obscurely stung. *Well, Julia could afford to have memories*.

Then suddenly she raised her head.

'Come here,' she said. 'I want you to see something.'

Desiree was surprised at herself. She had not shown anyone the shrine in her bedroom in a long time. And she had certainly not planned to show it to Laura.

Desiree disappeared into the bedroom for a moment, and rearranged a few things. Then she told Laura to come in.

Laura entered the room, looked up, and gasped. Two entire walls were crammed with photographs, floor to ceiling. She had never seen such a monument. She found herself relaxing at the sight of them. So there *were* memories here, after all.

She eyed the kaleidoscope of photographs carefully. First, she sought out the many pictures of Julia. How young she was – gaily-dressed, excited. And beside her in many of the photos was Desiree – dark, glowing, at ease. There were, Laura observed, no pictures of her father. Nor, of course, any of herself. She did notice, in the very center of one wall, a large blank space. She wondered if anyone had ever filled it, or whether someone had been taken away.

And then, at the very top of the grouping, she saw a black and white photograph of a little girl. She was about four years old. She was dressed as a fairy princess, complete with wand and wings. In her hand was a bulging Hallowe'en trick-or-treat bag, and on her face was a look of grinning anticipation.

Laura laughed aloud with delight. 'That must be you!' she cried.

'No,' Desiree told her. There was a strange note in her voice.

'But it looks exactly like you,' Laura pursued.

Desiree did not answer.

They had tea in the beige dining room, at the smooth white formica table. Away from the life in those photographs, Laura started feeling uncomfortable again. The atmosphere was as lifeless as a doctor's waiting room. She wondered nervously if she and Desiree would talk, and what there would be to talk about.

'Have you been sleeping?' Desiree demanded suddenly. 'You're much too pale.'

Laura looked up, startled. Desiree's eyes held hers intensely. For a second she was tempted to tell Desiree everything – about her father and the women, and last night's fight with Jeff. And then she dropped her eyes again, angry at herself for even considering such a betrayal.

'I'm fine,' she told Desiree.

'I see,' Desiree told her.

She poured more tea.

'It's English Breakfast,' Laura said in an inane attempt to cover the blank. 'That was my mother's favorite.'

90

'Yes,' Desiree said. 'I know.' She paused for a long time. 'In fact, I was with Julia the first time she ever tried it.' She regarded Laura. 'Do you want to hear the story?' she asked offhandedly.

'Yes,' Laura said.

Desiree poured more tea.

'We were rehearsing for *Promenade*. We were both nineteen – and a very young nineteen at that. Julia had never been to New York before. She had always heard about the Palm Court, and it was the first place she wanted to go.' Desiree shook her head slightly. 'I will never forget her dress that day – black, with a little white collar and cuffs. And she wore a silk gardenia.'

Julia's silk gardenias. Julia rose before Laura now – nineteen, in her black dress.

'It was a wonderful afternoon,' Desiree went on. 'A magic afternoon. We had eclairs – and English Breakfast tea. Julia had never been in such a glamorous place before and she loved every second of it.' Desiree laughed. 'And then the bill came. Julia had just gotten her first paycheck from the play, and she insisted on treating. She was very proud, very nervous about doing everything just right. I told her that the most elegant society women not only tipped the waiter, but they gave the Captain two dollars as well. Of course, Julia wanted to do that, too. She took out the money from her purse. As we got up from our chairs, a man came up to us and smiled. Julia leaned forward very graciously, and pressed the two dollars in his hand. She made the gesture beautifully. Then we walked to the door – and standing there, hand outstretched, was the Captain.'

Laura began to giggle.

'Yes,' Desiree nodded. 'Julia had tipped a guest.'

Laura and Desiree laughed and laughed, there at the

91

white formica dining room table. And then suddenly they were both weeping.

Laura felt no shame, no sense of strangeness. They wept soundlessly, did not attempt to comfort the other. Finally it was over.

'I've been feeling Julia's presence a great deal since she died,' Desiree said at last, in an altered tone.

Laura found herself tensing. 'You mean – like a ghost?'

'Something like that,' Desiree said.

'I don't believe in any of that,' Laura told her tightly.

Desiree shrugged. 'Your mother did, you know. Very much so.'

'Yes,' Laura admitted. 'I know. Though, it's kind of funny,' she added in a slightly higher voice. 'As it turns out, I actually went to see a psychic yesterday.'

She hadn't meant to tell that.

'I see,' Desiree said. 'And what did you think?'

Laura was silent. She could not frame any answer that made sense.

'I see,' Desiree said again. She sounded amused.

No, you don't see, Laura thought crossly.

The crossness and the silence smouldered in the air for a moment, and then as if nothing had happened, Desiree began to talk. 'You and I have known each other for twenty-three years,' she said. 'But we have never known each other at all. Would you like to hear about me?'

Laura was startled, touched, by the odd openness.

'If you'd like to tell me,' she said.

For an hour, Desiree talked. And for an hour, Laura listened.

'I was seven when my mother deserted me,' Desiree began. She spoke with very little emotion, but with a sharpness of emphasis that excoriated the memory like a carving knife. 'I remember the day she left. It was

92

winter, and I had come in from skating. I had a little fur muff on. And in it I had hidden a present for my mother – a pretty rock I had found. She liked little things like that. She met me at the door. She was in travelling clothes, and her suitcases were in a pile. She was normally very pale, but that day her face was red, under her red hair. It looked very strange to me. I asked if she had a fever, if she were going to the hospital.

'She knelt down beside me and said that she was going away for a little while – not to the hospital, but to her sister's. And that she would be back soon.' Desiree smiled wryly. 'I will never forget how hard I tried to talk her out of going, coming up with reason after reason why she shouldn't go, and all the while, that very solid pile of suitcases stood there. Mocking me and my efforts. She was going, and that was the only reality. I believe that was the moment I decided to become a playwright,' Desiree went on lightly. 'For a playwright can achieve all the alternate realities he desires.

'Her taxi came and she kissed me goodbye. It was not until I went back into the house that I took off my muff and realized I had forgotten to give her the little rock.' Desiree shut her eyes. Under the grey eyeshadow she wore, the lids seemed very fragile. 'For some reason, this was unbearable to me. The rock not given, the last message of love undelivered.'

Laura felt sick and sharp with pity. She could see the muff. The little stone.

'She never returned,' Desiree went on briskly. 'She did not go to her sister's. It was to another man, of course. My parents divorced. I never saw her again. We were a prominent family,' she added lightly, 'and it created quite a stir in the newspapers.

'So I lived with my father,' she went on. 'Or, I should say, I lived at my father's house. He was not often home.

93

He was very wealthy, very handsome, and he encountered many draws more potent than a cross-eyed daughter.' She laughed. 'I did benefit from his homecomings, though. He brought me back wonderful presents. I especially liked the pony.'

Desiree stirred sugar into her tea with a strange, mesmerized movement.

'Once, when I was twelve, he promised to take me to Europe with him. I'll never forget the excitement I felt. I planned, I packed three suitcases, I read all about the places we were going to visit. My father was away – the night before we were to set sail, he came back to the house. He saw all my preparations and started to laugh. He said he couldn't believe I had taken him seriously. That he was going to Europe, but with a girlfriend.' Desiree put the spoon carefully down. 'I didn't unpack my suitcases,' she said quietly. 'We lived near the Hudson River. I threw them in the river, one at a time, and watched them sink.'

Laura could say nothing.

'He was killed when I was sixteen. They said it was a drunk driver. I was never quite convinced.' She paused for a long time. 'I saw the body,' she added expressionlessly. 'It was hard to imagine my father less than spotless but there he was, on the street, covered with blood. It's strange – how that one moment seemed to re-touch all the earlier images.'

Laura remembered her own father in the hospital, the day Julia had died, and the shock of seeing him in a rumpled suit. She closed her eyes. She felt like sobbing and sobbing, and throwing herself ridiculously on Desiree, saying that she understood.

Desiree was still talking, in that same low voice. 'After my father died, the court sent me to boarding school. I hated it there. I had no friends. I did nothing but stay in my room and write. In my Junior year, a literary magazine called *Nimbus* sponsored a contest for young playwrights. I made myself enter the contest. Three weeks later, they wrote to me and said I had won. First place, nationwide.'

'Fantastic,' Laura said.

Desiree smiled oddly.

'Fantastic,' she echoed. Then she shook her head, still smiling. 'But it was not so fantastic.' And her next words burned into Laura like quick-lime. 'For you see, Laura, there was nobody left for me to tell.'

Then, abruptly, Desiree stood up. The poignancy sheered instantly from her. 'It's getting late,' she said briskly. 'I have a dinner engagement at seven. I have to start getting ready.'

She walked Laura to the door, and said goodbye. And Laura left.

All the drive home, Laura's mind flowed with Desiree. All these years, and she had never realized. All these years, and she had never dreamed what Desiree was; never dreamed that Desiree Kaufman could ever touch her like this. Laura felt dazed, overloaded with images. The father. The pony. The pretty little rock. The blood on the sidewalk. *There was nobody left for me to tell.*

Laura reached Santa Monica. On an impulse, she pulled next to the flower shop on the corner and went inside.

'I'd like to send a dozen roses to this address,' she told the salesgirl. 'And here's the message: "Congratulations on winning the playwriting contest. And I'm here for you to tell." '

A few blocks away from her apartment building, Laura started to feel anxious about going home. The whole experience with Desiree, so overlaid with emotion and revelation, now drained to absolutely nothing. Reality – the fight with Jeff, and having to face him again – now came back into painful focus. Her heart began to jar uncomfortably.

She took the stairs rather than the elevator, but inevitably she arrived in front of her apartment. The closed door looked ominous. She listened, but could not hear any sounds from within. Finally, she put her key in the lock and pushed open the door.

And to her joy, she was met with cleanliness, music, and the smell of roses.

'Oh!' Laura sighed. She felt as grateful as Dorothy, opening that grey Kansas farmhouse door and finding herself in Oz.

'Jeff!' she cried.

But when he came out of the bedroom, Laura could tell instantly that she had been wrong – none of this was for her.

'Where the hell have you been?' he asked tightly. 'I had to get this goddam place cleaned up by myself. My parents are coming in fifteen minutes.'

Laura looked at him, aghast. 'Your parents?' she gasped. 'Why didn't you tell me?'

'Because you were out,' he told her bitterly, and added, 'Probably seeing your psychic.'

Laura stared at him helplessly.

What horrible timing, she thought. *It's cruel. It's spiteful. Why do his parents have to come tonight?* She knew what evenings with the Kennerlys always did to Jeff. *Oh, I wish we hadn't had that damn fight*, she mourned. She wanted to rush to Jeff, hug him, remind him that they were a team and that nothing his parents could do to him mattered. So she started towards him, but as she passed the coffee table, she happened to glance down at the flowers on the table. They were tagged with Jeff's mother's name.

And she wanted to cry out, 'Why don't you love *me* enough to buy *me* roses?'

She turned without a word and went into the bedroom.

'How nice to see you, Laura,' chic, petite Sarah Kennerly said coolly. She looked with pained politeness at the black pantsuit.

'Nice to see you, too,' Laura said, her throat dry.

'Have you been working on a new little storybook?'

'Yes,' Laura answered in a rush. 'It's about a French hippo called Philippe, who thinks he's – '

'Jeff, darling!'

Jeff came into the room. Sarah Kennerly closed her eyes and gave herself to the rapture of hugging her son.

'Laura! How are you? Great to see you!'

Mac Kennerly, a large, expensive-looking man, followed his wife into the apartment.

'You're looking absolutely fabulous,' he told her heartily.

'Thank you,' Laura said uneasily.

When she had first met Mr Kennerly, she had liked him. She had been so grateful for his easy friendliness and had thought that, unlike his wife, he was on her side. But a few months ago, during a fight, Jeff had enlightened her – he had said that his father had told him that Laura was an absolute joke, and that nobody could understand what Jeff even saw in her.

'Well,' Sarah Kennerly straightened up and beamed at Jeff. 'Let's have dinner!'

They got into the grey limousine the bank had provided.

There wasn't room for all four in the back, so Laura offered to use the jump seat. Her offer was accepted.

She perched queasily, listening to the three Kennerlys talk about things back home in Colorado. She wondered why it worried her so that Jeff had never invited her back to Denver, to his house and places of the past. *Because they're not important enough to him, that's why*, she told herself staunchly.

They went to the Mandarin. It was not a happy choice. Mr Kennerly didn't like the table. Mrs Kennerly didn't like the sake. Mr Kennerly sent the soup back. Mrs Kennerly found the orange beef inedible. Jeff sat there sullenly. And Laura chattered like an idiot.

The evening resembled Quasimodo – every moment bulging with a thousand innuendos, jealousies, dislikes.

'When are you moving back to Denver, Jeff?' Mr Kennerly came to the point at last. 'The business is getting to the stage now where I could really use you. What do you say?'

But no one said anything. Frantic fantasies began to surge through Laura's head. *Why doesn't Jeff tell him that he's never going into the damned business?* she thought hysterically. *Why doesn't he say, "I'm an actor and a good one, and why can't you bloody well accept that?"* And she looked over at Mrs Kennerly eating her vegetables with downcast eyes like a malevolent cow. *She's loving it*, Laura thought. *She doesn't have to get involved; she can just be a martyr and enjoy her son's throwing his life away on a rotten career and a rotten girl. And she should be so proud of him! She should be so proud of him! And I'm the worst one of all*, Laura told herself despairingly. *Why am I letting them do this to Jeff? Why don't I just turn the whole table over in their laps? They didn't like this table anyway – and Lord knows they hate the food.*

'And that little Annette Pervald would certainly be glad to see you, Jeff,' Mrs Kennerly added thoughtfully. 'She came out this season, and you won't believe what a beauty she's turned out to be.'

It was at this point that Laura excused herself and went into the Ladies' Room and cried for fifteen minutes.

'And we're all of us nice people,' she was wailing to the restroom attendant, throwing out her fifth sopping Kleenex. 'Really we are. But I just can't help hating them so much. And you can't imagine how much they hate me. It's like we're different species. It's like an ostrich trying to talk to an amoeba. It's just impossible.'

The attendant watched her with black, impassive eyes. 'I'm sure I don't know, miss,' she said, and looked with a sigh at the little change dish by the sink.

'And it's just so damned miserable,' Laura whispered. She looked through her purse but she could not find a quarter. With narrowed eyes, the washroom attendant watched her leave.

When Laura came back to the table, she could sense that some sort of scene had occurred in her absence. Mrs Kennerly's eyes were red, Jeff was even paler than before and Mr Kennerly was more booming.

'Laura, you're really looking great,' he burst out suddenly, as though this was the first time he had seen her all evening. 'Isn't Laura a great-looking girl, Sarah?' he demanded. Then he paused and added sadly, 'I just wish she wore a little more eyeshadow.'

This was too much. Laura began to rock with wild, uncouth laughter. The three Kennerlys stared at her, ostriches at an amoeba. Then Jeff said suddenly, 'For your information, I wouldn't love her if she did.'

And he pulled Laura to her feet and they left the restaurant.

They were in bed and had lain there without speaking for half an hour. Finally Jeff cleared his throat.

'I'm – sorry about all that,' he said in a low voice.

'Forget it,' Laura rushed in. 'Your parents just want what's best for you.'

But she knew that Jeff was apologizing for a lot more than the evening, and her heart rushed towards his in a glowing wave.

'So – can we two be friends again?' he asked, like a gruff little boy.

'We're friends,' she answered him softly.

She looked at him lying there, and was filled with the perfection of him and of her love for him.

'There's only one thing that bothers me,' he said slowly.

'And what's that?' she asked, knowing that she would see to it that it never bothered him again.

'That psychic.'

She almost laughed aloud. She had forgotten all about him.

'I understand that you went on account of your father – but you've got to promise me you'll never see him again.'

She smiled. 'That's a real easy one,' she said. 'I promise.'

He smiled also. 'Then I've got something for you,' he told her.

He reached over to the bedside table and gave her the earrings from Robinson's.

She was so grateful and so happy and so excited that,

watching her, Jeff thought, *I would have bought them if they'd cost a thousand dollars.*

And he pulled her to him and began to make love to her.

At three in the morning, Blake woke up and couldn't breathe. The very darkness was striving to suffocate him, a hairy black hand over his throat. He reached for the phone and knocked it over. He pulled it up again by the cord, and felt in the darkness for the button that would automatically re-dial the last number he had called.

The phone was picked up on the second ring, and the voice was a knife that instantly broke the death-clasp of the darkness.

Chapter Six

Even the first touch of morning sun was cruel against Desiree's face. She liked the night hours; candle-light, starlight. But light by itself was too naked a word. The bed felt unpleasantly hot around her. She had been having dreams again – dreams of him – and she could still feel the yearning of them in the dampness of the bedclothes.

She lay for fifteen minutes more, feeling the sun grow inexorably brighter. She straightened the bedclothes around her, and felt that the dampness had dried. No trace of those dreams was left now. Although she knew it was no use trying to get back to sleep, she did it anyway. As she did every morning.

By her bed, her humidifier hummed helpfully, but the sound was irritating, not lulling, and Desiree switched it off. The silence created was awful. She switched the machine back on, smiling wryly. She had not realized how used she had become to that humidifier – both the hypnotism of its sound and the illusion that it would keep her face young forever.

She lay flat, her head touching only the edge of her hypoallergenic pillow. She had lain that way when she had been a child, in the days when sleep had come so effortlessly. Then she reached over to the bedside table, picked up her ice-blue sleep mask, and put it over her eyes. With it on, the daylight disappeared for Desiree, but she still felt it just outside the fence of plastic, waiting to pounce.

Today she must start the new play.

The little thought dropped into her mind like a cyanide tablet. Desiree tore off the mask and sat upright, gasping. And the perspiration started again, dampening her Natori nightgown.

Nonsense, she told herself, the way one would tell a child who is afraid of shadows. *There is nothing to be frightened of.* She had written many plays. There were still people who thought she was the best playwright in the country.

Rising quickly from the bed, Desiree went over to her huge walk-in closet. It had been beautifully arranged several years ago by a professional decorator, and Desiree saw to it that the organization was maintained. Dresses and trousers hung, grouped by color and style, sweaters lay in fragrant nests of cedar chips. The few out-of-style clothes she had saved for sentimental reasons were stored discreetly at the back. On one of these shelves was a silk gardenia that had belonged to Julia.

One whole wall of the closet was taken up with gym equipment – the personal massage table, proportioned to fit Desiree's body, the slant board, the Stairmaster. Desiree pushed past these now to a small brass trunk. And from it she pulled three worn leather scrapbooks.

She had not looked at them in years.

Strange, but she felt almost furtive, holding them now. She did not even wish to take them back into the bedroom, but sat down on the floor of the closet and opened them there. It was a shock to see how yellowed the pages had become. *Acid from the smog*, Desiree told herself firmly. *Not time.*

She turned the pages. There were programs from award ceremonies, reviews of her plays; xeroxed copies of interviews, newspaper photos of herself. How terribly young she looked.

There were no reviews of her last four plays in the scrapbook. What was the sense in keeping them, after all? Desiree did not believe in dwelling on the negative. And yet – how strange. Every word of those reviews was simply there in her memory, growing there and clinging.

Damn. Damn.

Angrily, she pushed the books back into the chest, and then moved the chest back behind the massage table. She left the closet swiftly. She would feel better once she got out of the house. Once she got to the gym. Quickly, she dressed in her hand-painted designer warm-up suit. There. She did feel better – hadn't she known she would? Triumphantly, she started to leave the room, but halfway out the door, she stopped. Her glance had fallen onto the photographs covering the walls. Unwillingly, irresistibly, she was drawn backwards to them. She was annoyed at herself for letting this happen. She had been doing too much of this reminiscing lately – far too much.

Desiree thought of yesterday's visit, and how she had made the images of the past dance like little manic marionettes for Laura. It had been quite a show. She found herself wondering why she had told Laura so much.

I didn't have to. A lot less would have spellbound her.

She guessed it had been the playwright in her responding to an audience – any audience. And there was always something especially gratifying about being admired by a young person. But that was not all there was to it, Desiree felt uncomfortably. It was also something to do with Laura and the look – almost Julia's look – that had come at times into her eyes.

Sentimental idiot! Desiree thought impatiently. The truth was that she had gotten real comfort from that look, and she had gotten real comfort from telling Laura all those stories. Stories she had wanted to tell no one else in years. And there were so many more of them. Perhaps she would ask Laura back to tea next week.

Something strange is developing here, Desiree thought. *I wonder what it is.*

She found that her eyes had tears in them. She walked over to the wall of pictures and touched them with hands that were very cold. She found herself looking first at the pictures of Julia — the ones Laura had been looking at yesterday. And then she moved onto the pictures of Leo. There were three of them — one taken on their wedding day, one from the fifth anniversary party, and one on holiday in Greece. Desiree went up to the last one, and scanned it closely. She had never before noticed the way he was looking at her in that picture. It created chills that raised the fair hair on Desiree's arms. *I would kiss the ground fasting for another look like that*, she thought. But at the time, she had taken it all as her due. Just as she had taken the brilliant reviews, the awards.

Desiree put her hands over her face. *What on earth is the matter with me today?* she wondered wearily. *I'll feel better when I get to the gym.*

It occurred to Desiree that it was a trifle sad that all the pictures she cared about were twenty-five years old. She smiled wryly. That would be a nice touch in the new play. A character who lives a life populated entirely by old photographs. And then Desiree's eyes fell upon the center of the wall, which was blank. She took from a drawer the picture which she had removed yesterday, and she put it back. It looked incongruous with all those other fading pictures — this one was new; brash and

105

alive and bursting with vitality. She had clipped it from *People* magazine two weeks before.

Desiree found herself smiling. Suddenly there was a pump of excitement working in her body. What did it matter that she hadn't heard from him in nearly a month? What did it matter that her friends said he was seeing Andrea Galanos now? Andrea Galanos was a little nobody; he would tire of her in a week. And nobody ever tired of Desiree Kaufman. *I am a survivor*, Desiree thought. That pleased her. She leaned near the humidifier. A survivor with soft cheeks.

Who knows? Maybe he's tired of Andrea Galanos already. Maybe I'll get a call from him today.

Yes, she thought. She could feel it. Today was going to be fine. All kinds of possibilities were taking shape. She was off to the gym now. She would work at the new machines. And the play?

She would begin the play tomorrow.

Jeff left early the next morning for a meeting with his agent. Laura lay in bed, watching him dress.

'Get my grey suit back from the cleaners,' he was saying. 'And could you pick up some mailing envelopes at the stationers?'

She regarded him in silence, superimposing over this preoccupied, business-like man the image of the consuming lover he had been the night before.

What do I mean to him, these mornings after? she wondered. *Does he love me just as much, or is it all different?*

Jeff kissed her on the top of the head and left.

Laura worked all morning on her new story about Philippe, the French hippo. It was going pretty well, she thought. It was amazing that even when everything else was so unclear, she was still able to write her stories and draw her pictures. Well, she guessed her mother had been right. She was at bottom still a child, writing books for herself.

But when the pages were finished, so was the sense of accomplishment. She felt drained, depressed. The day lay before her like an over-exposed photograph, blurred, unreadable.

She decided to take a drive. She dressed and got into the car. She turned on the engine, having not the slightest idea where she was going. When she reached Wilshire, the light turned green. She made a right turn instead of a left, simply because it was the easiest thing to do. She kept going down Wilshire, and finally the road dead-ended. She had reached the ocean.

Laura parked the car, and walked along the little seaside park. The benches were filled with the homeless – street people whose lives lay in unfinished chapters. She felt frightened. They seemed like a vortex, drawing her in to the point where she could not even bear to look at them. But there was one young woman she could not help seeing for her hair looked just like Laura's own. Laura shivered. She should have gone to the Santa Monica Mall, to the pier – anywhere but here.

This is ridiculous, she thought firmly. *These people have nothing to do with me. I will go down to the beach. I will find a smooth white patch of sand. And I will just sit there until I feel safe again.*

And she started down the hill.

On the beach she found a wholly alternate collection. Lovely young girls on spring break from High School, completely happy because they were completely absorbed in themselves. Laura listened to their dramatic talk of parents and teachers and the boys who were expected to come to the beach that afternoon.

It was heedless and hard and charming – and it made Laura lonely for the dream of being sixteen years old again.

But why? she wondered. *I was never like that.*

Those girls were as far from her as the homeless up there on the hill.

She lay down, anonymous, on the sand. Unquestioning, cool, not particularly welcoming, it accepted the imprint of her body as it accepted the imprint of everyone.

Unconnected, she thought. *I am unconnected.*

She went to sleep.

'Laura! Laura!' came into the unconnectedness.

She thought it was a dream. But when she opened her eyes she found him standing next to her, kicking sand all over in his excitement.

'What are *you* doing here?' she asked, too groggy for surprise.

'I was out jogging. Good for the build.' And he patted his puny chest and microscopic muscles triumphantly.

'I'm so glad to see you,' he told her. 'You've got to come back to my apartment. I've got something special to show you.'

He knelt beside her, and beamed at her expectantly.

Laura looked at him, amazed. The change in him was incredible. Gone was all the madness. His hair was spiking every which way, and his face was smudged with sweat and sand. Today he was no more than a child-like figure of fun.

'I can't,' she said.

'Oh, but it'll only take a minute,' he pleaded, smiling.

She looked up at him sharply.

Oh, what the hell, she thought suddenly. She had had such a depressing, eerie morning. In some weird way, this felt almost like a rescue. A bit of company for a few minutes, a cup of tea.

And then Laura stopped herself short. What was she thinking of? This was not company. This was Christopher Garland.

'I'm sorry,' she told him coldly. 'I really can't.'

His face looked suddenly embarrassed, blank, stricken – the way it had when she had refused his blessing the other day. The memory of that made her flush.

'Please,' he said quietly.

'Oh, all right,' she told him edgily. 'But just for one minute.'

When they reached the apartment, Christopher went into the bedroom.

'Close your eyes,' he told Laura and he brought out the surprise.

Laura opened her eyes, and smiled.

It was an old still from *I Love Lucy*.

She took the picture from his hand and looked at it. What memories came. Sitting in her father's den, doing her algebra homework, watching the old RCA set, and laughing at Lucy's escapades. It had been her nightly ritual for years, as much a part of her life as Sunday hair-washing and the Brentwood Mart.

She touched the photograph gently. And it all came back to her – what it had been like to be sixteen. Not the alien adolescence of those girls she had seen on the beach today, but *her* sixteen – her own stubborn, precious, iridescent sixteen.

It was like a sudden little gift of re-connection.

For the next half hour, she and Christopher topped each

other with *I Love Lucy* memories. Lucy as the Wicked City Woman. Lucy and the Grapefruit. Lucy and the Transatlantic cheese. Lucy and Bill Holden and setting her nose on fire. They recited scenes of dialogue; they capped each other on trivia. They laughed and laughed and laughed.

Finally, Laura lay back on the sofa, with an aching groan.

'No more,' she told him.

Christopher smiled at her. 'Would you like some tea?'

'No,' she said. 'I'd better be going.'

'Just one cup,' he told her.

She paused. She knew she shouldn't stay, but this floating feeling of having laughed was still with her, and she didn't want to let go.

I've been having fun, she thought, amazed. *I've been really having fun.*

'All right,' she said.

She watched him make the tea.

She thought of the last time she had been in this apartment; thought of Christopher's pale angry face saying, *It's not your father who's easily manipulated by the wrong people. It's you.* The finality with which he had slammed the door behind her. The finality with which she had driven home. Yet, incredibly, here they were now, drinking tea.

'Isn't it strange?' she blurted out. 'Your chancing on me at the beach the way you did.'

Christopher sighed. 'Oh, Laura,' he said with amusement, 'I didn't think *anyone* believed in coincidence anymore – not even you.'

She let that pass.

He was looking at her closely.

'What's wrong?' he asked gently. 'Why are you so sad today?'

'We've done nothing but laugh for the last half hour,' she reminded him sharply.

He shook his head. 'I asked you, why are you so sad?'

She persisted that she was not sad. But he would not look away from her. And finally she added, in a lower voice, 'I guess it's just that – life's so complicated.'

'Life's not complicated at all,' he said. 'It's we who choose to complicate it. And usually we do that to make smokescreens. So that we can keep from facing the real simple issue.' He put down his teacup. 'And what's the real simple issue, Laura?'

She dropped her eyes.

'I guess,' she said in a small, foolish voice, 'I guess it's that Jeff won't ask me to marry him.'

And then she felt angry at herself and ashamed.

But Christopher made no response at all. It was as if he hadn't even heard. He took another sip of his tea, looked out of the window. And then suddenly he stood up.

'I almost forgot,' he said. 'I have something for you.' And he went into his bedroom. He came out a minute later, holding out a little package. 'All wrapped up for you,' he grinned, 'for when you *accidentally* came by.'

Laura unwrapped the package. Inside was a little gold and turquoise ring.

She drew back. 'What is this?' she asked.

'It's Carmen's ring,' Christopher told her. 'She came to me the other night and said she wanted you to have it.'

Laura blinked. 'Who's Carmen?'

'My teacher.'

Laura took the proferred ring, held it for a moment. It was a beautiful ring. She would love a little ring like this. Then she jerked back to the reality of who was offering it to her, and she handed it back to Christopher.

'I can't accept this,' she told him. 'I don't even know your teacher. Why should she want me to have her ring?'

Christopher shrugged. 'I haven't a clue. She just said, "Give the ring to Laura." '

He kept smiling at her as if in some private joke and Laura felt suddenly out of her depth, not equal to pursuing it.

'Well, tell her I said thanks, anyway.'

At this, Christopher burst out laughing, and Laura suddenly understood the private joke.

'Carmen's dead, too, isn't she?' she asked angrily.

'Yes,' he said.

Her voice rose. 'First my mother, now Carmen. What is this? Are you some kind of cosmic host to ghosts?' She glared at him. 'We were having a nice time. Why did you have to go and spoil it by starting in with this crazy talk again?' She felt ridiculously disappointed, out of control. 'I want to go home.'

Christopher hurried over to her. 'Wait. Please,' he said quickly. 'Just let me explain.' His face was anxious and upset. 'And then you can go home.'

Laura looked at him narrowly.

He sat next to her on the couch. 'What I'm saying is not crazy talk, Laura,' he told her. 'What I'm telling you is the truth.'

She watched him. Once more his eyes were growing opaque. Chills breathed over her.

'Bodies die,' he said. 'But consciousness has nothing to do with the body. Consciousness is energy; and energy can't be destroyed. It just changes frequency, that's all. That's all death is – a change-over to a new frequency.' He shrugged. 'It's so simple, really. But most people seem to have such a hard time with it. They get so focussed in on the frequency of this one reality that they filter out all the others. But, believe me, they're

112

there.' He smiled. 'And very reachable. Once you learn how, you can travel to all kinds of planes of existence. Why, just yesterday,' he went on, leaning forward eagerly, 'I visited the most extraordinary system of reality. Where language was expressed in terms of pure color.'

There was a long pause.

Laura swallowed. She was at a total loss. 'How interesting,' she said at last.

She could not stop staring at him, and his opaque eyes.

'Have you always been like this?' she blurted out.

Christopher grinned at her. 'Nuts, you mean?'

They both laughed.

He shook his head, and settled back against the sofa. 'No. Before I met Carmen, I was a so-called normal human being – about as spiritual as a frankfurter. But the day I met her, everything changed. My whole world turned upside down. The spiritual search became the only important thing in my life. I quit my job, gave up my condo, ended up losing most of my friends.' He laughed, shrugged. 'Quite an adjustment. I studied with Carmen until she died. And now that she's gone, I teach others what she taught me.'

'And what's that?'

'Don't worry,' Christopher twinkled. 'I'm not going to tell you. Let's just say, certain principles. Certain principles of life.'

'I see,' she said again.

There was another long silence.

'But I want you to know something, Laura,' he told her unexpectedly. 'Before I gave it all up, I was the best photographer *The Hollywood Reporter* ever had. I really want you to know that.'

She felt oddly touched.

'I'm sure you were,' she said.

Then she looked at her watch. 'I'd better go,' she told him. 'Or I'm going to hit killer traffic.'

She stood up. Christopher stood watching her. Laura felt suddenly shy.

'Well,' she said formally. 'Thank you for –' She thought of all that had gone on in the visit, and finished simply, 'Thank you for showing me the Lucy photo.'

'Won't you let me give you a blessing this time?' Christopher asked her.

Laura looked at the vial of oil on his countertop. *Oh, what the hell*, she thought. *What harm could it do?*

'Okay,' she said.

Christopher beamed. He drew a little triangle on her forehead with the oil, whispered some words, and gave Laura a hug.

She left him and went outside. The sun had come out, and it sailed on the water, like a set of tiny golden boats, in a dancing race.

On the drive home, she thought about Christopher. That ridiculous body in those Bermuda shorts. The MGM studio mug. Carmen's ring. *Your mother's no more dead than you are . . . Yesterday I visited the most extraordinary system of reality. Where language was expressed in terms of pure color . . .* The way they had laughed over Lucy and the meat freezer.

How bizarre it all was. Laura shrugged. But somehow it had turned out all right – somehow it had managed to change the whole day. A feeling of peace floated about her, and she kept smelling the sweet oil Christopher had put on her forehead.

It wasn't until she was pulling into the garage that she remembered her promise to Jeff that she would never see the psychic again.

The phone was ringing when Laura reached her apartment.

'Hello?'

It was Desiree. She sounded very odd.

'I got your flowers,' she merely said.

But Laura could feel the emotion blasting through the phone wire.

'Laura,' Desiree added, in the same muffled voice, 'I'd like to see you again, please.'

She sounded as timid as a little girl. Desiree Kaufman, timid!

Laura smiled. 'Of course,' she said.

'When?'

Laura looked at the clock. She had had that whole bizarre adventure by the beach already and yet it was only four o'clock.

'What about right now?' she asked impulsively.

'Make it sooner,' Desiree told her.

Laura kept breaking into smiles all the time she was dressing. *Who would have thought it a month ago?* she wondered. *Desiree Kaufman dying to see me. Spending the afternoon with a mad psychic. Yes, she was definitely going to hell in a handbasket, and fast.*

Then she got a little chill.

And wouldn't her mother have loved it.

Desiree's house seemed less unapproachable, more organic, that afternoon. Perhaps because the fire was lit. It murmured in tongues, and its shadows softened the angles of the room. Laura and Desiree sat side by side at the coffee table and drank from a Lalique decanter of sherry. The bouquet of flowers from Laura shimmered, full of messages, on the table. Neither Desiree nor Laura spoke much.

Then Desiree stood up.

'There are some things I want you to see,' she said abruptly. She stood up and went over to her bookcase. Methodically, she began to take things down. She set them in piles before Laura and gestured to her to look. Here were all the things that were not on Desiree's walls, impressive things, public things – an invitation to a gala at the White House; a fan letter from Tennessee Williams. Awards, certificates, reviews of her plays.

Laura was impressed, and touched that Desiree cared enough to want to impress her.

Then, in the corner of one bookcase, she saw an unexpected sight – her own small row of children's books.

'Desiree!' she said in wonder. 'I didn't know you had these.'

'There's a lot about me you do not yet know,' Desiree said.

And going over to another bookcase, she pulled down several volumes. 'And now these,' she told Laura. 'A new threshold.'

She handed Laura scrapbooks and albums of photographs.

Laura drank more sherry. She looked at everything Desiree showed her. She looked very carefully. Picture after picture. Image after image. Desiree as a child, somber in a flashy rabbit coat. Desiree with her father; he looking at the camera, smiling; she looking at him, unsmiling. Desiree at fifteen, at her boarding school – strikingly ugly, the forehead too wide, too white; the black hair blunt.

There were school report cards, a pressed flower from her father's grave, a toy rabbit she had loved as a child. Each one a lightning flash, illuminating the past for just a moment.

And there were many pictures of her husband Leo.

'I was only five when he died,' Laura said. 'I don't remember very much about him. But he came into my bedroom during a party once. I remember that. He was very nice. He sat on my bed and told me about koalas.'

'Yes,' Desiree said. 'He thought you were charming.'

'I didn't know that,' Laura told her.

She felt suddenly heavy. That there had been someone in her life, however tenuously, who had liked her, and she had never known.

'He was very handsome,' she added, looking at another picture of the slender, blond man. 'I never realized how good-looking he was. He was a movie star, wasn't he?'

'A minor one,' Desiree told her. 'He looked too much like James Fox. There wasn't room for two of them.'

Laura nodded. 'Were you married a long time?'

'Yes,' Desiree said abruptly. She paused, and then added in an even voice, 'Then he came to me one day and told me he had fallen in love with someone else. It was another man,' she added.

Laura looked away.

They don't tell you these things when you're a child, she thought.

'He died in my arms in the hospital,' Desiree said with a small bitter pride. 'He wouldn't even let the other man in the room.'

The sherry was weaving thick bands of emotion through Laura's head.

'Would you show me more?' she kept asking. 'I want to see more.'

Laura was never to forget the feeling of that afternoon – the feeling that she had magnets all over her body, drawing the images in. The words on the letters seemed newly written, the ink still wet. The tears on the pages were still fresh, and the photographed images began to

117

seem like they were starting to move. And Laura felt that it was not Desiree's life she was reliving, but her own.

But there was one question still unanswered.

'Why did you never have any children?' Laura asked.

There was a pause so long, so severe that Laura grew uneasy.

'But I did have a child,' Desiree said at last. 'You saw her picture yesterday.'

The little girl in the Hallowe'en costume.

Desiree was looking out at the terrace. 'Robin died when she was twelve,' she said. 'She was at boarding school in Lausanne. There was an epidemic of tuberculosis.'

Laura looked at the pot of flowers, raunchy and life-affirming, on the coffee table. She kept looking at them because there was nothing she could think of to say to Desiree. Then Desiree turned from the terrace and looked at Laura sharply.

'No,' she said. 'It wasn't tuberculosis. Robin committed suicide.'

Laura looked up from the flowers. Somehow she had known even before Desiree spoke that this was what she was going to say. Laura thought of the exuberant little grin and the fairy princess wand, and she started to cry.

Desiree came over to Laura. 'You are the first person I have ever told,' she said. 'Even her father didn't know. Even your mother didn't know.'

Then she went over to a drawer, found something within it and brought this one final article over to Laura. It was her daughter's suicide note.

Laura read the little note three times. Then wordlessly she kissed it and handed it back to Desiree.

She stood up and said she had to go home. She and

Desiree hugged each other at the door. The shock of it was so intense that Laura backed off. She and Desiree stared at each other.

'You feel like my daughter,' Desiree said.

'You feel like my mother,' Laura whispered.

Chapter Seven

It was seven o'clock. Blake Alden was dressing for the premiere of the new Ray Abbott movie. He was not looking forward to it, but attendance was mandatory. Dwaine Meyer, the producer, was a friend. Besides, Blake thought wryly, this town being what it was, if he *didn't* show up, who knew what rumors would start? That he had been incapacitated by a stroke, that his new picture was being shelved, that he and Dwaine were on the outs . . .

Sometimes Blake found it astonishing that he had spent the last forty years of his life in Hollywood.

As he combed his thick ginger hair, he found himself remembering the old days. Remembering what premieres had been like, back in the Fifties. God, they had been wonderful. Sometimes he had started getting dressed as early as two in the afternoon because he simply couldn't wait another moment. The premiere, especially, for that Cary Grant movie . . .

Blake checked himself. What was the point of remembering? Cary Grant was dead. And he was seeing the new Ray Abbott film tonight.

He chose a pair of gold cufflinks shaped like seashells and inserted them into the pleated silk shirt that had been custom made for him in Hong Kong. It was the first time he had worn a tuxedo since Julia died. The last time he had worn it, it had been too tight. Now it fitted perfectly. That was a pleasant surprise.

Maybe the evening wouldn't be so bad, after all. He

thought of people he might well run into – a deal or two that might be discreetly nudged forward. And, of course, there was the lady in question. He still had to play things delicately, but if she were there tonight . . .

Suddenly, Blake found he was looking forward to the evening very much.

He reflected on his mirror image. In his tuxedo, he looked ageless, emblematic – the very symbol for joy and success. He realized with a sudden shock that for the first time since Julia had died, he was feeling alive again. Fiercely, flowingly one-hundred per cent alive once more. Blood had finally returned to the sleeping limbs. It seemed incredible, a huge personal victory. But it was his. Blake Alden was back.

Unexpectedly, he found himself thinking of that psychic – what had his name been? Christopher. Christopher had predicted it. That in two and a half months, Blake would get through the hell and be himself again. Interesting.

For an instant, Blake was tempted to call the psychic again – just to see what he'd say about the new developments in his life. And then, frowning, he stopped himself. What was he thinking of? That afternoon had been an isolated, never-to-be-repeated moment in time.

Blake shook his head, remembering some of the psychic's other predictions. What psychologists those people were. They read your clothes, your face, chance words and they got you hoodwinked into thinking they could see so much. Poppycock. Hard to believe, really, that he had actually gone to see a psychic. Well, it just went to show what trouble he had been in after Julia died. He guessed grief made babies of us all.

Anyway, that was behind him. He had landed into the present. The safe, sane present. Where nothing could touch him.

Blake looked in the mirror again. *Not bad*, he thought. He looked powerful, stable – he looked like a survivor. He smiled at his reflection – at the lean freckled face, at the alert green eyes. It was a strong, positive smile. He turned to see himself from all sides. Then he put his hand into his pocket to see how that angle looked.

There was something in his pocket. He pulled it out. It was a cocktail napkin covered in Julia's writing.

'Miss No-Talent!' the paper chortled.

Memory crashed. There had been some girl in some showcase production they had gone to see. And Julia's nudging him, giggling, giving him the note. Horribly shaken, Blake tore the napkin up. It fluffed to useless bits at the first touch and he threw it away.

There was a tentative little knock at the door. Coco came in to turn down the bed. Seeing him in his glory, she burst out, 'Oh, Mr Alden, don't you look nice tonight!'

He steadied himself against the dresser. He was very white.

'In the future,' he told her icily, 'would you please take the trouble to remove items from my jacket pockets before you steam them out?'

'You're late,' Jeff said, opening the door.

'I'm sorry,' Laura apologized hurriedly, 'but I went over to Desiree's house. We had the most incredible afternoon. And, oh, Jeff – I've got the most wonderful idea!' Then she looked at him, startled. 'Why are you wearing a tuxedo?'

'Because tonight's the Ray Abbott premiere,' Jeff informed her.

Laura's hand flew to her mouth. 'Oh, my God,' she said. 'I forgot!' And I meant to go to the beauty shop.'

She touched her head anxiously. 'Does my hair look okay?'

'As a matter of fact, no,' Jeff said. 'It looks like it got run over by a tank.' Then he added in a burst, 'I do think you could try a little harder.'

Laura flushed. 'I'm sorry,' she said.

'You'd better get dressed,' he answered.

She drew a bath, and dumped three capfuls of her most expensive Pavlova bath oil in the water. Her hair might look awful, but at least she'd smell good. Then she lay down in the tub, and closed her eyes.

She wouldn't think about the damned premiere. She wouldn't think about Jeff being annoyed.

She would think instead about her wonderful idea:

Daddy and Desiree Kaufman.

The idea had burst upon Laura the moment she had left Desiree's house that afternoon. Had just whispered itself, complete, into her mind. Daddy and Desiree.

Laura shivered with excitement in the warm water. It was sheer genius. And the more she went over it, the more perfect the picture became.

Point Number One – Desiree had been Julia's best friend. She would always honor Julia's memory and would even, by all those years of association, almost *be* a continuation of Julia.

Point Number Two – Once Desiree was in the picture, Laura could stop worrying about her father and other women. The threat of some little tramp re-decorating Julia's house in Chinese Modern would be gone forever.

Point Number Three – Her father and Desiree were completely compatible. They were both artists. They were both achievers. They had both known tragedy. They had the same love of Hollywood, the same past.

And Desiree, with her elegance and flair, would be a wonderful hostess at his parties.

And Point Number Four – Laura loved Desiree. She truly did. God, it had come fast, but she felt it was solid. She remembered the shock of emotion that had gone through her when they had hugged good-bye that afternoon. It had been overwhelming.

Laura rinsed her back thoughtfully. She remembered her recent wretched drive through Bel Air and her agony at the possibility that her father might re-marry. But all that was changed now. Now that Laura had chosen the woman herself, it was a whole different proposition. She felt in control – in control again, for the first time since her mother had died. And what a heavenly feeling it was.

Now, how to get them together? That was the next step . . .

'Laura! What the hell are you doing?' came Jeff's irate cry from the living room. 'We're late already!'

She leapt from the tub.

The premiere was held at the Pantages Theatre in Hollywood. Ray Abbott was the number one box office attraction and the atmosphere sparked with excitement. The darting flashbulbs made it seem lighter than life; the newsmen with their microphones made it seem noisier than life; the glaring red carpet and the array of sequined dresses made it seem more vivid than life.

Jeff and Laura pulled up in front of the theatre. The valet parking boy was young and very nervous. It was probably his first night on the job, Laura guessed – and he was probably a would-be actor, too. *Well, bless him*, she thought, helping him help her out of the car.

She followed Jeff down the red carpet, cordoned off by velvet ropes. She felt very shy. She glanced hastily at the hordes of people watching the scene. Their faces were inscrutable behind the flashing bulbs and extended autograph books. *But what are they thinking? What are they thinking about us?* Laura found herself needing to know. *Do they imagine our lives are better than theirs because we can go down the red carpet and they are not allowed?*

There was one skinny little boy who stood at the very edge of the cordon. He had dark, carelessly-combed hair and huge, delighted black eyes. With every movie star who walked by, a fresh-minted flush came onto his cheeks. Laura smiled, watching him. He made her think of someone. The question teased at her. Who was it? Of course. He looked like Christopher Garland.

'Hey! Isn't that the guy on that commercial?'

Jeff had been spotted.

'And who's he with?'

'Nobody.'

Laura felt herself blushing as wine-red as her silk dress. She could only hope that Jeff hadn't heard.

Everyone was coming up to Blake. It was his first big evening out since Julia's death.

'You look great,' they told him. They said it with some surprise, genuine gladness, and just a little disappointment. 'You've never looked better.'

Blake knew it was true. The softly glazed mirrors lining the theatre lobby kept sending back their reassuring reflections of a man whose wife had recently died, but who had never looked better.

'Oh, Mr Alden – we met at Buzz Talbot's party . . .'

Women were coming up to him, all yielding, all perfume. Blake remembered some, pretended to remember the rest. He took several phone numbers. He put them in his tuxedo pocket where Julia's little napkin-note had been.

He searched around the room. Yes, she was there – in gold chiffon. She looked beautiful. He looked away.

Jeff and Laura were standing together. *He's looking around, I'm looking down*, Laura thought. *Is that observation profound or stupid?* But she didn't have the opportunity to decide. Just then, a reporter from *Entertainment Tonight* came up to Jeff, and he moved away from her.

For lack of a better activity, Laura wandered over to the buffet table. She was on her fifth tasteless canapé when there was a sudden shrill cry behind her.

'Laura! Laura Alden! I can't believe it's you!'

Laura looked up apprehensively as an unknown person approached – a thin, curly-blond-haired young woman in a white silk cowboy suit and hat. She embraced Laura, smelling ponderously of Giorgio perfume.

'It's Mimi! Mimi Craddock!'

Laura blinked confusedly. She vaguely remembered a Mimi Craddock from High School, but that Mimi Craddock had been about forty pounds heavier, with no bosom, and lank and dank dark brown hair.

'Yes, it's really me!' Mimi laughed at Laura's non-recognition. 'Oh, Laura, it's so unbelievably fantastic to see you again!'

Laura smiled back but there was some memory trying to jell. Some reason she wasn't glad to see Mimi Craddock. But the reason shredded apart, even as she tried to probe it.

'Well, wow. You look just great, Mimi,' Laura said, trying to make up for the five years she hadn't given Mimi a thought. 'What have you been up to?'

Mimi groaned. 'I'm trying to be an actress,' she said. She rolled her heavily-mascaraed eyes. Then she added seriously, 'But you know how it is, Laura. It's impossible to get anywhere unless you know somebody.'

Laura felt obscurely embarrassed. *I know plenty of somebodies*, she thought, *but have I gotten anywhere?*

'And what about you?' Mimi asked. 'What are you up to?'

'I'm writing and illustrating children's books,' Laura said.

'Oh, wow!' said Mimi. 'That's so great. Have any been published?'

'Four,' Laura said modestly.

This time the 'Wow' reached new decibels.

'I'll buy them for my niece,' Mimi told her. 'I'll tell her I know a famous author.'

Laura smiled a little uneasily, not sure whether Mimi was putting her on or not.

'And is there a man in your life?' Mimi went on to ask.

This was safer ground. Laura pointed out Jeff, still talking to the reporter.

'Oh, my God. Oh, my *God!*' Mimi's eyes were omnivorous. '*Him?* The guy who does that *commercial?*'

The shock in her voice, although completely understandable, was, all the same, Laura decided, a little unflattering. She found herself flushing.

'And what about you?' she got off the subject quickly. 'Are you seeing anyone?'

Mimi made a face. 'Lots of people,' she shrugged. 'No one special. But I keep on trying – you know me!'

No, Laura thought, looking at her. *I don't know you. I haven't seen you in five years, and I never knew you then, either.* And that nagging half-memory returned.

'Are your dad and mom here tonight?' Mimi asked.

'My father's here,' Laura answered, and then she added, 'My mother died a few months ago.'

'Oh, that's right!' Mimi said, her eyes flying open sympathetically. 'I was so upset when I read about it in the papers. In fact, I was going to write to you and say how sorry I was, but I had no way of getting your address.'

Only the telephone directory, Laura thought.

The lights in the theatre lobby began to dim.

'I think we'd better take our seats,' she said crisply. 'It looks like the movie's about to start.'

But Mimi wouldn't go until she had gotten from Laura her telephone number, and a promise that the two of them would get together very, very soon.

Laura looked around for Jeff. He had left the reporter, and was now ringed by beautiful ladies, of all shapes and types. But his charm made no distinction among them – he was making them all laugh equally. Laura sighed. She felt jealous, hated herself for feeling jealous, hated herself even more for not having gone to the beauty shop this afternoon.

And then, past Jeff, she saw her father. Around him were also women grouped, swaying. Laura waved at him. He returned the wave vaguely, pre-absorbed in all the feminine attention.

Oh, Desiree, Laura thought longingly. *Why aren't you here?*

And suddenly, a wish granted, there she was.

'Desiree!'

Laura ran to her, snatched at her. Desiree wore a long pale gold dress, and Laura hugged her, loving the feel of the warm sequins against her skin. *They were like Desiree*, she thought extravagantly, *sharp and shimmering and beautiful*.

128

'Desiree!' she gasped again. 'This afternoon, you never mentioned – how unbelievable that you're here!'

'Not so terribly unbelievable,' Desiree said, amused. 'Considering that I have gone to every premiere known to man for the last twenty-five years. I am like a crab canapé – I am a fixture.'

'Are you here with anyone?' Laura asked.

Desiree paused for a fraction of a second. 'No.'

'Well,' said Laura, plotting quickly, 'after the movie, I want you to come out for an ice cream soda with Jeff and me.'

'You may be interested to know that I gave up ice cream sodas the same day I gave up playing hopscotch. And that was several years ago.'

'Then a coffee,' Laura insisted, laughing. 'Or a brandy. But you're not escaping.'

'Houdini is my middle name,' Desiree said, 'but very well. I'll meet you in front, after the film.'

We're halfway there, Laura thought giddily. *Now for Daddy! This is working out quicker than I ever hoped!*

She caught up with her father as he was going into the theatre door. She pushed her way through the group of scented women. She could feel their hostility.

'Daddy,' she said loudly.

She was amused to see how quickly the hostility disappeared.

'Daddy,' she said, using her most irresistible little-girl voice, 'could you come with Jeff and me for ice cream sodas after the show?'

She waited for him to say yes.

'Sorry, honey,' he said. 'I can't.' And he walked down the theatre aisle and to his seat.

Oh, well, Laura thought, feeling like a fool in front of all the watching women. *Next time.*

129

Jeff was furious when Laura told him that they were going out after the show with Desiree.

'Don't you think it would have been just a little considerate to have checked it out with me first?' he asked her coldly.

Laura bit her lip.

'I'm sorry,' she said. 'I guess I got a little carried away – I was so glad to see Desiree.'

Jeff looked at her as if she had rocks in her head. 'But you just saw her this afternoon,' he reminded her.

The Ray Abbott movie was terrible; and the little jaunt to C. C. Brown's was a total disaster. The table was too tight, the room was too hot, the sodas were too sweet.

And the conversation was strangely painful. No matter what direction it took, it seemed there were murderous rocks and undercurrents. Jeff kept making needling jokes to Desiree about women who wore provocative golden dresses, and Desiree kept alluding to all the young actors of her acquaintance who had become instant stars (both critical and commercial) soon after graduation from college.

Laura looked from one to the other in bewilderment. Why, in God's name, were they acting like that? She kept trying to soften things, but it did no good. If only Desiree would show that other side of herself, she thought – the side she had shown that afternoon – but Desiree was unrelaxedly sharp that night. Next to Jeff's gold ironic ease she seemed like a maddening brittle wind chime.

Desiree and Jeff drank only a little of their ice cream sodas, but Laura worked doggedly through hers and felt sick.

The evening didn't last long.

130

'All right, Laura,' Jeff said. His voice was very controlled. They had been driving for half an hour. It was the first thing he had said since they parted from Desiree. 'What was all that about?'

Laura felt too queasy to make up any lies.

'What it was about,' she told him shrilly, 'is that I love Desiree. I want you to be nice to her, and I want her to marry my father.'

For one stunned moment, Jeff was silent. And then he exploded into a wild, endless battery of laughter. 'You're crazy!' he yelped. 'You've gone totally and completely insane!'

Laura burst into tears. 'How dare you laugh at me?' she cried. 'How dare you? You're always laughing at me! You're always thinking I'm crazy! Well, I'm not — I'm not!'

Jeff looked at her sidelong, concerned. 'Okay, Laura, okay,' he said soothingly. 'I'm sorry. Take it easy. I'm not laughing at you. Really I'm not. But, I mean, since you were two years old, you couldn't stand Desiree Kaufman — and now you want to marry her off to your father. Don't you think that's a little unusual?'

Laura took a deep breath. She knew that she had to tell Jeff the story, had to make him understand. Making herself speak slowly and terribly sensibly, she began. The extraordinary visits with Desiree, the letters, the photographs, the flowers, the incredible feeling of connection and the hug that had seemed so eerily like her mother's.

She was perspiring. She knew she was not telling the story well. She knew how ridiculous it must sound. But she kept on talking until it all had been told.

There was a silence that lasted a long time.

Finally, Jeff cleared his throat. 'You poor baby,' he said quietly. 'You poor, poor baby.'

131

Laura felt tears of confusion and hopelessness come to her eyes. 'Why?' she quavered.

'Oh, Laura,' Jeff sighed. 'You have no idea what bad shape you're in.'

'Why?' she asked again, more sharply.

'Let's take it point by point,' Jeff offered patiently. 'First, you're thinking that Desiree's like your mother. That's bullshit. Laura, they're absolutely nothing alike and they never were. How can you even compare them?' He shrugged. 'You're just so desperate to have your mother back that you'll take any substitute. In the state you're in, the cleaning lady would have done just as well.' He shook his head. 'And I hate to say it, but Laura, at your age, this is pretty pathetic. I mean, you're twenty-three years old. What do you need a mother for? I give you all the love you could possibly ever want.'

She sat mute with unhappiness.

Jeff took time out to curse at a red Mercedes making too sharp a turn.

'Next,' he went on, warming to the analysis, 'this business of your father and Desiree. It couldn't happen in a million years. I mean, no offence to Desiree Kaufman – she's a good-looking broad – but your father's got every twenty-year old starlet in town chasing after him! He's not going to waste his time on her.'

Laura still said nothing.

'And then of course,' Jeff went on, 'we have this sudden mysterious friendship between you and Desiree. Springing straight out of nowhere.' He laughed. 'Laura, Laura, I can't believe you could have grown up in this town and still be so naive. Don't you get it? Desiree doesn't care two fucking pins for you – you're just being used.'

Laura found her voice at last. 'Used?'

'To get at your father.'

'But you just said – ' she began bitterly.

Jeff sighed. 'I don't mean romantically. But, Laura, Desiree is a *playwright* She hasn't had a hit in a long time. Your father is a producer. She figures, "Here's a poor little girl who's lost her mother. What a great way to get my foot in the door." '

Laura exploded. 'That's a vicious thing to say!'

Jeff shrugged, his patience gone. 'Have it your own way,' he told her tightly. 'But you'll see that I'm right. Friendships don't spring up as quickly as all that, Laura. And the fact that you could never stomach Desiree Kaufman for twenty-three years should tell you something.' He gave a sharp little laugh. 'But who can blame her for trying? She's no worse than anybody else. Nobody does something for nothing in this world.'

Then what about you? flashed into Laura's mind. *You could have any girl you wanted. Why are you with me? Is it because my father's a studio executive and you're an actor?*

And she hated herself for even thinking that.

They went upstairs to the apartment. Jeff undressed and went straight to bed.

Laura went into the kitchen. She made herself some tea. Then she sat down on the living room sofa. She was very numb. She thought about all the situations in her life – about her mother, about her mother and father, her father and Desiree, Jeff and herself. But she could come to no conclusions whatsoever.

Then she put the empty teacup down. She went over to the desk and pulled from it a large envelope. The envelope had come from Julia's room and it was filled with letters. Letters Julia had kept in her desk for as long as Laura could remember, and had never let her see. 'Someday, when you're older,' she had always said, smiling, when Laura had begged. And Laura felt old enough tonight.

She read the letters, for the first time, in the moonlight. They were love letters. Letters that her father had written to her mother. Letters Julia had written to him through their courtship, through their marriage. They were beautiful letters, saying every loving thing. Tears dripped down Laura's cheeks, staining the pages. She thought about her parents, their shadows stretching back through the years; mingling, calm, inevitable. Inevitable.

She thought of all the old stories, the saga of how they had met, their first date, the tale of their wedding day. It was like watching a wonderful old movie for the twentieth time. It was so safe, so smooth, in the past. But the present was so terrifyingly jangled. She closed her eyes.

I am frightened, Laura thought. *I am so frightened, Mama*.

Everything was confusion. She couldn't stand it anymore. Everything in her whole life. Goddammit. Was there nothing she could do to clear up the chaos?

And then she opened her eyes.

Chapter Eight

Laura knocked on the sea-wind-worn black door. Her hand against the wood was like a nervous spasm.

He opened the door for her, and awkwardly she came in.

He gave her tea, in the MGM mug.

Then she sat down on the couch. Christopher sat on the chair, looking at her, waiting for her to speak. Laura felt peeled, embarrassed.

'I'm not even sure why I'm here,' she said finally. He did not help her out, still said nothing. 'In fact,' she added, 'maybe I should just leave. It was ridiculous of me to have called you. You know I don't even believe in any of this.'

Christopher smiled.

'You don't owe me any explanations,' he said. 'But as long as you're here, why don't you at least stay for the reading?'

She watched, inert, as he reached for a small tape recorder. And into it he put a cassette. 'Ask me anything you like,' he told her. Then he leaned forward and took Laura's hand. 'But don't ask me anything you don't really want to know the answer to.'

An hour later, the tape clicked to a stop. Christopher leaned over and turned the recorder off.

'Well,' he said. 'That's that.'

He looked at Laura. In a huge effort, she stood up. Her bones felt fragile. Her head hurt. 'Well,' she said slowly.

Christopher looked up at her. 'Please think about the things I said.'

She stood in further silence. She just wanted to be out of there.

'And listen to the tape.'

He opened the tape recorder and handed her the little cassette. His hands were cool, remote.

He opened the front door, and smiled at her. 'Thank you for coming by, Laura. I'll see you soon.'

She gave a dry little laugh. 'I don't think so,' she said.

It was four o'clock. The traffic along Wilshire was stifling. Laura could not concentrate. She kept drifting – across the yellow divider line, past the faces of startled, furious motorists.

She felt terrifyingly disconnected, empty. She looked down at the tape Christopher had given her. *No*, she thought sharply. Then she watched as her hand crept over to the cassette. *No*, she thought again. And she watched herself pick the tape up and insert it into the deck.

And she listened as the sound of the voices filled the car.

'*I wanted to ask you about a woman. Her name is Desiree Kaufman. I've known her all my life, but since Mama died, these strange things have been happening.*' Her voice hesitant, embarrassed. '*It's as if we're somehow – connected.*'

'*Yes. It has to do with your mother.*'

'*What do you mean?*'

'*Have you ever heard of counterparts?*'

'*No.*'

'*People assume there's one soul per body, but that isn't true. Every soul, for the purpose of greater growth and development, creates different personalities and*

136

sends them onto the physical plane. These are called counterparts. I sense this was the case with your mother and Desiree. Very often counterparts live at the same time, in the same city, sometimes in the same family. There is a great bond between them. At some level, each counterpart knows everything about all the others. Often they will even share a particular trait.'

Uneasily, Laura remembered the hug that had been indistinguishable from her mother's.

'Counterparts wasn't really what I wanted to ask you about,' she told Christopher hastily. 'It was something else. I know that my father and Desiree would be perfect for each other. I have this plan to get them together. And I wanted to know if you think it will work.'

There was a long pause.

'No, Laura. The relationship with Desiree is there only for you. It would never work with your father. It would be dangerous.'

Laura could hear her voice shaking with disappointment.

'But that's ridiculous. How can you say that? You don't even know Desiree.'

Christopher sounded impatient.

'All I know is that if you push it, it's going to blow up in your face.' There was another long pause. 'Your father will marry again, Laura. Someone you introduce him to, as a matter of fact. But it won't be Desiree Kaufman.'

Agitatedly, Laura pushed the fast-forward button on the tape deck. Then she stabbed at the play button again. Christopher's voice was still and clear now.

'. . . something. Your mother was a very advanced soul, Laura. You are not her daughter for nothing. And it was no coincidence that you met me – or that Carmen offered you her ring. You've got an extraordinary destiny to fulfil. One day, you're going to be very important to the world.'

Laura's nervous laugh.

'Well, children's book writers are sometimes rich and famous, but I don't know about important!'

'I didn't say you would be important as a writer.' Christopher's voice was gentle. 'You're going to give all that up soon, anyway.'

'What?'

'You're going to be a teacher.'

'A teacher? Teaching what?'

A pause.

'Teaching what I teach.'

Laura shivered. Why was she even listening to this? She banged her finger against the fast-forward button once more. And again her car slipped across the yellow line. Again the honks, the curses.

'No,' Christopher said. 'You and Jeff will never marry.'

When she first heard it in his apartment, it was as if she had been struck. And hearing it again in the car, it was as if she had been struck a second time.

'When is he going to leave me?' she got it out at last.

'He isn't going to leave you,' Christopher said. 'You're the one who's going to leave.'

And then Laura's sudden joyous spurt of laughter.

'You must be totally crazy!' she cried.

And Christopher had laughed, too.

'That could well be true,' he told her.

Jittery, Laura pulled the cassette out of the player. She held it in her hand for a moment, not knowing what to do next. Then abruptly she opened the window and flung the tape outside. She watched with satisfaction in her rear-view mirror as it bounced once, twice, and ended up, finally invisible, by the side of the road. She found she could concentrate on her driving now.

The last time Laura had been to lunch at the Bistro Garden, she had gone with Jeff. They had come in to the restaurant, given their name, and the waiter had led them toward a charming table near the bar. But Jeff had refused to sit down.

'I'd like something on the patio,' he had told the waiter tensely. 'I requested something on the patio.'

'No, Mr Kennerly,' the waiter was suddenly equally tense. 'There is nothing available. I took your reservation myself. You did not specify.'

Laura could tell by the look on Jeff's face that he was close to shouting. She sprang in, saying that this table was perfect, that she had a cold, and didn't want to be outside, anyway. And she finally convinced Jeff to sit down.

But the lunch was horrible. Jeff knew that the table was not perfect, knew that the important people were seated in the patio, whether they had specified or not. Laura tried her hardest to distract him, to praise, to flatter, but it wasn't working. Finally, she gave up and they ate in near-silence.

She looked at the crowded patio, crammed with umbrellas and geraniums and symbolism. *It's nice on the patio*, she thought, with irritation and with wonder. *But not that nice . . .*

Today's experience at the restaurant was very different.

Laura told the Captain that she was lunching with Desiree Kaufman, and swiftly she was led out of the main room of the Bistro Garden and through to the best table on the patio.

139

Desiree, already seated and wearing an impossible hat, was frowning at Laura as she approached.

'You're much too thin,' she said.

Laura felt comfortable being scolded by Desiree. It had the familiar rub of childhood about it.

'You sounded very mysterious on the phone this morning,' Desiree told her. 'You're not usually up to such almost literary standards of suspense. Even I, jaded as I am, was intrigued. What's going on?'

Laura felt at a loss. She hadn't meant to sound mysterious, and now, with Desiree staring at her, her eyebrows raised expectantly, she knew her story would sound terribly flat.

'It's just – well, remember that psychic I told you about? I went to see him yesterday. This time I had a reading.'

Desiree did not look disappointed. 'I see,' she said.

'He said some things,' Laura began carefully.

'What things?' Desiree asked her.

A warning buzz in Laura's head.

You and Jeff will never marry . . .

. . . but it won't be Desiree Kaufman . . .

. . . teaching what I teach . . .

'I don't even want to talk about them,' she told Desiree hastily. 'It was all pretty ridiculous. I mean, I *know* it's ridiculous. I don't believe in any of it. But . . .'

'But . . .' Desiree prompted, smiling.

'But – I can't stop thinking about some of the things he said.'

'Why?'

Laura frowned. She looked around at the sane, solid Bistro Garden, at the vivid geraniums, the confident body language of the diners, the self-satisfied look of the waiter pocketing his tip. Then she superimposed the image of Christopher Garland, white-faced, sitting in his trance as he did the reading. It was impossible to reconcile the two realities.

'Because I can't make it make sense,' she said. 'I can't make it fit in.'

'What's this psychic like?' Desiree asked.

Helplessly, Laura tried to sketch an answer. 'It's hard to say. One minute he'll be perfectly normal, even worldly, funny, smart. And then the next minute, this weird feeling – this atmosphere . . . His whole face even seems to change – his eyes, bone structure, everything. And the things he says.'

'Which you can't forget. It sounds interesting,' Desiree told Laura. 'When are you seeing him again?'

'Never,' Laura was firm. 'But – '

'Yes?'

She blushed.

'I was thinking maybe you could go see him yourself.'

Desiree looked at her hard. 'Why?'

'Well – I don't know, exactly. As a sort of second opinion.' Laura laughed self-consciously. 'When I hear you say he's off the wall, too, then I can just forget about everything he told me.'

Desiree shook her head. 'Sorry to disappoint you, darling,' she said. 'But I wouldn't do it for anything on earth.'

'Why not?'

Desiree smiled. 'What if he got *me* thinking, too?'

'Ready to order, ladies?' asked the waiter.

As the days went by, Laura got the distinct feeling that she had an invisible noose around her neck. More and more often the thoughts kept arising – Christopher's predictions about herself, Jeff, her father, Desiree – and tighter and tighter they twisted their skeins around her throat. It was getting hard to breathe.

Just wait, she thought lugubriously. *One morning they're going to come in and there I'll be, lying strangled mysteriously on the bed – with not a mark on me. God, what a* Twilight Zone *that would make.*

On Monday morning, Jeff had an early appointment with his trainer. Laura woke when he did, and went into the kitchen to make some tea. As she sat down at the table, the noose reappeared, tighter than ever, choking her so that she couldn't drink.

Goddammit, she thought, slamming down the mug. She had had enough. Enough of this insane noose. Enough of this wondering and worrying about everyone's future, Christopher and his ridiculous predictions. It was time she got down to something constructive. Something productive. Something that would help make the kind of future *she* wanted.

Like her campaign to get her father and Desiree Kaufman together.

Laura smiled. She could have sworn she felt the noose slacken.

As soon as Jeff went off to the gym, she went into action.

First, she telephoned Blake. 'Hi, Daddy,' she said plaintively. 'I'm just calling to say that I miss you. I haven't seen much of you lately. Could we have lunch together, maybe? Just the two of us?'

She sounded nauseatingly girlish to her own ears, but Blake fell for it completely, as she had known he would.

'Of course, darling,' he said. 'What about tomorrow?'

'Perfect,' Laura smiled.

'Do you want to have lunch here at the house?' Blake asked.

'No, no,' Laura said hastily. 'Let's go out somewhere. What about Kate Mantilini's?'

It was the closest place she could think of to Desiree's condominium.

'But it's always so crowded,' Blake said doubtfully.

'Oh, Daddy!' Laura wailed. 'Please! It's my favorite restaurant!'

She had never been there.

'All right,' Blake said. 'If you insist. I'll meet you there tomorrow at twelve-thirty.'

He hung up, smiling. One forgot, sometimes, what a sweet child Laura could be.

Laura hung up, also smiling. When it came to subtlety, the snake in Eden had nothing on her.

Then she picked up the phone and dialled the second number.

'Desiree, it's me, Laura,' she told the answering machine. 'It's urgent. A friend of mine is a Phys. Ed. major, and she's got a test coming up. She needs that Jean Sanders book that you've got – the one on fitness. She can't find it in any library, and she's in a panic. You're our last hope. As it turns out, I'm going to be in your neighborhood tomorrow, so could you *please* come to Kate Mantilini's at a quarter to one, and bring me the book. I'll make sure it gets returned to you.'

Oh, Laura, you're wasted in children's literature, she told herself, hanging up happily. *You should have been in the State Department.*

Blake came early to Kate Mantilini's. He was uncompromisingly distant and snappish, the product of a bad morning. Laura tried hard to jolly him out of it exactly the way her mother would have done, but she wasn't Julia and it didn't work.

Well, that's all right, she thought staunchly. *Desiree will manage.*

At quarter to one, Laura heard, rather than saw,

Desiree come in. She could hear the appreciative murmurs of two or three men at nearby tables, could hear the timpani of Desiree's high heels, the swish of her Perry Ellis skirt.

'Hello, my dear,' Desiree said with dry cheerfulness. 'The St Bernard has come to the rescue – Jean Sanders is in a barrel around my neck.'

A plant blocked her view. For several moments, Desiree did not see Blake sitting with Laura. Then the two of them looked at each other.

But why was this such a terrible mistake? Laura wondered confusedly, staring from one iced-over face to the other. *They've known each other for so many years – why are they looking like this now?*

But it was too late to do anything but go on with her plan.

'Won't you join us for lunch?' she asked Desiree weakly. 'We've only just started.'

'I don't feel like lunch,' Desiree said, not moving.

There was silence. Laura felt the panic of the actor whose lines had been forgotten.

'Have coffee with us, then.' Blake spoke at last.

Desiree glided down beside Laura into the booth, like a hypnotized cobra going back into its basket.

There was a terribly long pause.

'You're looking well, Desiree,' Blake said.

'Thank you.'

'How's your writing?'

'Brilliant.'

'Your health?'

'Impeccable.'

'Good.'

Desiree stayed only five minutes, drinking coffee she said was tepid, but which she refused to send back for a fresh cup. The strained, monosyllabic dialogue continued.

At last, Desiree finished the coffee and she stood up abruptly. 'Here's the Jean Sanders book,' she told Laura. 'No need to get up,' she told the seated Blake. Then she swept down the aisle of the restaurant. Again, as she left, there were approving murmurs from the surrounding tables.

Laura and her father sat without saying anything. Finally Blake coughed.

'I had a bitch of a stockholders' meeting this morning,' he said, and they talked about it for the rest of the lunch. Desiree's name was not mentioned. It was as if she had never appeared at all.

Mrs Warnakie, Blake's secretary at the studio, was retiring. She was given a farewell party, and Blake stopped in on his way home to attend. Mrs Warnakie was a meaty woman with glasses that rose to a menacingly sharp point on either side. She was excellent at keeping the wrong people out of Blake's office, excellent at manifesting the forbidding voice over the telephone. But when Blake walked in the meeting room where the party was being held, Mrs Warnakie was fussing, blushing, opening feminine packages containing perfume and silk scarves. He watched her, oddly touched, oddly depressed.

She had been his secretary for twenty-five years. They had come to the studio at the same time. She had been pretty in those first days. He remembered a little parakeet she had once kept in her office. Blake teased himself to remember its name. Dovely – that had been it. He felt obscurely pleased that he had been able to remember that – as though he had saved something from the trash.

Her office was bare now, punctiliously cleansed of twenty-five years. He wondered where the files, the scripts, the posters, had gone. To a studio vault, or had Mrs Warnakie taken them home herself? Was her cubicle in the studio now re-created in some little apartment somewhere?

It was hard to believe she was going.

Mrs Warnakie looked up then and saw him. 'Oh, Mr Alden!' she breathed. 'I'm so happy you could come.'

Everyone was looking at Blake. He answered her with an easy smile, and handed her her gift. It had been chosen by Alison, his secretary at home. He figured an Alison would know what a Mrs Warnakie would most enjoy.

With hands quick from years of typing, she opened the gift. Inside was a tangle of silk and lace. She pulled out the fluffy white blouse. Blake felt slightly foolish.

'Oh, Mr *Alden*!' Mrs Warnakie choked.

Then suddenly she came close to Blake and she kissed him. 'I've wanted to do that for years,' she told him, her eyes moist behind the killer glasses. 'And now I have.'

Blake left soon after, so depressed he could barely walk.

It was Sunday. The morning was bright and sweet. Laura and Jeff drove down Pico, to buy some bagels for brunch. As they passed the Good Shepherd Church, they heard bells ringing.

'Oh, look!' Laura cried.

It was a wedding procession.

Laura drained in every detail. The bride, plump and blond, her stiff shyness at comic odds with her gaily blowing veil. The little flower girl running amok with self-importance, clutching her damp basket. The groom, making panicky jokes at his own expense. The preacher, smiling.

'I wonder how long the bride and groom have been going together?' Laura murmured.

Jeff shot her an irritated look. 'I wonder how long the bride and groom have been going together?' he imitated her. 'Oh, God, Laura, will you please lay off?'

Laura flushed darkly. With irony, she remembered Christopher's prediction that she would be the one to leave.

'Well, tell me all about it. How you met, and everything.'

Mimi Craddock rolled her huge eyes. They looked suddenly like fish eyes, restlessly seeking for food.

'I still can't believe you're living with Jeff Kennerly,' she added.

When Mimi had called last night, insisting that she and Laura meet for lunch, Laura had felt a strong desire not to go. But she had finally agreed, and suggested that they meet at the Old World Restaurant on the Sunset Strip. *Even if the date is a disaster*, she reminded herself, *there's always the strawberry waffle*.

But the lunch was turning out to be an easy one. It was soon apparent that Mimi had no interest in deep conversation and Laura gave up the strain of being meaningful. She just sat back at last and listened to Mimi's relentlessly self-centered monologues about her life and times. It was all rather fun.

And Mimi was so agreeably flattering. Flattering about everything; the way Laura was doing her hair, Laura's career plans, Laura's new shoes. And now she was going to be flattering about Laura's having hooked Jeff Kennerly.

So, dutifully, Laura related the whole story of the

romance. And the more she talked, the more she saw looks of god-honest envy in Mimi's face, the more confident she found herself becoming. Confident about how much she and Jeff really loved each other. Confident about how solid a team they were. Yes, it *was* pretty romantic. It *was* a pretty special love – and a few occasional fights didn't spoil that a bit.

If any two people in the world are meant to be together, it's Jeff Kennerly and me, Laura thought with assurance and relief.

And then Mimi went back to the subject of her own life. But her flippant edge seemed to have dulled over dessert.

With eyes once again liquid, she told Laura how hard it all was. How hard it was trying to be a working actress, trying to look good without much money, trying to meet the right people.

'I keep thinking I should give it all up,' Mimi mourned. 'And do something like sell real estate. But in this business, there's always the chance that next week something will turn up. Maybe I'll even get a job on a soap. It's so hard to know what to do.' She laughed ruefully. 'Makes you wish you were psychic.'

And, to her own surprise, Laura suddenly found herself telling Mimi about Christopher Garland.

Why on earth am I doing this? she wondered angrily. She tried to stop, but Mimi had swallowed the subject whole.

'Laura! I had no idea you were into this kind of stuff!' she squealed.

'I'm not,' Laura said, red-faced. 'I don't even know why I mentioned it.'

'Well, it's fate that you did,' Mimi insisted. 'I believe in all the New Age things, and I've got to go see him. When can we go?'

'You can go whenever you like,' Laura told her shortly. 'But I'm not going with you.'

'Oh, but you have to!' Mimi wailed. 'I'd be too scared to go alone. Promise you'll come with me.'

Laura was embarrassed. 'No,' she said. 'I really don't want to.'

Mimi's voice rose. 'Laura, my whole career could be hanging in the balance. What conceivable harm could it do you?'

Her voice was so urgent that the diners at the adjoining table looked over in amusement.

'All right,' Laura said sharply. 'All right.'

She stared down at her coffee cup. *What a weakling she was*, she thought angrily. *Why did she ever agree? Now she would have to see Christopher Garland again. Damn. Damn. Damn.*

Mimi was appeased.

'As soon as I get back from New York, we'll make a date to do it.'

Laura was eager to change the subject. 'When are you going to New York?'

'Tuesday.'

'On your own?'

'No. I'm going with a guy. Ned Barry. Do you know him?'

Laura knew Ned Barry. She also knew his wife.

'Ah.' Laura tried to sound unsurprised.

'He's a producer,' Mimi explained.

And Laura understood fully.

She had another sip of her cold coffee.

Lunch was over. Laura wanted to split the bill, but Mimi insisted on paying, in so loud a voice that again there were interested glances from the neighboring tables. Embarrassed, Laura finally gave in.

149

The two of them stood waiting in the lukewarm sunshine for the valet to bring their cars.

'Well, where are you off to next?' Mimi wanted to know.

'I thought I'd drop by my father's house for a few minutes,' Laura told her.

She planned to go up to her mother's room and see if there were any more love letters.

There was a long pause. And then Mimi put an arm around Laura's waist.

'Gee, Laura,' she said in a tiny, breathless voice. 'Could I ask a really big favor?'

'What?' Laura turned to her uneasily.

Mimi's eyes were dark and rich. 'I was wondering if I could have a little something that belonged to your mother,' she said. 'Any old thing. A teaspoon . . . A package of playing cards. Anything.' She gave Laura a little squeeze. 'I admired her so much, you know. All those years in High School. She was kind of my idol.'

Laura was stabbingly touched. *I had no idea*, she thought.

'Of course, Mimi,' she said. 'Of course you may. In fact,' she added, 'why don't you come over to Daddy's house with me now? Follow me in your car. And we'll pick out something right away.'

'Oh, no,' Mimi demurred. 'I wouldn't dream of encroaching on your time with your father.'

'Don't worry about that,' Laura said. 'I'm just going to the house to get a few things. I doubt if we'll see Daddy at all.'

Blake was working, undisturbable, in his office when Laura and Mimi arrived. Mimi exclaimed so much over the hallway that Laura felt obliged to give her the full tour. It always made Laura proud to see her mother's decorating through another person's eyes, and Mimi was terribly and repeatedly impressed. But, Laura noticed, Mimi didn't comment on Julia's tasteful little touches – most of her raptures were saved for the spaciousness of the rooms and the size of the swimming pool.

The tour was over, and Blake still hadn't emerged from his office.

'Well, we might as well pick out your souvenir now,' Laura said, wanting to get her letters and leave. 'It's getting pretty late.'

'Oh, Laura,' Mimi said, turning pleading eyes on her. 'I hate to mention it, but I'm just dying of thirst. Couldn't I have a drink first?'

They were sitting in the library, drinking iced tea – Laura noticed that Mimi, for all of her professed thirstiness, had been satisfied with only two sips of hers – when Blake walked in.

'Hello, baby,' he said in surprise, and leaned over and kissed Laura. Then, looking up, he saw Mimi on the couch and he raised a polite, enquiring eyebrow.

'You remember Mimi Craddock, Daddy,' Laura said hastily. 'From my High School.'

Blake's memory was notoriously bad. Laura knew there was no way on earth her father would remember Mimi, but Blake was very gallant and assured them that he did.

I love Daddy so, Laura thought proudly a few minutes later, as Blake entertained them with scandalous stories of that morning's meeting with a popular actor. *He takes such trouble to entertain my friends*.

It was getting very late now, and Laura still didn't have the letters or Mimi's memento. She was afraid that mentioning the purpose of the visit would sadden her father, so she finally just rose, pretending she was going to the powder room.

'Please excuse me a moment,' she said.

She went quickly upstairs to her mother's bedroom. After all these months, it still smelled of Julia. Laura went to the desk first. As she had hoped, inside was yet another manila envelope full of letters, and she pulled these out with much excitement. And then she went to the bedside table. There, in the drawer, was the pretty little blue pomander Julia had loved. That would do perfectly for Mimi.

When she came back downstairs, the loot under her sweater, she found Blake and Mimi sitting silent in the library. Mimi was looking down, smiling.

'Hate to rush off, Daddy,' Laura said, 'but traffic's murder at this hour.'

Blake walked them to the front door. He kissed Laura and said to Mimi that it had been nice seeing her again. Mimi smiled once more.

When her father was safely back inside the house, Laura pulled out Julia's pomander, and, with ceremony she presented it to Mimi.

'What's that?' Mimi asked blankly.

'The memento of Mama's you wanted.'

'Oh,' Mimi answered.

She seemed touched by the pomander, but not, Laura thought, puzzled and a little hurt, quite as touched as she had expected Mimi to be.

Later that evening, Laura was able to reel in that half-memory of Mimi Craddock that had been eluding her since the premiere.

It was Laura's first day of High School. She was very nervous, very aware of being the new kid in the class.

It was gym-time. The girls lined up in rows on the field. In front of Laura was a very tall, rather heavy girl from an older grade. She turned around and looked Laura up and down. Then she narrowed her eyes.

'I hate you,' she whispered.

Laura shivered.

Well, people do change, she told herself.

Chapter Nine

'PROMENADE, by DESIREE KAUFMAN. *The Antioch Community Playhouse.* TONIGHT ONLY.'

The poster had been carefully done by a not terribly good student of calligraphy. Seeing it gave Desiree a sharp, rather awful thrill.

She sat down in the small auditorium. She had come alone; none of her friends even knew she was here.

On her right was a young couple. They told her they had come tonight for two reasons – the babysitter was available, and the man who did the lighting was a second cousin. And on Desiree's left was a skinny young man with glasses. He was there, he told her, because he believed Desiree Kaufman to be the best playwright in America.

The play began. Desiree was instantly sorry she had come. She very much did not want to compare this little evening in this little theatre with *Promenade*'s opening on Broadway all those years ago – but she could not stop herself. Like those little rocks that unfurl into palaces of coral at the bottom of a fish bowl, that other evening only grew more vivid, more resplendent, every second.

She was opening telegrams. Answering the door to welcome yet another bouquet of flowers. Walking into Sardi's. The room rising in a wave of love.

Tears came, did violence to her careful mask of make-up.

The young man on her left asked if she was all right.

'I am not all right,' she told him coldly. 'I am Desiree Kaufman.'

She watched her play. She had forgotten how wonderful it was. The lines of dialogue were brilliant and she wondered how they had ever come to her – and from her. She watched the actors. They were not good. *And yet*, she thought, *they are keeping my work alive – which is more than I will ever do.* And she felt a strange jealousy towards them.

When the play was over, after the applause had subsided, and just before the audience started to leave, the young man next to Desiree jumped to his feet.

'Ladies and gentlemen,' he said with a loud, shaking voice, 'I want you to know that the author of *Promenade* is here with us tonight.'

The audience murmured and peered, clapped again, demanded a speech.

The boy pulled Desiree to her feet. She felt sick. But she managed to make a little speech.

After the show, everyone gathered around and congratulated her. And wanted to know what she was working on now.

She fled finally through a fire door.

As Desiree reached the parking lot, the attendant came rushing towards her with a sweating, excited face.

'I've okayed it with the management,' he said triumphantly. 'Since you're Desiree Kaufman, you don't have to pay the $2.50 parking charge.'

It was her first High School reunion. From the moment the invitation came, Laura had thought of nothing else. Even though she had hated High School, she felt overwhelmingly excited about going back now. She had the oddest feeling that today was going to be important. Who knows? she thought. Some detail missed during those actual years of attendance – some tiny little arrow that she should have followed and didn't – might show up at the reunion. And this time she would be ready.

Laura dressed more carefully than she had dressed for the Ray Abbott premiere, and was ready half an hour too early. She looked in the mirror. Portrait of Young Woman attending her High School Reunion. She felt monumental, archetypal.

'You look beautiful,' Jeff told her.

By the time they reached Mapleton Drive, Laura was jittery, chattering, perspiring. Over and over, she went through the litany of girls Jeff would meet; their traits, their accomplishments, her memories of them.

They drove up to the familiar driveway, and turned in at the sign which read, 'Talbot School for Girls.' Jeff parked the car, took Laura's hand and they walked into the school.

The big brick building smelled exactly the same to Laura, sounded exactly the same. It felt very strange, like a time warp, entering it with a man, and not wearing a school uniform. She kept expecting to be pounced on and ladled out demerits.

Laura led Jeff to the Great Hall where the reunion was being held, and pushed open the heavy door. There in front of her was a roomful of strange grown-up women. Laura felt panicky; she wanted to turn and run. But Jeff pulled her inside the reunion.

'It's Laura Alden!'

Everyone rushed to Laura at once, laughing, hugging her. And she exclaimed, hugged back, introduced Jeff, said how glad she was to be there. But that was a lie. The whole thing was bewildering to the point of nightmare.

She kept staring around her. What an awful joke that everyone should all be so changed. Who were these

156

people, wearing adult clothes, talking about careers, showing pictures of their babies? What had happened to those other girls? Laura wondered bewilderedly. The old ones? The real ones?

She grew more and more unsettled as the hours went by. She talked with classmate after classmate, hearing about their lives – while in her head she saw them, classmate after classmate, as they had once been. Alison Brady, who was going to be a dancer, now married to an Oregon lumberjack. Vera Deutsch, the May Queen, a typist for a janitorial service. And someone told her that little Janis Page – 'Most Likely to Succeed' – was dead from drugs.

She tried to have it make sense but it wouldn't. All these lives which had been connected and now were not. What was the point? What was the goddam point of all those friendships, those experiences, those High School years? And of course there was no little arrow for Laura. No subtle little missed arrow which was going to change her life now. High School was over. What on earth had she been hoping for?

As Laura was leaving, a girl she didn't remember came up to her. 'Laura,' she said earnestly, 'congratulations on your great success in life. We always knew you'd end up somewhere really special.'

Baffled and drained, Laura got in the car and Jeff drove her home in silence.

The plan was that they would meet at twelve, at the perfume counter of Neiman Marcus, but Laura had been waiting for fifteen minutes and still Mimi had not shown up.

Finally, she came scurrying from the scarf department.

'Oh, Laura, I'm sorry I'm late. I just saw the most

gorgeous Anne Klein scarf, but the price was totally ridiculous. You wouldn't believe what those bandits were asking!'

'Too bad!' Laura sympathized.

'Why too bad?' Mimi asked in surprise. 'I got it anyway.' She motioned to the green Neiman Marcus shopping bag in her hand.

They went to the little coffee shop on the fourth floor. The conversation was vapid, as usual. *Why did I ever agree to come?* Laura wondered. *Why do I keep on seeing her?* She thought that maybe it was part of that whole High School syndrome, and still trying to find that stupid little arrow.

Pretty pathetic, she told herself angrily.

Lunch was over.

'Come on,' Mimi jumped up. 'They're having a sale downstairs. I really need some things.'

It amazed Laura, the things Mimi really needed. Silky beaded pajamas, stylish gowns in vivid clashing colors. And Mimi went through racks of clothes with the single-minded speed of a cotton picker, pouncing unerringly on the trendiest designers and the most fashionable materials. It made Laura feel very childish and unformed.

Well, we all have our fields of expertise, she reminded herself. *And I've got Philippe, the French Hippo.*

It wasn't terribly comforting.

Finally, they reached the front door of Neiman Marcus and said goodbye. Laura was a quarter of a block away, when she was stopped by Mimi's casual call.

'Oh, and don't forget, Laura,' she said. 'You promised to phone Christopher Garland and set up our appointment.'

Numbly, Laura nodded.

She walked the rest of the way to her car, her footsteps

158

keeping unwilling time to the name. *Christopher Garland. Christopher Garland*. It grew and grew, louder and louder, in her head. It was almost as if that had somehow been what the whole afternoon had been about – waiting to set the name Christopher Garland free again.

The library was under construction and Laura circled the parking lot six times, looking for a space. When finally one opened up, she shot into it so fast that she slammed into the curb.

She stalked into the building and headed for the Periodicals.

'May I help you?' asked a pleasant library voice.

Laura jumped, caught out.

'Actually, I'm looking for some old *Hollywood Reporter*s,' she stammered.

'What year?'

'Oh, I don't know. Maybe five years ago.'

'Are you in film school?' the librarian asked with interest.

Laura thought for a moment that it would be nice to say yes, and thus be able to live forever as a film student in someone else's mind.

'No,' she said. 'Just curious.'

Guiltily, she cut herself off. But still the librarian did not seem suspicious – still she did not forbid Laura.

'Right over here,' she said.

A few minutes later, Laura went over to the farthest library carrel, a stackful of *Hollywood Reporter*s in her arms. She sat down furtively and opened the first one. She had half hoped he had been lying about the whole thing, but there it was – his name on the inside cover.

159

She spent the next hour looking through the pictures he had taken. He had been present at everything. Parties, galas, openings. She found herself wondering if he had had to wear a tuxedo to these events. He probably looked very funny in a tuxedo, like a skinny little boy dressing up.

She traced his pictures through a year. She grew to see which angles he most favored, the way he liked to pose a group.

In the last issue she looked at, she came upon a photo he had taken at a New Year's Eve party – a photo of her parents. Blake was smiling, his hands outspread, either telling or reacting to a joke. And Julia – she was not looking at the camera; she was dreaming, gazing off.

In shock, Laura stared at the photograph. Julia had been there. Julia had been within feet of Christopher Garland. If only she had looked up, for just a second. Looked up at Christopher, met Christopher, learned to know him, laughed him off, warned Blake against him. Then all this never would have started.

If I could only get her to look this way now, Laura thought crazily. She tried by force of will to drag Julia's face toward the camera, toward Christopher, but the picture on the page remained a picture on a page.

Finally she returned the stack of magazines. The librarian did not look up.

She called him that night. So as not to leave any room for foolishness, she had written it all down beforehand, about Mimi and the reading, and a suggested day and time. With each ring of the phone, her heart thudded more heavily, more stupidly. She was angry at herself that this was happening. At the fourth ring, his answering machine picked up. Laura waited for the beep, but when it came, she froze and ended up not leaving any message at all.

She hung up the phone, feeling very flat. She stared at the unused carefully thought-out sentences she had written and crumpled the paper up.

Let Mimi call him herself, Laura thought. *Why should I have to deal with him at all? I'll give her the number and she can make her own appointment.*

She called Mimi, and Mimi answered on the first ring. But Laura hung up without saying a word.

She wondered why she had done such a stupid thing.

Jeff had an audition the following morning. He dressed for it carefully, even put on his lucky tie.

'How do I look?' he asked Laura.

'You're a work of art,' she told him earnestly.

Jeff frowned. It always made him uneasy when she got intense like that.

'I know you'll get the commercial,' she went on. 'Just go in with a positive attitude, and – '

Standing before the mirror, Jeff tuned her out. Why, he wondered, when he was the most nervous, did Laura always manage to say the most wrong thing? He glimpsed her anxious, over-expressive face behind his in the mirror, and he changed position so he could block it out. He loved Laura, but didn't she realize how this chatter, all this extravagance of gesture and phrase, were wearing him down? Especially when he was worrying about sticking out his fucking neck for a fucking audition. But no, she kept right on with her little pep talks, never noticing a thing.

He felt very remote from her. He found himself suddenly remembering a girl from Stanford – one he had met before Laura. She hadn't been very interesting after a while, but he would always remember her peacefulness. She had been white, plump, soothing – he thought of a Buddha carved out of rose quartz. Just to be near her was to feel centered. He had liked to touch the top of her smooth blond head. He had even had the fancy that that would bring him luck.

'And if you *do* get the commercial, then the first thing you'll have to tell your agent – ' came the relentless anxious wisdom behind him.

Yackety yak, he thought furiously. Then he felt guilty.

Quickly he finished dressing; quickly he kissed Laura goodbye. Experimentally, he put his hand on the top of her head for luck. But Laura's hair felt as wavy and wiry as a sea sponge churning in the ocean. He drew away.

I hope I helped, Laura thought mournfully, watching him go.

She sat back on the bed, feeling dark and flat.

The phone rang.

'Hello?'

'Hello. I'd like to speak to Laura Alden.'

It was a man's voice; disorienting, high-pitched.

'This is Laura Alden,' she said cautiously.

'Well, I'm calling from Special Memories, and I'm happy to tell you that your plane is ready.'

Laura stared at the phone. 'My *plane*? What plane? What are you talking about?'

The man was instantly keyed up. 'The plane you ordered – with the special banner. It's ready. You're next on the list. We're primed to fly. When do you want it?'

Laura smiled. *Of course! The special surprise she had planned for Jeff. God, it had been months ago. She had forgotten all about it.*

'Well, his birthday's not until the twenty-fifth,' she began, and then, as she remembered how tense Jeff had

162

been that morning, she cut herself off. 'No, I can't wait. Let's fly tonight!'

The man giggled, as excited as she.

Arrangements were quickly made. The little plane would be flying over the apartment between five o'clock and five minutes past five that evening.

Laura hung up, smiling.

'I'm sorry,' Joe Hyatt, the producer said, looking at the stills. 'It looked good from the pictures, Jeff, but now that I see you in person, it's no go. You're just not right for this set-up. The thing is, see, we need a kid.'

Jeff stared at him. 'And what exactly am I?' he asked.

The man stared levelly back at him.

'You're not a kid,' he said.

Jeff went into a bar in Santa Monica and got drunker than he'd ever been in his life.

He came home at ten to five. Laura was waiting for him.

'Well, well? Did you get it?' she demanded, before he was all the way in the door.

Her eagerness was agony to him.

'If you'd stop talking and simply take a look at me, you'd see that I didn't,' he said coldly.

She was instantly penitent. 'Oh, Jeff, I'm sorry. It's just that I was so sure. These producers – they're crazy. What exactly did the man say?'

But Jeff wouldn't tell her what the man had said.

There was nothing Laura could do. She just went over and held him. But his body refused to be comforted.

'Hey,' Jeff said suddenly, looking up and breaking from her. 'What the hell is that? It sounds like an air raid.'

For a moment, Laura was as puzzled as he – and then she realized. It was the plane! *What perfect timing*, she thought thankfully.

'I can't imagine,' she told him, trying to hide her excitement. 'Why don't you go to the window and see?'

Jeff went to the window. The plane was right overhead. 'I LOVE YOU JEFF KENNERLY' the purple banner trumpeted in letters of gold.

Jeff saw it. For a moment he just stared. *He really is speechless with surprise*, Laura thought proudly. *The way it happens in books.*

'Oh, my God,' Jeff whispered at last. 'It's some kind of practical joke.'

Laura looked at him in horror. 'Joke?' she said. 'Of course it's no joke.'

He turned to her. His eyes were braziers. '*You* did this?' he said dangerously. '*You* did this to me?'

She stared back at him, her mouth limp, empty of defense.

'I thought – I thought you'd like it,' she faltered.

He stared at her with sickened eyes.

'You thought I'd like it?' he repeated incredulously. 'Have you lost your fucking senses?' Jeff began to pace the living room. His voice rose with every sentence. ' "I love you, Jeff Kennerly," – on a *plane* – and you thought I'd *like* it!' He thought of the audition that morning, of the producer possibly seeing that plane tonight, and he wanted to run wild, crash around the apartment, crash into those seventeen glossy photos of that idiot Jeff Kennerly. 'Goddam it, Laura, why didn't you use your head? Why don't you ever use your fucking head? I'll be a laughing stock! Everyone is going to think it's a publicity stunt! Everyone is going to think I hired the goddam plane myself!' He ended on a scream.

Laura paled.

'I'm sure they won't,' she said quickly.

He slammed his fist on the table.

'Of course they will,' he hissed. 'Are you that naive?

164

Are you such a goddam ostrich that you never paid any attention to how this town works? Why don't you rent me a goddam billboard next?' He looked at her downcast head coldly. 'For five years, I've tried to build a reputation – a quality reputation – and you've ruined it in one night. Thanks. That's all I can say. Thanks a lot.'

Laura raised her head and looked at him. 'I was just trying to tell you that I love you,' she said.

The plane danced away into the night sky.

The next morning, in her sleep, she heard the phone ring and heard Jeff answer it. He spoke briefly and hung up. And suddenly he was bouncing on the bed, laughing, shouting at Laura to wake up, grabbing her by the wrist and making her bounce, too.

'Laura,' he hollered. 'I've gotten a call-back. They want me to re-audition for the series!'

She was too sleepy to take it in at once. She just kept staring at the shockingly happy face that had no connection whatsoever with the face of the night before.

'That's wonderful,' she told him finally.

Jeff jumped off the bed and walked excitedly around the small room.

'I'd given it up for lost,' he said incredulously. 'Even my agent said to forget it. I wonder what made them think of me again, after all this time.' Dizzily, he laughed. 'Maybe it was that goddam plane of yours, Laura. Hey – yeah! Maybe one of the producers saw that banner and said, "Jeff Kennerly! I remember him. He wasn't half-bad, was he?"'

'You're a doll, Laura!' he cried, coming back to the bed and grabbing her and kissing her. 'You're a gorgeous little miracle worker. I love you to pieces. And I love your fucking plane!'

Laura lay in bed for a long time after Jeff left. She felt very numb. Strange hostile waters were churning all around her. And the noose was back. The noose was killing her. Finally she got dressed and drove down to the beach.

When she got to San Vicente, she avoided it, and went down another street. *The last thing in the world I need is to run into Christopher Garland now*, she thought grimly. She parked on Ocean Avenue and went towards the sand.

She was instantly sorry she had come. The beach was very crowded. Even with the sky and the sea shaking freedom from all sides, Laura felt claustrophobic in the presence of all those aggressive, glistening bodies.

And then the sand thundered. Someone was running up to Laura. *Dammit*, she thought. *I knew it.* He had found her again. Her face grew very red. Her breath came very fast.

But it wasn't Christopher. It was a boy chasing after a runaway volleyball.

And Laura was absolutely shocked by the feeling that ran through her.

She was wildly, desperately moody when she came home. Senseless tears kept falling.

What was going on? she wondered. *What the hell was going on?*

To try and calm herself, she went over to the desk. She read the latest supply of love-letters she had gotten from Julia's desk. They were so very beautiful, those letters. That love.

But reading the letters made Laura even more frantic. She kept thinking of Jeff – the way he had behaved last night about the plane, and the quick turnaround this morning. And around that throbbing nucleus, a cluster of other images began to crystallize.

Jeff jeering at her the other night. Seeing the wedding on Pico. The night at C. C. Brown's. Jeff telling her she was sick because she missed her mother. Jeff so happy to show her the picture from the *Inquirer*.

And she found herself remembering other things – images from the past – memories she had hidden behind her for five years. Jeff shouting, Jeff pushing her away, Jeff crying out that she was stupid. Jeff fighting with her parents, Jeff putting down her children's books, Jeff telling her he didn't know what he saw in her sometimes.

She thought she had forgotten them, but she had not.

Laura sat still, cold. For five years, Jeff Kennerly had been the cornerstone on which her whole life had been based. But it suddenly all seemed like so much quicksand now. *Who was she trying to kid?* she wondered bleakly. Love with Jeff was not like the love she had found in her parents' letters. She saw, with sudden vision, that it had never been. That it would never be. And she grew terrified.

But there was also something else. A whole other crystal that had been growing and growing and was unstoppable. Some realization was crashing upon Laura – something that she knew she didn't understand, that she didn't want to understand.

She came upon a line in one of her father's letters. 'I think of you in all seasons, at all times. Everywhere you are with me.'

Christopher, she thought.

And Laura burst into sudden horrified tears. *Not that*, she thought, *oh, please not that*.

But it was that. And in one moment, her whole world turned completely upside down.

Chapter Ten

'Time to get up, Miss Kaufman.' In a whisper, Lily, the maid, apologized for the morning. 'It's nine o'clock.'

She came into the room, the breakfast tray as a peace-offering. After she left, Desiree studied it. White wicker tray, floral Portault linens, limoges china in the Artois pattern and the soothing breakfast colors involved with juice and croissant and coffee. It was really very pleasant, even showed talent. She wondered about Lily – was she an artist in her secret soul? Or, Desiree smiled grimly, is she just so afraid of me that she knows better than to bring me anything that is less than beautiful?

The morning paper was in the pocket of the tray. Desiree turned first to the Entertainment section, to see if there was any mention of him today. There was not. Then she turned to the news, but after a moment, tossed the paper aside. How badly it was written, she thought impatiently. The sloppiness of style upset her more than the contents themselves.

For a moment, she wished that she were the one writing the news. Yes. The fantasy intrigued her. Quickly, she re-wrote her life. Leaving Yale for journalism. The youngest, most trenchant reporter. Wearing a great deal of black. This character pleased her. And a newswoman's world would necessarily be linear – cushioned by busyness and fulfillable goals. No longer the maelstrom.

But, Desiree thought, biting into her croissant and watching the buttery crumbs drop onto the newspaper and distort the print, if she were a newswoman, she would not be eating this breakfast from the wicker tray at nine o'clock in the morning. It was really rather simple.

The phone rang.

'Hello?' Desiree said.

The voice on the phone was shaking.

'Desiree, it's Laura. I've got to talk to you.'

'Yes?' Desiree asked a little coldly.

They had not spoken since the disastrous lunch at Kate Mantilini's.

'Something's happened.'

'I assumed so,' Desiree said. 'I hardly thought you had called to tell me your dreams.'

Laura's voice became hesitant, incredulous. 'Desiree, I think – I think I'm falling in love.'

'Fallen,' Desiree said.

'What?'

'Already fallen,' Desiree repeated patiently. 'In love with the psychic.'

She enjoyed Laura's shocked gasp, and added smugly, 'I've seen it coming for weeks.'

'But how *could* you?' Laura demanded. '*I* didn't know until last night.'

'I'm a good playwright, my dear,' Desiree reminded her. 'Some say the best in the country. And this was all in the script.'

Laura laughed bewilderedly. 'Oh, it was, was it? Well, I wish you'd warned me. Oh, Desiree, isn't it insane? I can't tell you what I've been going through.'

She talked on, explaining, giggling nervously. Desiree listened for several minutes. The childish excitement in Laura's voice at once charmed and irritated her.

'Does he know?' she asked bluntly at last, tiring of the vagaries.

'No.'

169

'Are you going to tell him?'

'I can't,' Laura said after a long pause.

'Why not?'

'Jeff.'

'Ah, yes, Jeff,' Desiree said lightly. Perhaps the situation was not so unredeemably childish after all. 'Well, what are you going to do?'

'I don't know,' Laura told her tensely. 'I haven't the slightest idea. All I know is that the whole world's turned upside down. I just can't believe this has happened to me!' she cried. 'I never thought anyone could matter to me but Jeff. And a *psychic*. I feel so foolish – I feel so terrible.'

Desiree laughed.

'No, you don't,' she said.

There was a pause.

'You're right,' Laura admitted. 'Oh, Desiree,' she burst out. 'You don't think I'm an awful person, do you?'

'No,' Desiree said. 'I don't. But if you were, I'd love you just the same.' She smiled wryly. 'Perhaps even more.'

After they said goodbye, Desiree hung up the phone and lay back against the pillow. So Laura was in love. It made her feel strangely vulnerable, strangely lonely. She closed her eyes.

. . . *Through the darkness, a boy came towards Desiree.*

She recognized him at once, was grateful to see him again.

'*Here, Miss – you dropped your theatre programme.*'

And so it had begun. There had been wet-fire roses in the Arboretum that summer. She and he escaping from the others, going on long walks under the brooding, sticky trees. His curious mouth – like a red passionate gash in his face – closing over hers.

170

He had died at the end of August — a freak accident in a neighbor's swimming pool.

She had been fourteen years old.

Light was coming through the window, groggy and crazy through the slats of the Venetian blind.

Desiree returned to the newspaper and the croissant.

So Laura is in love, she thought again, turning the page. *She will end up breaking her heart, of course, but so it goes.*

It was the most enchanted morning Laura had ever spent. She went to Robinson's to buy new sheets. And Christopher Garland was woven through every thread of every sheet.

It was as if all her life she had been walking around in shoes with fifty pound weights attached — and suddenly they were off. A single step now took her not the familiar few inches, but giddy miles. The old bounds and bonds were simply not there anymore. She was a light traveller, leaping as you leap in dreams.

Christopher Garland.

He was the constant whisperer in her mind, spiralling her thoughts into configurations that left her breathless. Anything served to summon him — a car, a cloud, a profile. And once summoned, the thought gripped her whole body with wild, rushing excitement.

You're acting like an idiot, she told herself. *You're acting like a tenth grader. What is it about him that you're in love with? That skinny body? Those Martian eyes? That crazy philosophy?* But the scolding was short. Because she had never felt half so alive in her life.

She did not let herself think about Jeff.

Finally, Laura left Robinson's. She drove home, growing fuller and fuller with her secret every second. *I need to talk to Desiree some more*, she decided. *I'll go over there tonight, and we'll get everything sorted out. Jeff will be at the gym – I'll have a clear evening.* It was a huge relief, even in imagination, to tell Desiree all of what she was feeling. Desiree was a playwright. Desiree would be able to sift through it all – the euphoria and the guilt – and give her the next scene in the play.

Then, as Laura was heading down Wilshire, on an impulse she stopped and went into a stationery store. She looked for a marbled composition book, the kind she had used to keep a diary in when she was a child. It made her happy to buy it now. It made her excited to think what she might be writing in the pages.

Balancing her packages on her knee, Laura opened the front door of the apartment.

'Hi,' Jeff said.

'Jeff!' She looked up in shock. 'I thought you'd be out.'

She clutched guiltily at the new notebook, as though the diary were already complete within it. But he didn't even notice what she was carrying.

'Change of plan,' he told her, grinning. 'When I read in *T.V. Guide* what was on tonight, I cancelled my hand-ball game. Hurry up and sit down. You almost missed the beginning.'

'What beginning?' she asked, flustered.

'*Return of Spring*,' he said.

Return of Spring was Jeff's film debut – a movie of the week in which he had the third lead.

He patted the sofa. 'Isn't this great?' he said. 'On top of getting the call-back yesterday, it seems like an omen. And if the ratings are halfway decent, it could do me some real good.' He patted the sofa. 'Hurry up,' he said. 'I want you next to me.' Then he pulled two bags of popcorn from behind the couch. 'Look what I got for you,' he said. 'Store-bought wasn't good enough, so I

172

drove all the way to the movie theatre on Wilshire for these!'

Laura looked at the bags of popcorn.

'Listen, Jeff,' she said with trepidation, 'I have seen *Return of Spring* seventeen times. I know every line in it by heart – and besides, we have it on tape.'

'It's not the same thing,' he said impatiently. 'You know it's not. Now sit down and let's watch.'

With a grin, he grabbed her by the waist and started to pull her down onto his lap.

Laura felt trapped, guilty, angry. 'Don't!' she said, struggling. 'Jeff, I'm sorry. But I just don't feel like seeing it tonight.'

He let go of her waist abruptly and stared at her. 'What?'

She swallowed. 'I had plans to see Desiree,' she said weakly. Perspiration flew out of her like ineffective crazy little words.

'I didn't expect you home,' she threw sentences randomly into the silence, 'and I really need to talk with Desiree. I didn't know the movie would be on . . . If you could just have given me a little warning . . .'

Abruptly, Jeff turned his back on her.

She knew how hurt he was.

She looked over at him, sitting so uncomprehendingly and angry; looked over at the popcorn he had driven all that way to buy. She thought of Christopher Garland, and her heart leaked with guilt.

So she sat down on the edge of the couch to watch the movie. Jeff took her hand.

Sitting there, watching *Return of Spring*, Laura felt very fragile, very torn. The movie was a maudlin pot-boiler, but Jeff was brilliant in it. Gazing at him on the screen, several times she found herself thinking how absolutely beautiful he was. And then she would remem-

ber that this talented, wonderful person was hers, that
he loved her, that he had driven all that way to buy her
popcorn.

And then she would think of Christopher Garland.

Thoughts and emotions chased one another around
and around in her brain like Sambo's tigers.

The movie was over at last.

Laura cried at the ending, as she always did.

'You were better than ever,' she told Jeff, blowing her
nose.

'Thanks,' he said.

He kissed her lightly, and rose. He changed the chan-
nel and became immediately involved in a sports event.

Laura got up also. She felt headachey and upset. Crazily, she kept thinking that she could smell Christopher's
incense all around her. And a line from *Pippin* kept
rolling like a wave in her brain. *There's one thing to be
sure of, Mate – there's nothing to be sure of.*

Desiree, she thought desperately. *I've got to get to
Desiree.*

She cleared her throat. 'If it's all right with you, Jeff,'
she said, 'I'd really like to go see Desiree now.'

'Sure,' Jeff told her, his eyes on the set. 'Go anywhere
your little heart desires. Kill the bastards!' he shouted
cheerfully at the screen.

Laura drove down Doheny. The evening was cold, red
and glistening, like the edge of a broken wine glass.

As she reached Desiree's house, she saw that the windows were dark. *Damn*, Laura thought. *She's gone out.
I should have called before I came.*

As a last hope, she checked Desiree's garage to see if
the car was there. But the garage door was closed. *That*

was strange, Laura thought, frowning. Desiree usually kept her garage door open.

Still Laura went towards the apartment. She climbed the steps and knocked on the door. There was no answer. She knocked more sharply, rang the doorbell. The resulting silence made her feel foolish.

She stood there blankly. She did not want to go back home, did not want to face a television-drugged Jeff and those lines from *Pippin* banging in her brain.

I'll go somewhere for coffee, Laura decided at last. *And I'll leave Desiree a note saying I'll be back in an hour.*

She rummaged through her bursting purse, but she could not find anything to write with. Then her hand scraped against something metallic. She pulled it out, hoping it was a pen, but it was a key. The key to Desiree's house. *In case you ever need a place of refuge*, Desiree had smiled.

Fate, Laura said to herself, and triumphantly she inserted the key into the lock. Then she moved into the house and flipped on the hall lights. There was no pen on the table. *I'll try Desiree's bedroom*, Laura thought. And she pushed open the door.

It all happened very fast, incoherently, gracelessly. The frantic twistings of the bedsheets. Desiree rising, naked and damp. The palette of fury, shock, embarrassment in her eyes. The man caught between the bed and the door, trying to cover himself.

It was the first time in her life that Laura had seen her father naked.

She shut the bedroom door on the frozen tableau, and ran, sobbing, from the apartment. Halfway down the front steps, she tripped and she fell like a child on the sidewalk.

'Stay right there,' a voice whipped.

At the top of the stairs was Desiree. She came relentlessly down. Wearing nothing but a blowing sheet, she looked immense, emblematic. Laura stayed absolutely still, watching her. The blood running from her knee was the only motion in the scene.

'How dare you?' Desiree asked in a low, cold whisper. 'How dare you come to spy on me?'

Laura swallowed, painfully. 'Jeff was right,' she jerked out. 'You were just using me.'

At that moment, a van drove by. The two boys inside caught sight of Desiree naked under the sheet, and they hooted with rapturous disbelief. Desiree and Laura did not even hear.

Desiree stood for a long time, wrapping Laura in flame with her eyes.

'You stupid little girl,' she said. 'You have no problems at all in your life – not one. You know nothing of the world. You know nothing about suffering. You know nothing of what life is about, so how dare you presume to judge me?'

'You used me,' Laura repeated thickly. 'Just to get to my father.'

Then Desiree dropped her eyes. Laura no longer felt on fire.

When Desiree spoke again, it was in an altered voice. 'Yes,' she said. Her tone was considering now, cool. 'Perhaps you're right in part. Perhaps I did start out with that in mind. Certainly the only reason I asked you to tea that first time was because of your father.' Then she raised her eyes again. 'And why not? Why not try to get close to the daughter of the man I love?'

'But I thought you loved me.' Messy tears were running down Laura's face. 'You said you felt I was your daughter – and it was all a lie.'

Desiree gave a frozen little smile. 'Was it?' she asked.

She straightened up. 'No, Laura,' she said, and her voice was chillingly soft. 'What was between you and me was real. All of it. It was not something I chose – becoming a mother is not exactly convenient at my age – or even something I can explain. To be whimsical, we'll say Julia arranged it for both our sakes. But the truth is, I love you. You are as much a part of me as your mother – or your father. Perhaps even more so. Believe me or not as you choose.'

Laura lay still a long moment, while Desiree stood motionless above her. The sheet raged in the wind. Then Laura reached up her arms, and Desiree came down. She hugged Laura and kissed her on the hair with strong, feisty pecks. And underneath the strength of her arms, Laura could feel how much she was trembling.

They were sitting close together on the steps, hidden by the portico so that they could no longer be seen from the street. The sheet was shared evenly over their shoulders. The outdoor carpet oozed the dampness from the past week's rain, and Laura's knee was a bloody mess – but neither she nor Desiree wanted to move.

'Why didn't you tell me?' Laura asked.

Desiree smiled wryly. 'I wanted to wait until I was sure you would understand.'

'I understand,' Laura said. 'Now that I'm over the shock, I even approve. In fact,' she admitted, 'the truth is, I was trying to set you and Daddy up myself!'

Desiree laughed. 'Yes, of course, that lunch at Kate Mantilini's. I should have guessed what was going on. Something that clumsily contrived could only have been a Laura Alden production.'

Laura laughed too, ruefully.

'You say you understand,' Desiree went on musingly. 'You may approve, but you do not necessarily understand.' She moved restlessly under the sheet. 'I met your father twenty-seven years ago,' she went on. 'He was the first man I ever loved.'

It came as a surprise to Laura. And some prim, child-part of her felt violated. She had never considered the fact that, before her mother, her father could have ever loved anybody else.

'We talked about getting married,' Desiree went on, 'but I wasn't ready for that. I was too young, too ambitious.'

Storms from various dangerous winds were blowing about Laura. Sensing them, Desiree smiled again. 'And then, one night at my house, your father met your mother,' she said distinctly, 'and that was that.'

Laura nodded, satisfied. But then another wind overtook her. 'But you and Daddy – ' she faltered.

'There was nothing between your father and me,' Desiree told her firmly. 'For twenty-seven years we met at parties, danced on occasional New Year's Eves. Your mother was my best friend, Laura.'

'Did she – '

'No,' Desiree said. 'She didn't. And why should she?' Then her voice became very slow, very mesmerized. 'But maybe she knew all along, Laura. Because after she died, something very strange happened.

'I had seen nothing of your father since the memorial service. Rumor had it that he had started dating women – the predictable ones, nothing serious. Then, one Tuesday night, I went alone to Matteo's. And your father came in. He was also alone. I looked up and saw him.' She laughed grimly. 'It really does happen this way sometimes. Like in a bad novel. It was truly like a lightning bolt. And the feelings were there again, as if they had never left.' She shrugged wryly. 'I'm entirely convinced Julia engineered the whole thing herself. She always did have rather a ghastly sense of humor.'

178

'And Daddy?' Laura paused.

'Yes,' Desiree nodded. 'He came over to my table. We were together that night. We were together all the time after that.' She sighed. 'You have no idea of the machinations that went on – the machinations to keep you from finding out. "She'll be so upset. She'll never understand," your father kept saying. Shows how much *he* knows.' She gestured towards the two of them with a smile. 'I guess only your psychic friend could have foreseen you and me out here with this damned sheet!'

It was with a chill that Laura suddenly thought of Christopher Garland and his prediction about her father and Desiree. That it was a relationship which was doomed.

'And now what?' she asked quickly. 'Now that I know? Are you and Daddy going to get married?'

Desiree stiffened. 'One forgets sometimes that, under those childish looks of yours, there beats an equally childish heart. No,' she said, 'this is not a fairy tale. We are not going to get married.'

'But why not?' Laura persisted, stung by the sarcasm.

'My dear Laura,' Desiree told her grandly. 'I have spent the last fifteen years perfecting the details of my life. I am not now about to have them upset by marrying any man, especially your father. We dine at different times.'

She's lying, Laura thought with clarity. *This is all a lie.*

And then suddenly Desiree began to cry. A small, bitter, hopeless crying that sounded as if it had been there forever. Laura watched her in horror. In that one moment, Desiree changed forever in her mind. The chic, the briskness, the knife-edge were blunted beyond repair, and she saw only a lonely woman sobbing in a bloody sheet.

'Desiree, Desiree,' Laura murmured, aghast, so sorry she had seen.

'I love him so much,' Desiree wept. 'So much, so much. And it's over.'

The nakedness was terrible to witness.

'What do you mean, it's over?' Laura gestured bewilderedly towards the house. 'I mean, just now, you and he – '

Desiree shook her head impatiently. 'He came over to see me about a project,' she said in a low voice, 'and he was a little drunk. Things got started. That was all. It wasn't the way it was before – it hasn't been that way in a long time.' Mascara clawed blackly at her cheeks. 'I don't know what happened, Laura. I don't know what changed him. But it's over.'

'Well, maybe not,' Laura said with bleak hopefulness.

Desiree grew angry again. 'What do you know about it? I know every starlet he's seeing now. I know where he goes and who he goes with. The romantic doings of the great man are duly reported in the tabloids,' she said drily, 'and what tidbits they fail to pick up on, my friends are only too happy to supply me with.'

'Oh, Desiree,' Laura whispered mournfully.

Suddenly, Desiree grabbed at Laura's hands. 'I can't stand it, Laura. I love him so much.'

Baffled, miserable, ineffectual, Laura patted her hands.

'Please help me,' Desiree whispered. 'Please help me.'

The words fell, finite and heavy. 'But I can't,' Laura jerked out. 'There's nothing I can do.'

'You're his daughter,' Desiree said.

I wish I'd never come here tonight, Laura thought.

'Please help me get him back.'

'I can't,' Laura was about to say again. And then she was filled with a terrible anger against herself. She hadn't been able to keep her mother alive. She hadn't

180

been able to drive the car. She hadn't gotten Jeff to marry her. She hadn't been able to save herself from the psychic.

But she was stopping the tides now.

Damn Christopher Garland and what he had said. Desiree was perfect for her father, and he was perfect for her. She loved Desiree. She was pledged to Desiree. And she would fight every force in the Universe to make sure this relationship worked out.

She held Desiree's hands. A sudden feeling of strength, of sureness, came flowing from her. 'Of course I'll help you,' she heard herself saying. 'You can count on me, Desiree.'

Desiree looked up into Laura's face. 'Thank you,' she said.

Laura was suddenly exhausted. 'I'd better get going now,' she said, rising. 'It's been quite an evening. Give my love to your admirer,' she added lightly, gesturing toward the house. 'If you like, you can tell him I never saw his face.'

Chapter Eleven

I am sitting in my pajamas at the breakfast table writing this. Birdie keeps jumping up to attack the pen. It feels really strange to be keeping a journal again.

It's so hard to start – what should I put down? So much has happened. It's incredible that my handwriting is exactly like it was in college – the last time I kept a journal. But nothing else is the same.

I've thought so much about the Daddy/Desiree situation. I've caught a cold from sitting on her steps that night and somehow that's managed to make the whole thing seem more real. But I am still so haunted by what happened. I wish I had never seen it. It was something I was not meant to have seen.

I've talked to her every day since. It's been very uncomfortable. Now that I know the secret, it's all she talks about – how to get Daddy back. We come up with all these different ploys. I even find myself telling her all kinds of little details Mama used to share with me about Daddy. How Daddy hates strong women. How Daddy loves patterned silk stockings. Hoping that will help Desiree get him back. I wonder if I should feel disloyal to Mama by giving away these little tips. I don't think so. There is that strange, fantastic connection between Desiree and Mama, after all.

I've seen Daddy only once since that night. I was nervous about seeing him, knowing we would finally have to face the issue, but, incredibly, we didn't. Daddy talked non-stop about a deal he's making, and he never even mentioned the other night. I thought maybe, in the shock of the moment, he didn't even realize it was me coming into Desiree's bedroom. But that's insane – of course he realized it was me.

Things are so awkward – have always been so awkward – between us. Surface talk only, all the real things never getting said. Does Daddy even notice? Or does he think we *are* talking about the real things? I don't know. I wish we were close enough so that I could just come out and say, 'What's going on with you? What's going on with you and Desiree?' But I can't. I just can't. Could any daughter? All those years of embarrassed silence between us. Misunderstandings. Being the child. Mama being the go-between.

It's too late to change all that, but I do wonder. What would he say if I told him, 'I want you to marry Desiree Kaufman?' And what would he say if I told him that I've fallen in love with a psychic?

Which brings me to a whole other damned tangle.

I've given the Christopher situation more than enough time to go away, but it's just getting more and more intense. I feel like the Haunted House ride at Disneyland. Every room with a ghost – and they're all Christopher. I wake up and he's there. All day he's there. He's like a curtain between me and everything else. Jeff keeps asking me if everything's all right. I don't know what to answer.

I keep waiting for it to get diffused, but it doesn't. I see that I've got to do something. I can't let myself go off the deep-end over this. I keep asking myself what it is about him, but I don't know. There are only a few things I'm sure of. That this is madness. That it's delusion. And that it will eventually go away. I just have to find a way of seeing him again in the meantime.

Finally made up my mind to act. I called Christopher up. I told him I wanted to take one of his private metaphysical classes. He didn't ask any questions, didn't even seem surprised.

I start the first class on Monday. I feel so relieved – at least something is in the works at last.

I heard a song on the radio today. I think it was one of Dan Fogelberg's. It started out, 'Changing horses in midstream gets you wet and sometimes cold. Changing faces in the middle of a dream gets you home.'

That song sounded like an omen. I've been feeling so guilty since this whole thing started. Guilty towards Jeff for trying to think of ways to see C. Guilty towards C. because of why I'm taking the classes. But I see now that I must do this. Get this issue resolved, one way or the other. And maybe the song is right – sometimes, to get home, you have to change faces in the middle of a dream. But I don't think things will come to that. I'm sure I'll be over this soon, neither Jeff nor Christopher will ever know, and then I'll quit the classes.

My first session with C. So nervous when he opened the door, afraid he'd take one look at me, and see through everything. But he didn't. He was very calm, said how glad he was to see me. And still not one word about why I had decided to take the classes.

We talked a few minutes before the session. He was adorable. He showed me this spice rack he'd bought. He said he had to return it to the store because it was defective, but it turned out he'd just hung it upside down.

Then we had the session. It was very strange. He started off with his theory of life – that our beliefs create our entire reality. That there's no such thing as accident or luck or even outside influences. That every single thing we experience is the direct result of what we believe.

Then he burst out laughing. At my expression, I guess. He said obviously I wasn't convinced. I said his theory did seem a little naive. I mean, sure I have plenty of beliefs, but they're based on years of experience. He said I had it backwards – that the beliefs had come first, and had created the experiences. I said, 'You make me sound like God.' And he said, 'You *are* God.'

That made me pretty nervous. There are not many things in life that I'm sure of, but this is one – that I positively, absolutely am not God!

The session went by fast. With him talking like a teacher in school – nothing personal at all. When the hour was up, he gave me a quick hug and sent me on my way.

Thinking it over now, I feel frustrated. This kind of session was not at all what I had in mind. The things he tells me, I've no use for, and no progress is being made in the emotional area. I've got to start getting through to C. on my level, not his. But I see no opening for me to do that unless I keep on with these sessions. So I guess I've got no choice.

And, in spite of everything, it's worth it – the feelings are still there, more than ever. I've never met anyone like him in my life. The feeling of peace that comes from him.

And I keep thinking of the Dan Fogelberg song, that changing faces in the middle of a dream gets you home.

So I go back next Monday.

FRIDAY

Life on hold. I told Jeff I was depressed and he said 'Life's a bitch, and then you die.' Deep inside, I guess he's right. Mama dying. Daddy getting older. Desiree so unhappy. Even the good things – like Jeff possibly getting the series – somehow don't hold up. And nothing happening for me. And yet, God only knows, I'm one of the lucky ones.

Thought about C. and his beliefs. Does he really think that if Jeff and I didn't believe life's a bitch and then you die, it wouldn't be like that? But it is like that.

SUNDAY P.M.

Had a bad fight with Jeff tonight. I made him a meatloaf and he hated it. He told me I was totally inept. Went through all the things I couldn't do. Said he did everything, and gave everything, and that I was a parasite. I feel so angry; it is so unfair and untrue. Birdie got nervous and started meowing. Jeff said he couldn't stand Birdie, that he was going to kill her. He actually caught her and started to open the window to throw her out. I grabbed her back and we're both tugging at her. It was ridiculous. We both started laughing.

We made up and J. apologized. He said he'd had a bad day (he found out the producers are still auditioning for the series), and that he hadn't meant anything he said. But I feel so shaky. The way his feelings for me change according to his mood. I am loved only if he gets the audition. No, that's not being fair to him. Of course he loves me. And most of the time he's wonderful. But it's just sometimes I feel we speak two different languages, and everything we say has to be translated into a third language before the other can understand it.

I am going through my recipe book again, but really the meatloaf wasn't so bad.

Depressing session with C. He asked me how my week had gone, and I somehow ended up telling him about the fight with Jeff. He got very angry with me. Asked me if I had no self-esteem at all. Because if I did, I wouldn't put up with this ridiculous relationship one minute longer. Ridiculous relationship?! I thought of how every woman I knew would love to be in my shoes.

He told me he wasn't talking about the way the world sees things. He was talking about spiritual frequencies; that Jeff and I were on two different ones, and that he was pulling me down. That the fact that I stayed with him was only a reflection of my terrible beliefs about myself, and that all the important work I had to do in the world was in jeopardy unless I let go.

It's just ridiculous. It's apparent to me and to everyone who knows me that getting involved with Jeff was the luckiest thing that ever happened to me. He was just in a bad mood last night. What am I supposed to do? Leave him because he was mean to the cat??

C. just kept on getting more and more worked up. That the longer I stayed with Jeff, the worse the situation would get, and that my only hope would be to leave him right now and be entirely alone.

I couldn't believe that. Alone? Throw my whole life away? Jeff is the only security I've got. I kept thinking of Mimi, that pathetic girl without a stable relationship. No way, no way, no way.

I got terribly upset. Christopher asked me what I was so afraid of. I said I wasn't made to be alone. He said we are never alone. He said that each of us is an infinite universe, but that I never would discover this about myself as long as I was with Jeff. He said that relationships are illusions, and that everything has to come from within yourself in the first place. That if you think you're getting anything from anyone else, it's delusion. And that the minute you look to someone else for safety, you're doomed. You've given away all your power. That it's only when you know you can stand totally alone, that you can have happiness with another person.

Well, sorry, but I'm just not made that way. It was bad enough that my mother had to die – and now I'm supposed to give up Jeff, too? No, thanks. I said I had a headache, could we please change the subject?

So he went onto other things – and they were just as crazy. How the whole relative world is just an illusion, and that we're like characters in a play, and that we chose the play before we were born. And that we each chose our particular play because we have these particular challenges to work out, and that we've probably been working on the same ones for thousands of lifetimes. I get so nervous when he goes on like this. Does he honestly expect me to believe it? That I've been around for thousands of lifetimes? That I chose my parents? That Jeff's been threatening to throw Birdie out the window since the days of Ancient Greece?

C. hugged me again at the end of the session, but he seemed real remote and tired. I'm getting nowhere fast.

LATER

I feel so torn. On one hand, I sincerely think C. may be more than a little insane. On the other, there's that something about him – that incredible peace. I just can't help being drawn to him more and more. I almost wish I could believe in his theories. That would forge bonds and make us close, but I'm too honest to pretend. On the other hand, if I let him know exactly how ridiculous I think it all is, he probably wouldn't let me take sessions anymore. So I've got to go along with it to some extent, even do the homework he's given me, crazy meditation exercises and belief lists, etc. And sooner or later, I'm bound to wear him down.

The most unbelievable session. I came in; C. grinning at me, very mischievous. He said, 'I know you didn't believe a word of what I said last week,' (the reincarnation issue) and told me that he was going to try and prove to me that he was right. I said it would take one hell of a lot of proving, and we were laughing.

Well, he hypnotized me.

It wasn't what I thought it would be like. I just felt very relaxed. I kept saying, 'This isn't working,' and finally he said, 'Then try to open your eyes,' but I couldn't.

First he told me to imagine I was sitting on a bench overlooking a valley. The valley was filled with clouds, and one rainbow. He told me to slide down the rainbow into the valley. I saw myself doing it. Then he said, 'Look down at yourself. What do you see?'

And this is incredible. I looked down and I wasn't looking down at myself.

It was someone else. A young woman, around nineteen, with long blond hair.

It was quite a shock.

C. kept asking questions. What was I wearing? What was I doing? Where was I? What was my name?

And the strange thing, I knew all the answers. I could see my dress so clearly, the way the buttons were covered and everything. I knew I lived in Germany – I could see all the cobbled streets. It was like watching a movie about the nineteenth century, but at the same time I was in the movie.

Another strange thing was that I was very unhappy. I had just been to a well, getting water, and now I was going home. I just got more and more weighed down. I went home. Everything went blurry for a little while. Then I was standing by a window. There was a little bird in a cage behind me. Then a man came into the room. It was my husband, and I was scared of him. He was a very tall, important businessman. He didn't look like anyone I've ever seen in this life, but I knew in some weird way, the instant I saw him, that he was Jeff.

I didn't even wait for C. to get me out of the damned hypnosis. I sat right up on the couch and opened my eyes.

LATER

Can't get this afternoon out of my mind. Of course I don't believe in reincarnation, but the thing was, what happened today seemed so real. That's what I can't get over. I don't know what to think. I wish I could talk to somebody.

LATER

Ended up talking to Desiree. I can tell she's worried about me. She said, 'Just remember – you're out to seduce this psychotic psychic – for God's sake, don't start believing him.'

That made me feel better. Makes me remember who I am, and why I'm going to C. in the first place. Let's get this seduction show on the road! Next time, I'll wear my white t-shirt with no bra. Maybe that'll do it.

MONDAY

Life: Life is a cooperative, not a competitive, venture. Individually, we create our personal experiences based upon our beliefs. Together, we create world events based upon our most powerful mass beliefs. The world outside is the cumulative result of the world within all individuals. It is a physical replica of humanity's combined inner beliefs and expectations; a mirror of what we are at any given time.

God: Many of us have been told to worship God, but few of us have been told to worship the god within us. But it is impossible to worship any God or truly love anyone, if you don't first love and worship yourself. That's because you can only give to others what you possess yourself.

Evil: Evil is not a cosmic force or devil, responsible for sinful, malevolent actions and the woes of the world. Rather than a hellish power, evil is the ignorance of the laws of nature that causes the individual to harm others and poorly create his own life. On a global level, evil is the mass ignorance that causes humankind to violate the natural law, thus creating negative world conditions.

Took this notebook to C.'s today. He asked what it was. I said it was a sort of a journal of our sessions. He was so funny and vain – said he'd always wanted his wise words immortalized. So he dictated the above. Kindly disregard.

Today's session went by so fast. I left, feeling depressed and a little cheated. I look forward to seeing Christopher all week, and when I do see him, it's nothing but listening to him talk metaphysics for a whole hour. No chance to get to know him. No chance to get him to fall in love with me.

LATER

Had an incredible brainstorm. I'm going to call up C. and find some other way to see him this week.

TUESDAY

Did it. I called up C. and lied through my teeth. I said that my car had to be taken into the body shop, about two blocks from him. And that I would have a free hour before they could fix it, so would he like to have lunch with me? He said he'd love to. I am so happy.

LATER

Am even happier. Hid my car a few blocks from C. and walked over to his apartment. We went to the Brasserie on Main Street. He was just adorable. I kept laughing at his various absurdities, and he looked at me very seriously and said, 'I love to make you laugh. It's one of my favorite things in life.'

It was all so wonderful. I feel so euphoric. We were together for over an hour. Talked about everything in the world. Except metaphysics, thank God! My feelings are so strong; it's all I can do to keep them hidden. Will he ever fall in love with me? Today was a good start, anyway. I will never forget it; the wind, the sun on the water, C. in his pink t-shirt and dirty tennis shoes. And my feeling so happy.

LATER

What if he *does* fall in love with me? What would I do then? Well, I'll worry about that later.

THURSDAY

I got a fan letter today from a seven year old boy. He said I was his favorite writer, and that my books 'help him with all his life.'

It made me want to cry. But then I get scared and I think how can I help anyone else with his life, when my own is in such a mess? But maybe that doesn't matter. I wrote him back and said I would keep on writing books, and keep on trying to help with all his life.

SATURDAY

Jeff and I fighting a lot. He keeps saying I've changed, that I'm not there for him the way I used to be. And I feel so nervous in his company. Like he's a loud noise constantly breaking in on things.

I've also thought a lot about lunch with C. the other day. I'm starting to feel scared. I wonder what I'm doing to myself. I think I'm in this a lot deeper than I had let myself realize. Yesterday when I was driving, I imagined myself telling the whole story to a friend, asking for her reaction. If I were that friend, I'd be frightened to death for me. Just the bald facts of the story sound like I've gone totally around the bend.

The fact is, this lunch took place entirely because of me, and my lies about the car. The fact is, the only reason I see C. at all is because I said I wanted to take the sessions. The fact is, C. has never once made any kind of move to see me or to push the relationship forward. The fact is, it isn't a relationship.

And yet it gains more power for me every day.

THURSDAY

Desiree called up this morning. She sounded very depressed. She wanted to know what was happening with Daddy. I've got to start helping her there, like I promised. I went over to his house. He wasn't in, and I looked around his office. There were all these messages on his desk, from all these women. I felt so bad for Desiree that I ended up stealing the messages. I figured, if it was something important, the women will call back. And if they don't, so much the better. But I can't worry too much about that. I want Desiree for Daddy, and anything I can do to weed out the competition is fine.

I miss Mama so much. I wonder what she would think

about all this. Christopher and Desiree and Jeff and Daddy. I wish she were still here. I wish I could still talk to her.

SATURDAY
Went into Port O'Call today. I saw this precious little limoges box, shaped like a chair. I got all excited; I thought, that's Mama's Christmas present! And then I remembered that she's dead. Made a real fool of myself in the store.

MONDAY
I feel very, very strange. Went over to C.'s for my session. He was in a really up mood and kept trying to make me laugh. But I was hostile to it. Finally he asked me what was wrong. I told him about seeing the little chair at Port O'Call. He said not to be sad about Mama, and went into detail about her experiences on the Other Side. I couldn't help it. I blew up at him and said that all his ideas were just bullshit. That he didn't understand the first thing about pain and missing anyone. That if he had ever lost anyone close to him, he would watch his precious philosophy crumble to pieces. He said, 'Just a minute,' and he went into the other room. He came back with a newspaper clipping from a few days ago, an obituary about a woman up in Oregon who had died of cancer. I said, 'Yes, so what?' He said that that was his sister.

LATER
I just can't get it out of my mind. How could he have been like that – so calm and so cheerful – and his sister had just died? He told me there was no miracle in it – that it was all due to what he understands to be true

about life. And that I could have it all too, if I would just stop being so stubborn.

I keep thinking that if I see him long enough, I'll expose him as a fraud, or catch him in the act. But it's not working out like that.

I stopped at Port O'Call on the way home, and, crazy as it sounds, I ended up buying the little limoges chair. Merry Christmas, my Mama, wherever you are.

TUESDAY

Went over to Daddy's today. To spy for Desiree again. She had heard he was seeing a dancer from a Variety show. I was able to find the girl's picture in his desk, and a love note. Took them, gave them to Desiree.

I don't know what she does with the information, but she feels she needs to have it. It's a little creepy but what can I do? I guess I shouldn't really be spying on my father but I don't care. The end will justify the means – he must, and will, end up with Desiree.

Besides the love note was really stupid – and all misspelled.

WEDNESDAY

Jeff and I have been fighting so much. He's so constantly cynical, constantly grumpy. I just can't help being on edge; can't help comparing him to C. I just keep thinking of C, wishing I could see him. Wanting another dose of his tranquillity. I don't know if I can even wait till Monday. Maybe my car could have another breakdown?

Spoke to Desiree. Told her how frustrated I was feeling about the Christopher situation; that no progress seemed to be made. She asked me how I acted with him, and I told her. She said that I have been doing it all wrong. That I have been thinking of C. as a spirit, not treating him like a man. She said that men like chal-

195

lenges. And that my problem was that I wasn't a challenge – that in just listening obediently to everything he told me, I was just like all his other students. She said I ought to shake him up, make him more aware of me as a woman. And that that way, things between us will get on a more emotional level; not just the student/teacher thing.

Well, I'll certainly give it a try. Maybe there's hope at last!!

MONDAY

Feel like hell. Went to see C. I did what Desiree suggested. Disagreed with every word out of his mouth. He was very patient, answered all my arguments. But ten minutes before the session was supposed to end, he stood up and asked me if I wouldn't mind leaving. He said, 'With this attitude, I wonder why you bother coming here at all.'

I've ruined everything.

LATER

I ended up going to the library. Believe it or not. Got out seven books on Metaphysics. My plan is to read them and call C. with some questions. I hope that will smooth things out between us. I can't stand to have him angry at me.

WEDNESDAY

Have read all the books. They're as crazy as hell. Kept wondering, as I turned the pages, what am I doing, reading this stuff? Even Mama, at her worst, wasn't reading books like this! But I have to admit, they were kind of fascinating. And I was surprised to see how many of the things that C. has told me about beliefs and the soul keep coming up. I thought they were his home-grown ideas, but apparently not.

LATER

Put in my call to C. Left a message on his machine, telling him I'd been reading all these books, and saying I had a few questions. Hope he'll realize that that's an apology. Hope he calls back.

LATER

He called just now. Jeff answered the phone. When I heard C.'s voice, thought my heart was going to bounce out of my body. He sounded incredibly sweet. He said, 'I know you can't talk now, so I'll answer your questions next time I see you. But I just want to tell you how much I appreciate your call. I know what you were trying to do, and I thank you for it.'

So relieved and happy – felt like I was melting. After I hung up, Jeff was looking at me strangely. He asked me who had been on the phone. I said it was an old friend of my father's. Jeff said, 'Well, I hope he never calls again. I really hated the sound of his voice.'

SATURDAY

Went to Dalton's. Went to the Metaphysical section and bought a few more books. What the hell. It can't hurt.

WEDNESDAY

Not much to write. Situation pretty unchanged. Jeff and I still fighting, and I'm still not getting anywhere with C. At least the children's book is going well – I think it will be my best. Nothing new with Desiree.

Found a great metaphysical bookstore on Melrose called the Bodhi Tree. Have been spending a lot of time there. But the smell of incense gets into my hair. Jeff even noticed. I told him it was a new shampoo. He said to please not use it anymore.

TUESDAY

Had an embarrassing experience. Went back to the Bodhi Tree, and got a nosebleed, of all things. Before I realized what was going on, I'd dripped blood on half the Zen section. Couldn't stop it – didn't even have a Kleenex. Finally went to the manager – he was really nice. He gave me cold towels, tissues until it went away. We got to talking – he said he's been in metaphysics for years. He even goes on pilgrimages to places like India and Santa Fe. I said I didn't believe in any of the New Age stuff, and he laughed and asked me what I was doing in his store. I said I'd just dropped in to bleed. He recommended a book to me, Chris Stone's *Re-Creating Yourself* and when I went to buy it, the cashier told me that the manager had said it was 'on the house.' Thought that was so sweet.

SATURDAY

Weird experience. The dishwasher's broken, and I called in a repairman to fix it. He looked over at the bookshelf while he was working. He asked me if I was a New Age freak. I laughed and said, Of course not. He said, 'Well, lady, I just wondered. You do have three entire shelves filled with books on the occult.' I was shocked. But after he left I saw he was right. How strange. I had no idea I've been reading so much about all this.

Feel that things are getting a little out of hand.

I'd better start turning back.

SUNDAY

I got shaken up today. They played the Dan Fogelberg song on the radio again, the one that was my big symbol.

Well, it turns out I got the words wrong. Changing faces in the middle of a dream *doesn't* 'get you home.' Changing faces in the middle of a dream 'gets you *old*.'

I feel frightened.

I feel like I'm drowning.

What's going on? What's going on with me?

As Laura came in the door for her session, Christopher was sitting on the couch, waiting for her. He was holding a book.

'I found a quote the other day,' he said. 'Something from Narihira.' He opened the volume and read aloud, ' "I have always known that at last I would take the Path – but yesterday I did not know that it would be today." It made me think of you,' he said.

He was smiling at her.

The quote tolled in Laura's mind, chilled her. 'No, Christopher,' she said distinctly. She cleared her throat and looked up at him. 'There are a lot of things you don't understand about me. Things aren't exactly what they seem. I come to these sessions for reasons of my own, not for the reasons you think.'

His smile grew brighter.

'Can't you understand?' she demanded angrily. 'I'm not on the Path, never was, and never will be.'

And he burst out laughing.

Chapter Twelve

Blake's office at the studio had always been a source of dismay to Julia. It was filled with the plaid-covered blond furniture Blake had picked out when he was twenty-five and had never changed. Furniture that managed to clash with every carpet and every window treatment in every room it had ever been placed in. Over the years, Julia had regularly hinted, pleaded, threatened, that her next project was to re-decorate Blake's office at the studio. Time and again, in readiness for this event, she had bought preliminary items – leather desk sets at Aspreys, Klee prints for the walls. But Blake had always deflected her attempts. He made it into a joke, saying that the way Hollywood worked, by the time the decorating had been done, he would be on to a new job.

Blake wasn't sure why he felt this peculiar fondness for the studio office. Perhaps it was the cumulative effect – seeing that same furniture around him, year after year after year. The era at MGM superimposed over the era at Fox superimposed over the era at Warner's. Or perhaps because the furniture was the one touch of ugliness and of whimsy in his life, and he felt affection for just that reason. Or perhaps he just liked being reminded of being twenty-five again.

He sat now at his big wooden desk. Before this afternoon's meeting, he had just enough time to go through his list of calls. There had been twelve, since lunch. Five were from women. He concentrated on those.

It was interesting to Blake, reading the list. Each

name, tasted in his mind, yielded a whole array of varied sensations. The last one, especially. Even the name itself seemed to flirt with the page it was written on.

In the middle of the list of messages was the name 'Laura.' Laura. It was like a stone.

He had seen her only once since that night at Desiree's. God. That night. It made him squeamish even now to remember it. He couldn't believe Laura had been there in that bedroom. He had thought at first it was some trick, some hysterical prank of Desiree's.

How was he to have known they had become friends? As far as he had ever been aware, they had never even liked each other. And Desiree's babbled, disturbing explanation before she had run out the door to Laura – psychics . . . Julia . . . counterparts. Well, better to forget it all.

He had wanted so much to talk to Laura about it at their lunch – to talk about himself, about Desiree – but it was impossible. The channels of their communication did not extend that far. And there were certain things you simply did not discuss with a daughter, especially one like Laura, who had loved her mother so much. So he had said nothing at all.

Blake looked down at the page and read the message she had left. 'Laura sends love.' His thoughts then turned to the other female names on the list. How would he feel, he quizzed himself humorously, if any one of *them* had 'sent love?' Again, he went down the list, tasting out the various emotions that this message would have engendered.

And when he came to the final name, again there was that telling, delicate frisson.

There was a knock at his door.

'Come in,' Blake said.

'They're ready for you in the screening room, Mr Alden,' Paula, his new secretary, told him coyly.

Blake was about to feel annoyed by her tone, but then, as he noticed the lines around Paula's eyes and the increasingly desperate make-up and moisturizer job that tried to hide them, annoyance softened into pity. God knew, it was a hard thing being a woman over twenty-five in this town.

Blake had taken Paula out to lunch once, her second week on the job, just to be kind. But she had dressed so carefully that he had realized the invitation had meant too much to her. And so – again out of kindness – he had not asked her out again.

'Tell Buzz I'll be right there,' he told her.

He walked down the corridors. They were hung with poster-sized photographs of that season's stars. Lord, they were all so young, so endlessly energetic. Blake found himself wondering where the photographs of last season's stars were stored.

He reached the screening room. He was the last one to arrive. He greeted the others, saw an unfamiliar face, looked questioningly at Buzz.

'Blake, meet Anthony Allbright. We're bringing him in on the new Eliot Fletcher project. He's got some exciting ideas.'

Blake nodded. So this was the one everyone was talking about – the Junior Executive to watch.

Allbright rose. 'Hello, Blake.'

It amused Blake the way Allbright took his hand with such an aggressive, fresh and yet respectful grip. He must have been practising that one at home.

The movie began. After a few moments, Blake buzzed the engineer. 'John,' he said impatiently, 'I can't hear a word. Could we have a little more sound?'

The volume was increased to the maximum. As Blake

202

turned back to the screen, he caught the small, meaning-ful smile that Allbright gave his associate.

Blake Alden's a deaf old man.

Blake flushed for a moment in the darkness, but then he let it slide away. What the hell – who cared what Allbright thought, anyway? Cocaine or ego – one or the other would get him. And he would be gone in less than a year.

Blake settled back to watch the movie. He thought no more about the Junior Executive and his tiny smile.

Desiree opened up her packages from Bullocks before she was all the way inside her house. *I have grown to shop with more passion than I write,* she thought wryly. First, she unwrapped the Gucci scarf she had bought herself. Yes, it would do fine. Elegant, chic, expensive and signature – all those good things. She put it in her scarf drawer without further interest. Then she unpacked the next bag. She laid the outfit on the bed and looked at it, smiling.

The moment she had seen this Vicki Teil dress, she had thought of Laura. Not Laura as she currently was, not Laura as she saw herself, but Laura as Desiree imagined she could be. The black drape chiffon would look striking with that red hair, and the low, Thirties' waistline would be impish, seductive. Give Laura a little life.

The dress had been ridiculously expensive, and Desiree usually managed to get her designer clothes wholesale, thanks to Jean Torrey, her personal shopper, but on an impulse, she had bought Laura the dress. Now, she had only to find the right shoes and purse to match. She smiled again as she thought of this coming Christ-mas, the festively-wrapped boxes, and Laura opening them.

She can wear it New Year's Eve, Desiree thought complacently.

As Desiree repacked the dress and turned, her glance fell on her photo wall – and in particular on the picture of the little girl in the fairy princess Hallowe'en costume. Cautiously, Desiree went up to the photo of her daughter.

Robin would have been twenty-seven now. Tall, dark-haired, possibly with Leo's bone structure. She would have been very beautiful. And the black Vicki Teil dress would have looked wonderful on her, too.

For a second, Desiree was overcome. She sank on the bed and put her hands over her eyes. *A nice touch for the new play*, she taunted herself cruelly. *A woman without a daughter, obsessed with someone else's. How touchingly neurotic.*

She put the new dress away. As she was closing the closet door, she heard the phone ring.

For a moment, it was like winning the play-writing prize again – with no one to tell the news to. And then Desiree remembered that there was Laura.

She dialled the number impatiently, and willed Laura to be home.

Laura was home.

'Hello?'

'A man has contacted me,' Desiree told her without preamble. 'I met him at an opening last week. He wants me to turn *Ace of Clubs* into a movie, and he wants me to write the screenplay. Sole credit, major distribution, and a lot of money. I think he's in love with me, and I'm sure he's Mafia.'

'Oh, Desiree!' Laura's voice cracked with the earnest weight of her delight. 'How wonderful! Tell me everything about it!'

204

Desiree felt warm with the pleasure of the reaction. She told Laura the details of the phone conversation, and Laura was thrilled.

'I'm going out with him tonight,' Desiree said. 'He wants to discuss it over dinner. Should I wear the green or the gold?'

And they talked about that, deeply.

'And what about you?' Desiree asked finally. 'What's going on with you?'

'Nothing new,' Laura sounded suddenly weary. 'Still the same. In every particular.'

'I see,' Desiree said, and they hung up soon afterwards.

It kept recurring to Desiree, as she went about her day – that note of strain in Laura's voice. It unnerved her, made her feel frustrated. She found herself worrying, growing more and more impatient. When would Laura wake up and get over the damned psychic? she wondered. Really, this ridiculous crush had been going on far too long. When would Laura finally realize what a hopelessly inappropriate situation it was?

For a moment, Desiree wondered what Julia would have done. But she could come up with no answer. *Well, it's my burden now*, she thought wryly. And she wondered how, and at what point, she should interfere. But at the thought of actually doing so, to her surprise, she felt her resolve slacken. When it came down to it, she realized she could not bear to be the one to wake Laura out of her happy delusion.

Let Jeff do it, she decided finally. He was bound to find out about this sooner or later. Let him handle it. And the playwright in Desiree gave a grim smile at the possibilities of that scene.

She did not ask herself how much the reason for her non-interference in Laura's affairs had to do with herself and Blake Alden. It was sometimes better not to delve too deeply in these matters.

Besides, she had her own life to attend to. The Mafia Man was picking her up in twenty-five minutes.

Desiree stood before the mirror, massaging Tabu into her temples, her springing hair. She watched the reflection of the bedroom behind her. Its starkness, as always, soothed her. She wondered what the Mafia Man would say about her condominium. So often men found it hard to say anything at all. Probably, she thought, he would not even notice the place. But he would notice the dress. Of that she was certain. She was glad she had worn the gold.

They were going to dinner at a new restaurant on Pico, to discuss more fully her play and its potential for a movie.

Desiree smiled. The man liked her play. He liked her even more. He wanted her play. He wanted her even more.

She shrugged. So far she had managed to keep him completely at a distance. She could feel his frustration. And it was, yes, a little exciting.

Desiree found herself wondering if she would keep him at a distance tonight. She sat down on the chair. Maybe she would not, she thought slowly. The excitement grew.

To her surprise, she found she was truly, urgently looking forward to the evening ahead. It was the first thing in a long time that had kept its shape, that had not been drained of color. It was something vivid, possibility-filled, and totally independent of Blake Alden.

God help me, I am getting over him, Desiree thought exultantly. And it was high time. High time that he be diffused and made to disappear. Desiree was too good an observer of herself not to realize what her obsession was doing to her. Little Laura may be a slave to infatuation, but I am not.

Yes, she thought again, looking at Blake's picture on the wall. She felt strong tonight. Strong enough to battle even the pull of Blake Alden.

If the Mafia Man made a move, she would play.

The restaurant was Cajun. It had been written up as a 'Best Bet' the week before, and was predictably packed by the predictable packs. It was wildly noisy. Desiree felt irritated by the ambience – the cramped tables, the bad art on the walls, the over-zealous waiters, the endless specials. She sat on her uncomfortable chair, under the unflattering light, and listened to the Mafia Man talk.

He did not appear even to notice the restaurant. He was telling her about his hobby. He had, he said, the largest private collection of Wild West memorabilia in the country. He listed his inventory, his face shiny with mastery. He made Desiree think of Gatsby, throwing down his shirts on the bed before Daisy.

Inwardly, she sighed. The Wild West had never been her favorite period.

What did interest her, however, were the Mafia Man's stories of how he had acquired the artifacts – the underground deals, the secret trips, the armed competition, and the fact that he had never been bested.

'Are you this ruthless about everything you want?' Desiree asked him, smiling.

He had been about to answer, when he saw her look across the restaurant. And what she saw was Blake Alden sitting at a corner booth, with his arm around a young blond girl.

Nina was thrilled with the restaurant. It amused Blake, made him feel protective, to see how eagerly she scanned the door for in-coming celebrities.

He watched her as she watched. There was, he couldn't help noticing, a curious contrast between the skin around her eyes – unlined and fresh – and the expression within the eyes themselves.

The dress she was wearing was very tight, very sexy. He put his hand over hers. She squeezed it in a gush of emotion. Blake smiled.

She wanted, he knew, the ingenue part on his new series.

'Are you enjoying yourself?' he asked her.

'Oh, yes, darling,' Nina said breathlessly.

Blake started to tell her the funny story about the first time he had ever eaten Cajun food – during the War when there had been a shortage of beef.

'What war?' she interrupted him, puzzled. 'Oh, you mean the Vietnam War. God,' she laughed. 'I was just a baby then.'

Blake stared at her. A strange drowning feeling was in his throat. 'No,' he said slowly. 'It was another war.'

But she didn't hear.

'Oh, my God,' she gasped. She had turned into a pulse of excitement. 'Isn't that David Angel at the bar?'

Blake looked over. He saw a crowd of young men standing there, all equally sullen-looking, all equally ill-groomed, all equally qualified to be David Angel. He could not in the least tell which one of them was the star. Oh, but in the days of Old Hollywood, you would have known in an instant. The way they moved – and dressed. The way cigarettes were lit, hair tossed back.

A longing, a missing, flowed over him. A longing for every single thing that had been and wasn't anymore.

Nina was watching him apprehensively. 'Is anything wrong?' she asked delicately.

'I was just thinking about Fred Astaire,' he told her. 'I remember once when we were doing a picture together – '

For an instant, Nina frowned. 'Who's Fred Astaire?' she asked. Then illumination came. 'Oh, I know. He's the guy who's dead. I read about him in *People Magazine*.'

Blake stared at her for a long moment. 'Yes,' he said tonelessly. 'He's the guy who's dead.'

There was a wet bar in the limo, and Desiree poured out yet another Scotch and soda. The sips dulled her.

The Mafia Man put a heavy white arm around her neck. It felt like a boa made of dead python.

'You've been acting funny for the last half hour,' he told her. 'Is something wrong?'

'Nothing at all,' Desiree smiled superbly.

The arm tightened, grew yearning. 'What a woman you are,' he murmured. 'Desiree. A mature woman like you is what a man like me needs. Those other guys – they disgust me. They should have their balls torn off. Those old letches. Always after the young girls. Did you see, in the restaurant? That beautiful young girl – that innocent young girl with the face of a saint – and Blake Alden, with his hands all over her?'

In a fuzzy dream, Desiree raised her arm. And in a fuzzy dream, she slapped his face as hard as she could.

In a second, her neck was between his huge hands, and the expression on his face woke her right up.

I am about to be killed, she thought detachedly. '*Playwright strangled in limo by jealous would-be lover.' The papers will adore it.*

Then, with a look of disgust, the Mafia Man flung

Desiree away to the far end of the seat, and turned his back on her. She looked at that back. Looked at it for a long time.

Well, so much for Ace of Clubs *being made into a movie,* Desiree thought wryly. *What the hell anyway.*

She poured herself another Scotch.

The morning was rainy. Laura had woken up with a new slant for Philippe, the French hippo. She was sitting at the table, making sketches, having difficulties, and longing to be rescued.

The phone rang. It was Desiree.

'Can you come on over right away?' Desiree asked.

Laura was immediately delighted. But then, as she heard more of Desiree's conversation, the delight faded.

'I'll be there,' she said.

Desiree kept pouring coffee, agitatedly, relentlessly.

'If you could have seen her, Laura – that smug, fat little face, like a peony. The way she kept looking at him.' *And the way he kept looking at her,* she did not add.

'Oh, Desiree,' Laura said nervously. 'I'm sure it was nothing. Maybe it was a business dinner. Maybe she's up for a part.'

Desiree snorted. 'And I can guess what part she's up for.'

Laura laughed, again, nervously.

'Her name is Nina Gibson,' Desiree said. 'I was able to find out that much. She's from Seattle, and she's a highly untalented actress. But I need to know more. See what you can find out.'

Laura's heart sank a little. Damn. She was starting to feel so guilty. She wished there were a way she could get out of it. But a promise was a promise. And she couldn't let Desiree down.

'Okay,' she said resignedly. 'I'll find out what I can.'

Later that afternoon, Blake was safely away at an executive meeting, and Laura was prowling around his office. *Nina Gibson*, she thought bleakly, and looked around without much hope for information. She went through her father's desktop. No photos, no love-notes. And then she came upon his weekly schedule. She saw there was to be a dinner party on the following Tuesday. The name Nina Gibson was on the list – and under it was her own.

Laura smiled with relief.

Desiree laid the strategy over the phone.

'Tuesday night? All right. First of all, I want you to wear your white. It's not really the right season, but no matter. The point is to look young, and to make the person you're with look old. And the person I want you to be with is Nina Gibson. All evening. Talk to her. Sit next to her at dinner. Find out all about her. Find out her weaknesses. Don't let your father near her. And for God's sake – outstay her.'

Desiree hung up the phone. *You're shaking like your grandmother*, she told herself unpleasantly. She looked at herself in the mirror. She did not savor the image there – the banished dowager queen and her last desperate ploy. Attractive in a Robert Bolt film, perhaps, but a trifle overblown for everyday life.

For a moment, Desiree felt demeaned, pathetic, and then the other concerns rose clamoring again. Could she trust Laura with the instructions? she wondered. Or was Laura too easily swayed? If Nina Gibson were nice to her, would she give in?

Desiree felt clawed by frustration and apprehension.

She did something she hadn't done in ten years. She lit a cigarette.

Laura sensed which one Nina Gibson was, the moment she entered her father's living room. And she hated her on sight.

There was no doubt that the actress was beautiful. And there was also no doubt, at least in Laura's mind, that everything about her – the sheer white blouse with lace appliqués, the clinging long hair, the floral perfume, the windchime earrings – had been chosen with the specific intent of winning Blake Alden. And the actress manner, so fluttery, so feminine, so soft, was so everything that Laura's father most enjoyed. *Of course*, Laura realized, *when you spend two seconds looking into her eyes, you got the real story*. But Laura was only too aware of the fact that Blake Alden didn't like to spend two seconds looking into anything.

Nina leaned over and kissed Blake on the lips. Laura began to perspire. She looked around at the drawing room that her mother had decorated with such lavish love. Every antique table, every limoges box, every fresh-cut rose seemed to scream, *Get this imposter out*.

And I will, Laura thought grimly. It was no longer just for Desiree.

She started to head in Nina Gibson's direction, to dilute the intimacy with Blake, but she found herself firmly held back. Frail, ancient Anthony Lewis, who had been cameraman on her father's first movie, was holding her with a surprising and rather creepy strength.

'I had a stroke,' he said. 'Why didn't you come see me in the hospital when I had my stroke?'

Laura felt shaken. She let herself be led to an antique sofa, let herself be told about the stroke.

Across the room, she could see Blake and Nina on

another similar sofa. Things were lively on that love seat – a lot of laughter, Nina protesting, Blake teasingly insisting upon some point.

'And when my doctor saw the first set of test results – '

Laura did not turn away from Anthony's defeated red eyes, but she willed her ears to travel across the room to Blake and Nina.

'You must remember her – you met her at my party,' Nina was insisting. 'My best friend. Well, it's all come out. She's left her husband and a ten month old baby – to follow this lady guru through India!'

Her enjoying, scandalized voice, Blake's amused response.

'Sounds pretty far gone,' he said. 'Well, anyone who gets mixed up in the occult has to be pretty neurotic to begin with. And you say this is your best friend?' The teasing note was back. 'What's that expression about birds of a feather? Are you planning a trip to Delhi yourself in the near future?'

Again, her squeaks of denial, the laughter.

Laura sat stiffly. She felt her face grow hot. What, she wondered, with dread, would her father say if he knew about her? Would she be 'pretty far gone,' too? It was a sickening thought. She imagined being, some night, discussed at just such a cocktail party '. . . and then Laura Alden met this *psychic*, from the *beach*, and you wouldn't *believe* what happened . . .' and it made the wine she was drinking twist around in her throat.

Anthony Lewis' dry, heated hand was on hers.

'And then when he saw *those* set of test results, that's when he said, "We're putting you in the hospital." '

It was a relief to turn back to his misery.

At last dinner was announced. Laura stood up quickly, recalled once more to her mission of shadowing Nina

Gibson. But there were placecards, and she found herself seated at the far end of the table, next to Jeff. Nina was beside her father, and so Laura had no chance to interfere with the actress's mealtime performance.

But, just wait, she thought narrowly, watching Nina Gibson flutter and feint around her father, *just wait till round two*.

'Chicken breast, sir?' Matthew, the butler, asked Jeff.

'No,' Jeff answered tightly.

You'd think that just once Laura's father would remember that he didn't eat chicken.

The anger built and built. Why did Laura's father insist on inviting them to these fucking evenings, anyway? The same guests, the same stupid conversations, and always someone asking, 'And what are you working on now?' You'd think it would occur to Laura's father just once to invite someone who could do Jeff's career some good but no, time after time the same old dinosaurs creaked on over – cameramen, writers from the ancient days of Hollywood. Laura kept saying she thought it was wonderful that her father was so loyal to his old friends. Well, that might be so, but Jeff could think of a few other words to describe it.

And especially tonight. Why did there have to be a dinner party tonight? He had met this girl in the gym last week, only casually, of course, but he had promised to hear her read a scene before her audition, and she had mentioned that she'd be home this evening.

Blake stood up. 'If everyone's finished with dinner, let's go into the screening room. We're running *The Uninformed*.'

Jeff swore softly. 'Let's get out of here,' he whispered urgently to Laura. 'I hear it stinks.'

He started to pull Laura up, but she resisted.

'I can't leave yet,' she told him agitatedly.

He stared at her. 'Why not?' he asked.

Her eyes shifted away from his. 'I – I'd just like to stay a while, that's all,' she said, flustered.

He knew she wasn't telling him the truth, and he started to get angry. But then he remembered the girl at the gym.

'All right,' he said suddenly. 'We won't argue. You stay if you want to. But I really want to leave.'

'Sure, Jeff,' Laura's face was relieved. 'You go on and do whatever makes you happy.'

He smiled. 'Lucky thing we came in two cars,' he said lightly. 'I guess this was meant to be.'

He kissed her on the top of the head, explained to Blake he had an early casting call and needed sleep, said goodbye to the dinosaurs, and left.

But going down the drive, the anger against Laura returned. Goddammit. What the hell was so important that she had to stay at her father's house and see the fucking movie? He was getting really worried about her. Nothing she did seemed to make sense anymore. Well, one of these days, when he had a little more time, he would get to the bottom of it and straighten everything out. But in the meantime, he thought, taking out the piece of paper with the girl's address on it, he would give help where he could – where it was appreciated – and listen to that little blond actress read her lines.

It was Round Two.

The guests went into the screening room. Laura waited to see where Nina Gibson was going to sit. Nina chose the top row, on the aisle, and she sat down gracefully. Laura raced up there also, almost breaking a leg, and flung herself beside the actress. Blake looked a little surprised by the seating arrangement, but he sat down on Laura's other side without comment. Laura felt very victorious.

But five minutes into the movie, the tide turned. Nina retaliated. She started craning her head, making little noises of despair.

'Are you all right?' Blake finally asked.

'I can't see the screen!' Nina whimpered, sounding near tears.

Laura clenched her fist. The screen was, at the most, ten feet in front of the woman's face.

Blake was very protective. 'Why don't you come sit on my other side?' he suggested. 'There's a perfect view from there.'

Daintily, Nina stepped over Laura, and sat beside Blake. She took his hand and squeezed it. Laura sat grimly back in her chair. So much for Round Two.

After the movie, the guests started leaving. Nina didn't leave. Laura didn't leave. Nina ate a chocolate. Laura drank more cold coffee. Finally all the other guests had gone, and the two women were alone with Blake. The three of them walked to the porch. Blake began to glare meaningfully at Laura, but she pretended she didn't see.

Finally she said, 'Daddy, do you mind if I stay awhile? I really need to talk to you about something.'

'Couldn't it wait until tomorrow?' he asked her.

'No, not really,' she said.

There was a long, full pause. Finally Nina said, 'I really ought to be going, anyway.'

'No, no,' Blake said, but she smiled, kissed him delicately on the cheek, and left. Cold in her victory, Laura watched the enemy drive off in her red Jaguar.

'Well,' Blake said impatiently, turning to Laura. 'What's so important?'

Laura just stared at him. Her mind froze over. 'I – I

don't think I want to talk about it after all,' she stammered finally.

Blake turned away from her. Laura could tell how angry he was. She left immediately afterwards.

Jeff came into the apartment at quarter past twelve. Laura was in bed.

'You asleep?' he whispered.

'No,' she said.

'I went to visit some friends,' he explained. 'How was the movie?'

'Terrible.'

The boniness of her back as she lay in bed startled Jeff. 'Hey, baby,' he said to her softly. 'You all right?'

Laura burst into tears.

'What's wrong?' he asked her, concerned. 'Come on; tell me. You've been keeping too much from me lately. Come on, honey. Tell me.'

She turned over and stared at him.

But she could tell him nothing.

WEDNESDAY

I couldn't sleep last night. When Jeff asked what was wrong, there was nothing I could say, no place I could have begun. Desiree? Christopher? I feel so alone. Alone with all the mistakes I've been making. And seeing that woman in Mama's place at the table.

LATER

I feel terrible. Daddy just called. He asked me in future to please stop interfering in his private life. He sounded so angry. I apologized, but I had to tell him how I felt about Nina Gibson. He interrupted me – said he was old enough to choose his own company, and that it was none of my business.

Ha, ha. Now that I think of it, this is the closest thing to a real discussion that we've had in years.

It just gets worse. Told C. about the dinner party and what I had done to Nina Gibson at the screening. He was just furious. Said he'd known something like this was going on, but didn't think I'd sunk so low already.

He kept talking about the Flow, the Flow, the Flow, and how if we try to thwart it, like I'm doing, everything ends up in disaster.

I tried to explain how I'd felt seeing that woman, how I was honor-bound to help Desiree. And he told me to shut up. That I had absolutely no right to do what I'd done, that I was the most manipulative person he had ever met. That I felt so powerless in my own life that I had to interfere with everyone else's. And that Desiree was a menace – that she had no right to ask me to. He said that Daddy was strong and smart, that he knew exactly what he was doing with Nina Gibson and everybody else, and to just leave him alone. And that if it weren't Nina Gibson, it would be someone else and did I intend to devote the rest of my life to sabotaging Daddy's girlfriends? I said, yes, if necessary.

I hate even to write what he said next. He looked at me and shook his head and said, 'People like you are dangerous.'

I just feel so awful.

That I'm dangerous.

I keep thinking. Maybe he's right. How I'm fooling C. into thinking I'm taking these sessions for good reasons, when really I'm just trying to get him to fall in love with me. And all that spying for Desiree. And how I'm not telling J. about C. And how I'm trying to thwart the Flow.

Damned right I am. Who the hell cares about some stupid Flow? And who the hell cares what Christopher thinks about me?

FRIDAY

I had lunch with Desiree today. I said I had something to tell her. That though I wanted her and Daddy to end up together as much as ever, I had decided that it was wrong for me to interfere anymore. I was so afraid she'd get upset, but she only said, 'I see.'

I thought it was all all right. But as we were leaving, she said, 'I assume Christopher Garland has had something to do with this new resolution of yours.' I lied and said no. She said, 'I see,' again, and I knew she didn't believe me. Then she said, 'Oh, by the way – there's something I've been meaning to ask you. Exactly what sort of things does Christopher teach you in your sessions?'

It was awful. If you could have seen her face – heard her voice. She was so horrified by everything I told her. '*This* is what he's been teaching you – *this*? "Each human being is all-powerful?" Tell that to the starving African children. To earthquake victims. To Vietnam vets. "All relationships are cooperative?" Just try telling the Jews they asked for Hitler.'

And then she said about Christopher exactly what he had said about me.

That he was dangerous.

It shook me up so much, it's made me question everything. It brought up every old belief I've ever had – that metaphysics was the worst kind of heartless insanity.

Desiree said that she had known several people who had gone off the deep-end because of philosophies like this. She said that life was hard on just about every level you can name. There's disappointment, disillusionment, sickness and death, and the sooner we face up to this, and the fewer illusions we have, the better off we are. She said we are unhappy to the extent that we allow ourselves to be deluded: and the more quickly we become realists, the better, and that these metaphysical philosophies are just ways of avoiding the issues. She said she had been worried about me for a long time, felt I was going overboard, and now she was sure. She said I had to backtrack fast, or I was lost.

I just don't know. I just don't know anything.

NEXT DAY
Desiree just called. She said she met this Dr Hoch from the State Mental Institute at Camarillo. They were talking about philosophy, and Desiree mentioned C. And the doctor said, 'Oh, yes – I know Christopher Garland. He used to be a patient of mine.'

It makes you want to die.

FRIDAY
I called C. up and asked him point blank if he had ever been in Camarillo. He said yes. That he had checked himself right in. Back in the old days. When he had followed popular world views such as that the individual has no power, that people were made to suffer, that life is short and then you die. He said that was enough reason, right there, for any normal person to go crazy. But that once he found metaphysics, there was no reason to go back. He said he remembered Dr Hoch. That he was a nice guy, and that he used to wear chartreuse ties.

I'm not even sure what's sane and what's insane anymore.

LATER

Went out for a walk today. An old lady was waiting on the bench for a bus. She looked so scared. It was so strange. I just went over and I put my arms around her. She put her arms around me, and we just stayed there. Then I guess we both realized this bizarre thing we were doing, and we pulled apart and couldn't look at each other. And then her bus came.

LATER

I am so happy, so happy. Jeff said he's going to take me to Santa Barbara tomorrow for the whole weekend. I am so relieved. Not to have to deal with any of this stuff, anymore. Spent the day shopping for a new bathing suit. Heaven, heaven.

SUNDAY NIGHT

Very tired. The trip a bust.

Jeff and I did all the right things – galleries, nice restaurants, going to the beach. But something's changed, gone. I remember the first time we went to Santa Barbara, holding Jeff and wishing on a star. Wishing that every moment of my life could be this happy, and that every moment would contain this man beside me. And now I couldn't wait for the weekend to be over. It was such a strain to pretend. Trying to recapture.

Jeff was so sweet – he bought me a little music box, told me how much I meant to him. But it just didn't make any difference.

I feel so afraid. I don't know what's happening, but I do know it's happening fast. And last night, when we made love, the most frightening thing of all. For the first time, I couldn't get into it. I finally had to pretend it was Christopher I was with.

3 A.M.

I've made up my mind. I'm going to stop these sessions with C. before it's too late. Desiree's right. He is dangerous. It's all because of him that being with Jeff feels so meaningless now. I could deal with that if C. were in love with me. But he isn't – so why do I keep hanging on like this? It's sheer masochism. And I'm putting everything I have in jeopardy.

That expression keeps running through my head – *you can't run with the hare and the hounds both.*

On Monday I'll call him. I'll just say I can't see him anymore.

LATER
I can't do it.

SATURDAY
Went to the beach with Jeff. We took a walk along Venice Pier. I was thinking about Christopher. Then I looked up and saw him on the boardwalk. I thought my heart was going to explode. He didn't see me. He had on ridiculous bright orange and purple Bermuda shorts and pointy sunglasses. He was with a young blond guy. They were trying to ride skateboards, and falling off and laughing. I just kept looking at him.

Jeff saw me. 'Stop staring at that poor guy,' he said. 'He can't help the way he is.'

SUNDAY
Mimi Craddock called, wanting to know when we're going to see C. for her reading. We finally made a date for next Thursday. Damn. I just don't want to take her. Feel very uneasy about it.

A bad evening. Jeff heard Matt Tomlin is definitely going to get the lead in the series. We went to Daddy's for dinner. And all Daddy could talk about is who he's casting for this and that part.

On the way home, Jeff started screaming at me. That if I really loved him, I'd boycott Daddy until he helps Jeff. That Daddy's not helping Jeff is not only an insult to him, it's a slap in the face to me. That Daddy doesn't love me and never has.

Finally I started to scream back.

Jeff pulled the car over. He looked at me for a long time. He kept shaking his head and saying I had changed so much he wasn't even sure if he loved me anymore. Oh, God. Please let this be over soon.

NEXT DAY

Got chest pains in the night. Jeff took me to the emergency room. The doctor gave me Valium. He said it was all just nerves. Jeff very sweet, very apologetic. Felt the chest pains coming on again.

Something has to get resolved. Right now.

NEXT DAY

Can't even write. I'm too happy.

Everything is wonderful. Incredibly, totally wonderful.

Arrived at C.'s for my session. He opened the door, smiling. He said, 'Hi, how are you today?' I thought of everything that's been happening in my life, culminating in last night's trek to the emergency room, and burst into tears. Went totally berserk. Practically started beating up on Christopher. Screamed at him that he was driving me crazy. That I was so unhappy, and that he didn't care at all. That I was just another client to him, that he didn't give a damn about me, that he was the most bloodless human being I'd ever met. He stared at me, and I couldn't believe it.

He started crying.

Tears running down his cheeks. He said he was sorry – so sorry and that he thought I knew how he felt. That he loved me so much, that I was so precious to him. And there was no one in the whole world who was more important to him than I was.

And we're both standing there, hugging and crying.

He took me by the shoulders. He said, 'I want you to understand something. You are to me what I was to Carmen. I was her Little Prince. You are my Little Princess. You are the next link in the chain. And I never want you to forget that.'

And he kept holding me. His Little Princess. I can hardly stand it, it is so wonderful.

My head is whirling. There is so much to do, so much to look forward to. I feel saved – resurrected. And grateful. So intensely grateful. It's all starting at last; just as I wanted. Just as I knew it would. And soon it will turn into a romance. Soon he'll look at me the way I want him to look at me. And of course I have to tell Jeff – but not just yet. That's going to be so hard. And I want to have this moment of pure joy a little while longer. Such floods, floods of happiness.

Mimi twirled lipstick around her mouth for the fourth time, fussed, frowned in the car mirror.

'Oh, I'm so nervous,' she said. 'Do I look all right?'

How like Mimi, Laura thought, amused. *Just because Christopher's a man, she goes on automatic pilot. Is she ever in for a surprise.*

'You look gorgeous,' she said soothingly.

Poor Mimi, she thought. Let her put on all the make-up she wished. Christopher would look straight through the facade – through the flattering hairdo, the Anne Klein clothes, the over-earnest eyes – in two seconds flat. Laura hoped he would be gentle with Mimi – not expose her to herself *too* quickly. And then she grinned. *No*, she thought. *He'll be gentle with her, all right. Only I get the rough treatment – and that's because I'm the Little Princess.*

Laura smiled, thinking of her recent anxiety about introducing Christopher to Mimi. God, she realized, she had actually been jealous! What an insanely insecure little creature she had always been. And thank Heaven all that was over. 'There is no one more important to me than you,' he had said. And she would carry that sentence about with her always; a little golden bullet-proof vest.

Mimi put away the make-up, smiled at herself in the mirror. Laura watched her sidelong. It struck her for the third time during the drive that there was something different about Mimi today – a subtle change from her usual attitude. In spite of the protestations of nervousness, Laura knew that she really wasn't nervous at all. There was a certain smug calm about her. Something was definitely afoot.

Laura found herself suddenly very curious.

'So, Mimi,' she said casually, 'do you have a lot of questions to ask Christopher?'

Mimi smiled. 'No,' she said delicately. 'Only one.'

And again that look of mysterious confidence.

Fine, Laura thought. *Let her keep her little secret.*

They had reached Christopher's. Laura parked the car. Expressively, Mimi looked around. Seeing this, Laura felt a hot flush of protectiveness. *If she says one word about its being run down, or those dead flowers in front, I'll push her over the cliff*, she thought.

But then, as Laura started up the path to the house, all drossy thoughts of Mimi burned away. She was going to see Christopher. It was the first time they would meet since he had told her he loved her. She wondered if he was as nervous about the meeting as she.

Laura knocked on the door, smiling, his Little Princess.

The door opened.

'Hi,' she said.

'Hi,' he said.

Then he looked past Laura. Looked past her to Mimi. And Laura saw his face. *No!* she wanted to scream. *No!* It couldn't be happening.

There, on his face, as he stared at Mimi, was the look. The look he had never given her.

Christopher stepped forward quietly. He took Mimi's hand. 'Hello, Mimi,' he said. 'Aren't you lovely?'

And Mimi looked up at Christopher, smiling.

It couldn't be happening. It couldn't be happening.

Finally Christopher turned to Laura. His face redressed into its usual kind peacefulness.

'Hello, Little Princess,' he said.

She wanted to vomit. The very name stung her, mocked her hideously now. Yes, she flashed, it was perfect – a stupid, infantile name for their stupid, infantile relationship.

She stared at him, thinking with frantic fury of all her foolish hopes. The months and months of ruses. Her thousand pointless attempts to make him fall in love with her.

And all Mimi Craddock had to do was open the door.

Mimi Craddock! Laura raged in a fresh wave of pain. That this supposed God – this person she had thought was so pure and wise – could fall for someone like Mimi Craddock!

It was the most unbearable touch of all.

Mimi was giggling. 'Little Princess! How cute. May I be a Little Princess, too?'

Laura looked for a long ironic moment at them both.

'By all means,' she said quietly. 'This one just abdicated.'

At four o'clock, Jeff came home. He came in the door carrying a bottle of champagne and two dozen roses. Laura had been sitting at the dining room table, her head in her hands. She raised her head, stared, disoriented, at Jeff.

'What's happened?' she said.

'I've gotten the series, Laura,' he told her. 'I've gotten the lead.'

She made a sound, kept staring.

He was laughing, glowing. 'It wasn't true about Matt Tomlin. It's mine. All fucking mine. And that's not all,' he said, walking towards her. 'I've been thinking. I think it's time we got married.'

And he handed her the roses.

Laura looked down at them. The room grew out of focus around her. The flowers were so shockingly red they stung her eyes.

'You want to get married?' she whispered.

So it had come at last; the moment she had longed for since the first moment of the first day she had met Jeff Kennerly. But now that it was here, she was too drained to respond.

She was dizzy, panting, unable to concentrate. Jeff's face was bearing down on hers. 'Jeff,' she gasped, pushing him away, 'I need a little time.'

He stared at her, bewildered, cut. 'What are you talking about?' he asked tightly. 'I thought you wanted this as much as I did.'

'I wanted it more.' She began to cry. 'But I don't know anything now,' she whispered. 'I just don't know anything.'

Without a word, Jeff pulled the roses from her hands. He stuffed them in the wastebasket. As he walked out of the apartment, he turned back for a moment. 'Congratulations,' he said. 'You've just thrown your life away.'

Chapter Thirteen

Grimly, Blake hung up the phone. But the news he had heard did not hang up with the receiver. It whined incessantly in his ear like an operator's recorded message.

He wondered how best to deal with her. He didn't know. He thought of the last months, and searched frantically through them for clues, for fragments of Laura. But there were so few to find. First Julia's death, then Archie and the deal, then the women, had managed to block Laura from his view. Effectively and, yes, with his consent.

He got into his car and started furiously off. He realized, of course, stupidly, now too late, that it should have been otherwise. There should have been lunches, long father-daughter talks. Laura minded about the women; he had known that. He should have discussed them with her openly. He should have explained about that night at Desiree's. He shouldn't have yelled at her about Nina Gibson. Goddammit. He should have shown more interest in her children's books.

Blake cursed at an easy-going truck. He felt angry, caught-out, ashamed, guilty before Julia because he had not better looked after their child. But dammit – what was he supposed to have done?

What would Julia have done? What would Julia do now? Would she see the humour in it? Let it alone? Panic? Again, he didn't know.

Blake jerked around the truck and sped forward. He

drove rapidly, his black Bentley scattering the traffic. The image of Laura as a little girl bore down on him. She had been – what had he called her?

His little pixilation.

He had put her picture in a special frame of auburn leather – the color had just matched her hair. He loved it that they had the same hair – it was the great bond between them.

He found himself wondering if she knew how proud he had always been of her. He also wondered if she had ever guessed how often she irritated him with her timidity. Or how painful it was being with her after Julia had died. Or how at a loss he felt.

He hoped he was doing the right thing now.

Blake parked the car by the weed-strewn sidewalk, and, without waiting for the elevator, ran up the stairs to the apartment.

Laura sat cold and rigid on the bed. Meteors, was what came into her mind. She was ossifying like a meteor, plunging alone through space forever. The doorbell rang. She jumped up as if freed from a spell. She ran to the door, her blood racing drunkenly. Jeff was back. He had come back to her.

She pulled the door open, and stared at the figure outside.

'Daddy,' she said faintly.

She had never seen her father look so grim.

'Laura, we've got to talk,' Blake said.

She put her hands in front of her face. 'Jeff's left me,' she whispered.

Blake did not react at first. Then he reached over and patted her with mingled pity and annoyance. 'I'm sure he'll come back,' he told her. And then he added, 'But, believe me, if he doesn't, it's no great tragedy.'

He could not keep the scorn out of his voice.

Laura stared, disbelieving. 'How can you say that?' she demanded.

He was silent.

'You've never liked Jeff.' She pulled on Blake's arm wildly. 'Why? Why?'

And hearing the question, Blake suddenly realized exactly how much he had always loathed Jeff Kennerly.

He stiffened. 'I didn't come to talk about Jeff,' he told her coldly. 'That's your business, not mine. Now sit down.'

But Laura would not sit. She stood beside him, clenched. A meteor again.

'How long have you been seeing Christopher Garland?' Blake suddenly demanded.

The question shocked her. She stared at him. Stared at the growing anger in his face.

'What?' she asked dully.

He asked her again.

Finally, she told him. Hating herself for her stupid timid guilty voice. 'Since February.'

Blake made an exclamation of disgust. He paced the small room.

'My God, Laura,' he said. 'I couldn't believe it when I heard. What have you been doing? What have you been *doing?*' In horror, he gazed at her.

Numbly, she gazed back at him. What had she been doing? she echoed silently. What had she been *doing?*

'I can't understand it,' he said. 'You're smart. You're successful. You had everything going for you.' He glared at her. 'How could you let yourself get mixed up with a man like this? Have you lost all common sense? Don't you have any idea how dangerous these people can be? Look at Jim Jones! Look at Rasputin!'

231

The thought of Christopher Garland as Rasputin made Laura want to scream with aching, weeping laughter.

'No,' she choked. 'It's nothing like that. You don't understand.'

And then the realization, the ridiculousness, the unfairness, hit her.

'But Daddy,' she cried. 'You're the one who went to him first.'

Blake looked uncomfortably away. 'I'm aware of that,' he said coldly. 'It was a month after your mother died. I was in pretty bad shape.'

The sentence hung there.

'Well, I'm not in bad shape,' Laura said quickly.

Then she and her father remembered at the same instant that Jeff had left her. Laura bit her lip. Blake grew gentler.

'Come here, little pixilation,' he said.

She burst into tears.

He sat down on the sofa and drew Laura towards him. Blake thought, as they sat there, that her weight in his arms created a tenderness in him that no other woman, not even Julia, had ever caused. He thought of her again as that flame-headed five year old, and his chest squeezed.

'Look, sweetheart,' he said, after a long pause. 'I know we haven't been as close as we should be. And that's my fault. I guess I haven't been the greatest father in the world.' Without amusement, he laughed. 'Obviously I haven't been, if you need to go looking to psychics for guidance.' Then he took her hand and covered it with his own. 'But Laura, listen to me. This isn't the way. I promise you, it isn't. I appreciate what you're going through, and that you're searching, but you're not going to find any answers from a man like Christopher Garland. If you feel you need counselling, we can set you up with someone – someone real.'

Christopher, the unreal.

'Hey, look,' Blake went on. 'I met Christopher. I agree with you. He's a sweet guy. A real sweet guy. And I'm sure he doesn't mean to cause any harm. But this occult business – it's just escapism, Laura – pure delusion. First thing you know, you've lost touch with reality. And suddenly, you're off the deep-end.

'A guy like Christopher meets someone like you, someone in a very vulnerable position, someone who's lost, and for whatever reason – ego, greed, or maybe even because he really believes in the stuff he teaches – he tries to get control. And he gets it through any means he can.'

Laura said nothing, but Blake could see a response beginning to break in her face. He pressed on.

'Look,' he said. 'People have been searching for answers since time began. If Christopher were really onto the Truth, the only Truth, wouldn't we all know it? If metaphysics and spiritualism were really the answers, wouldn't everyone in the world be practising them? And if – '

'It's all right, Daddy,' Laura cut him off wearily. 'You don't have to go on. I'm not seeing Christopher anymore. It's over.'

She had said the words. The words of finality. And hearing herself say them, she cried and cried until the front of her father's shirt was wet.

I have nothing left now, Laura thought at last. *Including tears.*

Then she lay back on her father's shoulder. They did not talk about Christopher anymore. They just talked about easy things. Happy memories of Julia. Silly jokes.

'Laura, let's get closer,' Blake burst out suddenly.

'We've never been close enough, you and I. What was that your mother used to say? "Let's have a fresh start." What do you say to that?' His voice grew enthusiastic. 'Let's start doing things together. Going to movies. Taking trips, just the two of us. Maybe we'll go to San Diego for the weekend. We'll stay at the Hotel de Coronado. Remember what a great place that was?'

Laura remembered. She remembered going there with her parents when she was eight, so proud of her new blue bathing suit. She imagined what it would be like now, travelling with her father. The twenty-three year old, unattached, anxious-faced daughter. Running errands for Blake, arranging his appointments with the hotel masseuse and barber shop. Breakfasting with him in the hotel dining room, being told she wasn't eating enough.

Oh, Daddy, she thought. It would be so nice if she could go back to being that little girl in the blue bathing suit. But it was impossible.

She said nothing, only kissed his cheek. She lay against him for a moment more, and then suddenly she looked up.

'Daddy,' she asked quietly, 'how did you know I'd been seeing Christopher?'

He did not answer.

'Desiree told you,' she said in a low voice. 'She was the only one who knew. And she swore she wouldn't tell.'

But of course Desiree had told. Blake had probably called her up and said, 'What's going on with Laura, Desiree? I'm worried about her. Has she ever confided in you?' and Desiree, in her weakness, her desire to be important to the man she loved, had spilled it all.

'It wasn't Desiree,' Blake said finally.

And then Laura knew.

234

'Mimi,' she whispered. 'Oh, my God. Daddy, how long have you been seeing Mimi Craddock?'

She grew more and more panicky through every second of his silence.

'Since you brought her by the house,' he said defensively. 'I liked her. What's wrong with that?'

And Laura went cold with fury, remembering. How clearly she could see it all now. Mimi, begging to be brought to her parents' house, pretending she wanted a little trinket of Julia's. Mimi, asking for the tour, for the iced tea, which she never even drank, so that she would be sure to be seen when Blake came out of his office. Mimi, with that sly smile on her face when Laura had come back to the library. Oh, God, how could she have been so blind?

Laura pulled herself from her father's side and stood over him, raging. 'That cheap little tramp. How could you? How could you?' she demanded.

Coldly, Blake also rose. 'Laura, it's really none of your business.'

She swallowed, her throat raped with a surge of bile, her resolution not to interfere forgotten.

'It's my business because of Desiree,' she told him. 'What about *her*?'

Blake stared at Laura, bewildered. 'What *about* her?'

Laura flushed. Incredibly, he seemed to be serious in his surprise.

'What do you mean, "What about her?" ' she sputtered. 'That evening at her house . . . I saw you . . . You two . . .'

Blake shook his head and made a strange, bewildered sound.

'Oh, Laura,' he said. 'Are you actually that naive?'

He stood up and walked distractedly around the room.

Finally he came to a picture of Julia on the bookshelf, and he stopped. He picked it up, held it, looked at it.

'God, she was beautiful,' he said flatly.

Then he turned to Laura. 'Listen,' he said gently. 'Your mother had just died. I was lonely. I needed someone. Desiree was there. We had known each other a long time.'

Seeing Laura still look so puzzled by even these primer words, Blake began to grow irritated. 'There was never any question of its being serious,' he snapped. 'I took her out for a while. Like I took out a lot of other women. And that was all there was to it.'

Laura continued to stare at him like a cretin. *And that was all there was to it?* She wanted to sob with crazy laughter. She thought of all the scheming that had gone on – the spying, the stolen messages, the night with Nina Gibson, her grandiose promises to Desiree, and above all her absolute certainty that she, Laura Alden, was manipulating Destiny to perfection.

And that was all there was to it?

She was routed, pathetic, ridiculous.

And she suddenly saw something else – something that made her feel sick. She saw that, all along, what she had done had not been done for Desiree. Or for her father. It had been done for herself. Only for herself. So that the great Laura Alden could be in control.

Oh, God. What was that he had said? *People like you are dangerous.*

And then she thought of Desiree. 'But Desiree's in love with you,' she told her father quietly.

She waited for his face to change at this news, but it did not.

'I'm sorry for her, then,' Blake shrugged. 'Because I'm not in love with her.'

The embarrassing, the ignominious end.

'But you're in love with Mimi Craddock?' Laura asked him faintly.

Blake's laughter shot through the room. 'Give your old man some credit!' he protested. 'Of course I'm not in love with Mimi Craddock.'

Then he grew quiet. He looked down once more at the photo in his hand and he tapped Julia's face with his finger. When he spoke again, his voice was very soft.

'Listen to me, Laura. This lady here was the love of my life. The one and the only.'

He returned the picture to its place on the shelf. And when he looked at Laura again, there was an expression on his face that she had never seen there.

He's forgotten I'm his daughter, she thought. *And he's telling me the truth.*

'I'm never going to find another like her,' he said, 'so I'm not even going to try. But I'm sixty years old, Laura. And, unlike your friend Christopher, I've a sneaking suspicion that this life here on earth is all we get. So I'm going to make damned sure I have a ball with what's left of mine. And that means Mimi Craddocks and Nina Gibsons and nightclubs and dressing too young and whatever else makes me happy.' He laughed wryly. 'I know there are people who think I'm making a damned fool of myself – my daughter obviously included – but that's okay. Just wait till *you're* sixty,' he teased her.

Laura dropped her head. She didn't feel sixty. She felt six hundred.

'Forgive me, Daddy,' she said. 'I just didn't understand.'

Then each looked away from the emotion in the other's face.

The room was getting dark. Nightbirds began to sing – tentative, melancholy.

'Well,' Laura said wearily.

'Well,' Blake said, mocking her.

Sadly, they laughed.

'What are you doing tonight?' Blake asked her.

The Jeff emptiness hit hard.

'Nothing,' she said.

'Want to go to dinner with me?' Blake asked. 'I'll even spring for a movie.'

Laura shook her head, smiling. 'What a guy,' she told him lightly. 'But no thanks. Take one of your lovely ladies.'

'You are my lovely lady,' he said.

He looked at her for a long moment; wanting miracles for her, and knowing there were none.

He kissed her and was gone.

And Laura was left beached, surrounded by the sharp broken edges of things that had been.

For a while, she did mindless inconsequential tasks in the apartment. Straightened the pages of her new children's book. Tidied her scarf drawer. And, that accomplished, she could think of no other way to put off what she knew she had to do now.

She dialled the number and Desiree answered on the second ring.

'Desiree,' Laura said.

And she told her. Told her that the whole thing with her father was over. That the whole thing had really never been. That they had only been fooling themselves with hand-shadows of their own devising. Her voice slid up and down as she spoke, like a palm wet with perspiration.

Desiree did not say a word. Laura kept on talking, kept on crumbling more and more bits of what her father had said, and throwing them into this black hard pit of silence.

Then Desiree spoke at last. 'I see,' she said. She sounded very calm. 'Thank you so much, dear. You've made it all very clear. And something else is very clear, too. You vicious little bitch.'

Laura gasped, but Desiree shut her up. 'It was you,' she said. 'You who ruined everything. How could I have fallen for it? You've always hated me, haven't you? You were jealous from the time you were a child. You never wanted me for your father, of course you didn't. I was a threat, wasn't I? So you got close to me. Close enough to learn my secrets. And then you used them against me. Worked on your father. Discredited me.'

Laura was mouthing, 'No,' but the word was not coming out.

'What did you tell him, Laura?' Desiree was asking. 'What did you say about me?' And then she laughed. 'I've got to hand it to you, though. You fooled even me. You're brilliant. Absolutely brilliant. And very, very sick.'

There was a pause, and Laura ached with it.

'I loved you,' Desiree whispered bewilderedly. 'I felt you were my child. And you did this to me.'

Laura moaned.

When Desiree spoke again, her voice was changed. It was hard now, empty, almost off-hand.

'Oh, one more thing, my dear,' she added casually. 'Since we're being so honest with each other today, there's something I think *you* should know. Your father never loved your mother. He was unfaithful to her from day one, with every woman in town. In fact, we all used to laugh at Julia. Poor dear Julia.'

Laura lay in bed. Her brain was a minefield, ready to explode. No matter in which direction she tried to find safety, to take a step was to be destroyed. Everyone had been discredited. Christopher by her father. Her father by Desiree. Desiree by her father. And everyone had betrayed her. Desiree by her outburst. Christopher by falling for Mimi. Her father by being unfaithful to her mother. Her mother by dying. God damn them all.

There were no steps to be taken.

There were no thoughts that were safe.

So she would never move again.

So she would never think again.

She was all alone.

She wanted to scream and scream.

And then it came to her. The one thought, the one path. The one path that was beautiful and dependable and safe for her to tread forever.

Oh, God, what a fool she had been.

'Come back, Jeff,' she moaned into the bed. 'Come back.'

He came back at four in the morning.

'Of course I'll marry you,' she said as he walked in the door. 'I was insane. I'm not insane anymore.'

He walked over to the bed and took her in his arms.

It was dawn. Laura lay crumpled in sheets and the fading rainbow of love-making. Jeff lay beside her. She closed her eyes in relief and surrender, and ran her arms down his golden tangible body. She tried, for several moments, the game of matching her breathing to his, but his breaths wanted to be slow and deep, her own to be short and quick. Then she rolled onto her back and closed her eyes.

Mama, she thought. *Where are you, Mama?*

After a moment, Julia's image came into her mind – sitting in her purple caftan, having tea at the wrought-iron garden table.

'Mama,' Laura whispered, 'I've got something wonderful to tell you. Jeff and I are getting married.'

Julia poured the tea in silence. Her face was remote, as if she had not heard. And, concentrate as she would, Laura could not draw from her any reaction whatsoever.

'I just wanted you to be the first to know,' she said finally, into the emptiness.

And the picture faded slowly away.

Laura felt chilled. She pulled the covers up around her. *You are getting married*, she told herself solemnly. And then she told all her selves. Five year old Laura the tomboy, ten year old Laura with braces, fifteen year old Laura who thought she'd never have a boyfriend, twenty year old Laura who was sure Jeff Kennerly would never marry her. Told them all that this coming spring, she would be a bride.

A bride! she thought with a sudden surge. *A bride, just like my Barbie doll.*

I will be married with an antique veil. I will be married with a Cuisinart. I will be married with Martex towels.

Blake was working at his desk. Laura came into the room. She could tell how relieved he was to see her looking her normal self again.

'Hi, sweetie!' he said.

She went over to his desk. She stood beside him, looking down, smiling, as he looked up.

'Daddy, Jeff and I are getting married,' she said, and as she saw his sudden expression, she babbled on quickly. 'If you'd like a grandchild, better put in your order now,' she said. 'The boy or the girl model?'

'Are you sure about this?' Blake only asked her.

'Come on, Daddy,' she laughed uneasily. 'I've been begging the guy to marry me for the last five years.'

Blake smiled.

'Well, then, it looks like you got your way,' he told her. 'That's my girl.'

He was silent a moment.

'I'll give you a wedding,' he said. 'We'll do it up in style.' Then he laughed in a spasm of sadness.

'Oh, Laura, wouldn't your mother have loved all this? Can't you just see her? She'd be going crazy with this news – ordering flowers, sending out invitations, hiring whole orchestras.'

Laura thought of Julia, the way she had been in her mind that morning, pouring tea in strange silence.

'She sure would have, Daddy,' she answered him staunchly. 'She sure would have.'

Jeff's parents flew down the following evening. This time Laura had warning, and she made sure the apartment was beautifully clean and full of flowers. She even took the Currier and Ives print the Kennerlys had given her last Christmas, and hung it so that it was the first thing they would see when they came in the door.

Mr Kennerly was, as always, jovial, unreadable. Mrs Kennerly looked as though, since hearing the news, she had done nothing but weep.

The four of them went to L'Hermitage. Not a word was mentioned about the upcoming wedding until the wine was brought.

'Well,' said Mr Kennerly, raising his glass. 'Here's to you two. I can't say we're surprised, but we're both very, very pleased. Welcome to our family, Laura.'

Laura thanked him, kissed him on the cheek. She felt very tender in her triumph. She looked at this man and woman, knowing how they had fought against her for five years, knowing how awful this night must be for them, and quickly she changed the subject. Throughout

242

the remainder of the meal, she talked gently and respect-
fully about subjects of general interest, trying hard to be
a good winner, since they were being good losers.

But it was odd. The victory over Jeff's parents, now
that it had finally come, did not somehow mean nearly
as much to Laura as she had always imagined it would.

Mr and Mrs Kennerly had to get back to Denver the
next morning, so it was an early evening. Laura and Jeff
came back to the apartment.

'You were great,' Jeff kept saying to her. 'I can't believe
how great you were with my parents. I swear, you're
like a different person these days. I should have asked
you to marry me years ago!'

'True, true,' Laura told him airily. The whole evening
had been such a performance, and even now she could
not get over the feeling that she was onstage.

Jeff sat down beside her on the couch. He put his arm
around her shoulders.

'I still can't believe all this is really happening,' he
said.

'You mean us getting married?' she asked, smiling.

'Well, that, too,' he said quickly, and she knew that
he had really meant getting the series.

'I can believe it,' she told him staunchly. 'I've always
known you'd make it.'

'Have you?' he asked her, surprised. 'I haven't. Not at
all.'

And I never knew, Laura thought with a pang. *We've
been together all this time, and I never knew he felt
like that.*

Lightly, Jeff hugged her.

'But now that it's happened, everything's different.
The way I feel. The way everyone treats me. God, it's
incredible.' His eyes brightened. 'I mean, even my folks.

Did you see how they behaved with me this evening? All those questions about the show? Didn't you think they seemed impressed?'

Tenderly, as if he were a little boy, Laura assured him that indeed they had seemed terribly impressed.

'And, you'll see, it's going to make all the difference to us, too,' Jeff went on.

Laura pulled away slightly. 'In what way?' she asked him, her laugh a little nervous.

'In every way,' he told her firmly. 'You and I are finally going places.'

Going places, Laura thought. *And where does that mean we were before?*

Jeff laughed at her serious face. 'The first place being bed,' he told her, grinning, standing up and pulling her to her feet.

'In a moment, Jeff,' she told him. 'There's a call I have to make first.'

'Well, hurry up,' he said, and went into the bedroom.

She stood staring at the phone. Then she picked it up and dialled his number. She owed him that, at least.

She got the answering machine.

'Hello, Christopher,' she said. 'This is Laura. I'm afraid I won't be coming in for tomorrow's session.' She paused. 'As a matter of fact, I've decided to stop taking sessions altogether. Things have changed here – and I just don't need to see you anymore. I hope you understand.'

She hung up the phone and went over to the bookcase. One by one she pulled the metaphysical books from the shelf, and one by one, she threw them into the big trash container.

Then she went in to Jeff.

Chapter Fourteen

Telling the outsiders was perhaps the most fun of all. Sentimental friends of her mother's, fond relatives, jealous acquaintances of her own. It was fun listening to their endless babble of pleasure, envy, romance, predictions of bliss. It was the frosting on the cake – the ultimate, sugary, rich, emotional frosting.

And everyone called. The phone rang continually like a joyous churchbell.

One night, it rang very late. Laura picked it up.

'Hello?' she said.

No one responded.

'Hello?' she asked again.

Finally a female voice asked to speak to Jeff Kennerly.

'He's in the shower,' Laura told the voice. 'Can I help you? This is his fiancée.'

There was a high-pitched gasp from the other end of the line. Then the phone went dead.

Laura smiled a little bitterly.

They went to a jewellery store on South Beverly Drive. It was the fourth one they had tried. Jeff had been marvellously understanding about the importance of the ring to Laura – how it had to be the perfect one.

She saw it in the second trayful she looked at. That little fairy ring – white gold and yellow gold. She could hardly bear for even the salesman even to touch it. It was hers.

And one day she would give it to her own daughter.

Laura closed her eyes. Fiercely, she imprinted on herself all the details of this moment. *I will never forget this*, she thought. *The moment I chose my wedding ring.*

When she opened her eyes again, Jeff was laughing at her.

'You're a head-case,' he said – but he also said that the ring was indeed beautiful.

'And what about one for you?' the salesman asked Jeff. 'I believe we have a matching one.'

'Perfect!' Laura gushed, and immediately she realized she had said the wrong thing.

'No,' Jeff said. 'I don't wear jewellery.'

'Of course you wear jewellery,' Laura cried, looking in bewilderment at his gold I.D. bracelet and the chains about his neck.

'I mean, I don't wear rings,' Jeff said tensely.

The salesman immediately busied himself at the far end of the counter.

Childish tears leaped to Laura's eyes. 'You don't love me!' she cried. 'You don't want anyone to know we're getting married! That's why you don't want a ring!'

'Lower your voice,' Jeff told her, anxiously glancing around to see if anyone had heard the outburst. Shamed, Laura collected herself.

'Of course I love you,' Jeff went on in a low voice. 'It's not that at all. It's just – in this business – doing the series – people think of you differently if they know you're married. I mean,' he added hastily, 'everyone will know I'm *married*, but if they see a ring all the time – It just makes a difference, Laura. In the way I'm perceived. By the guys at the studio, by the public, by everyone. And at this point in my career, I can't afford to have *any* chips stacked against me. Understand?'

Laura understood. She nodded miserably.

He patted her shoulder briskly. 'So we'll just buy your ring for now, but don't you worry, the minute I can, we'll go out and buy me the biggest wedding ring you ever saw. Okay?'

The salesman miraculously reappeared, and sold them Laura's ring.

Leaving the store, Jeff spotted a couple window-shopping across the street. The man was in his late fifties, with an aggressive toupee and a dark silk Italian suit. And the woman was very young, in clothes that were very short and very tight.

A candle was lit behind Jeff's eyes.

'That's Lou Hinkle,' he said worshipfully. 'Our executive producer.'

Lou turned and spotted Jeff. He waved him jovially over. Jeff ran across Beverly Drive, without benefit of crosswalk, pulling Laura after him.

'Hello, Lou,' Jeff said casually enough, but Laura could tell how nervous he was.

'What a surprise seeing you,' Jeff said. Then he turned to Laura. 'This is Laura Alden. Laura, Lou Hinkle.'

Lou winked at Laura. 'I saw where you two were coming from. Shame on you, young lady. The poor guy gets a series, and you're right away suckering him out of some jewellery, huh?'

Laura tried to laugh appreciatively.

'Well, see you Monday, Jeffie,' Lou said, and patted Jeff's cheek. And he left without introducing the girl.

'God,' Jeff said slowly. 'Of all the people to show up. Can you believe it? I've only been talking about him non-stop all day!'

Have you? Laura wondered. *Yes, I guess you have.*

'Jeff,' she said suddenly, 'Jeff, why didn't you introduce me as your fiancée?'

247

He turned to her in surprise. 'Didn't I?' he asked. 'I thought I did.'

Laura found one change in her new life to be very unexpected and a little ironic. Her relationship with her father. She and Blake had suddenly become pals. They talked on the phone every day now, lunched once, even twice, a week. It was as if, now that the secretive shady things – Desiree, Christopher – had been dethroned, they could start the relationship afresh and be free to walk in the clear lit spaces at last.

Laura enjoyed the time with her father, enjoyed the freedom from hidden agendas and yet somewhere, secretly, there was a strange sense of hollowness. As if their closeness, now that it had finally come, was not so much a victory as a denouement. And that it was still, somehow, not quite real.

But that's ridiculous, she told herself stoutly. *What's happened is wonderful – we're relating on a new mature level. All that's gone is the melodrama.*

Neither she nor her father ever mentioned that hour in Laura's apartment, or the things that had been said then. And soon, that moment and all the revelation and emotion in it, came to seem to Laura like a stray outlying speck on an otherwise perfect graph – something to discount and forget about completely.

Though Blake rarely talked about his social life, Laura knew that he was still dating Mimi Craddock, and one night she had an idea.

'We ought to arrange a double date with them,' she told Jeff.

He looked at her quizzically. 'Why?'

'I just think it would be a friendly thing to do.'

But in truth, it was more than that. The idea carried with it the final symbol of her being adult – and her new, adult relationship with her father. All subterfuge, resentment, mourning for Julia had finally been left behind, and, Laura told herself proudly, she was ready to embrace the present in a frank, realistic way.

The four of them went to a French restaurant in the Valley. Laura and Jeff had never been there before, but Blake and Mimi were well known in that tiny dark place that smelled of wine.

The evening was not a grand success. The words that everyone chose to say seemed out of sync with everyone else's choices.

Laura spoke nervously, inanely, about the things she hoped to accomplish with her children's book.

Jeff spoke hardly at all.

Blake told a few jokes.

And Mimi chattered as maddeningly as a bee caught in a lace curtain.

Listening to her, Laura wondered how her father could stand it, but Blake didn't seem to mind at all. He was terribly, surrealistically courteous to Mimi, attentive to her requests, to her endless stories. In fact, he seemed very much like a man in love.

And yet two months ago, in her apartment, he had laughed to scorn the very idea of loving Mimi Craddock.

Laura felt chilled, watching them. Watching these strangers. What a fool she had been, to think that she and her father had been growing closer. So what if they talked every day? Real life, real feeling, real communication, had nothing to do with a telephone or a lunch-table. Things were no different now than they had been before. And she realized she understood him less than ever.

That afternoon in the apartment, I really saw him, Laura mourned. *And now he's disappeared again.*

After dinner, while Blake and Jeff dealt with the valet parking, Laura and Mimi were left alone for a moment on the sidewalk.

'Well,' Mimi said brightly. 'How's your friend Christopher doing?'

'I have no idea,' Laura said coldly. 'You probably know more about that than I do.'

'How should I know?' Mimi asked in surprise. 'I only saw him that one time.'

'Oh,' Laura said. 'I was sure you would go back.'

'Why?' Mimi asked.

Laura despised herself for her sudden hot flush. 'Maybe the way he looked at you,' she said bluntly.

Mimi was insulted. 'Him?' she scoffed. 'Really, Laura. He's not exactly my type.' Then she smiled. 'But he is a good psychic. He answered my question all right.' Slyly, she glanced towards Laura. 'It was about your dad, if you want to know. Tell me Laura, were you surprised when you found out?'

'No,' Laura answered her shortly, but she was no longer even listening. Her mind scrambled, teetered, challenged to absorb what she had just heard. So Mimi *hadn't* gone back to Christopher. Nothing had come of that look.

Laura felt strangely claustrophobic. She didn't understand. Could it possibly be that she had got it wrong this whole time? Had she simply been over-reacting that day? Had she even imagined that look? Oh, God, maybe if she hadn't left his apartment . . . maybe if she had called afterwards, demanding to know what his feelings for her were. . .

Stop it, she told herself angrily. *What the hell did it matter now anyway? Everything had worked out for the best. Absolutely for the very best.*

Jeff came home from the studio every night with new names and new stories. There were dinner dates with the new people, new clothes, new expressions in his speech. The director had been heard to say that Jeff's was the best performance in the show. And Jeff's name was apparently being mentioned in connection with a feature film. It was all going right, going exactly as Laura had always hoped it would. Her golden boy had at last come into his rightful golden kingdom. And any frustrations, misunderstandings, struggles, had been smoothed away.

What sort of sickie am I? she would wonder, looking at Jeff's satisfied face, listening to his satisfied talk. *What sort of sickie would be missing the old days?*

The era of the supermarket Corningware plates was over. Laura spent hours at Robinson's and Geary's, Bullocks and Neiman Marcus, choosing china, silver, linen to complement her new life. She did her shopping alone. There was no one she especially wanted to go with.

These were strange and draining afternoons. For some reason Laura found it hard to make even the simplest decision. For so many years, she had dreamed of getting married, dreamed of choosing patterns, pillowcases, cutlery. A hundred times since childhood, she had walked through these very stores thinking *Someday I'll have this . . . or this . . . or this . . . in my house.* And now the day had come – and the actual choice was being made. It was absolutely wonderful, of course, yet in a bizarre way it made her feel wistful. Wistful that all the possibilities, all the choices of the years, had congealed and narrowed into this One Ultimate China Pattern. Or this One Ultimate Glass. Instead of being a moment of fulfillment, it was a moment almost of diminishment.

'That's ridiculous,' Jeff said, when Laura told him about this feeling. 'Think of it this way. If you get the stuff home and you don't like the way it looks, you throw it out and get something else. It's as simple as that.'

Perhaps it was. Perhaps not.

She was watching the CBS Evening News when Jeff came home. He threw the door back like a cymbal clash.

'Guess what, baby!' he cried. 'We're moving!'

Laura glanced at the television, at the grave, flaccid-voiced newscaster and his bagful of international disasters. *And they called this news?.*

She switched off the set and turned to Jeff. 'What did you say?' she asked incredulously.

He paced the room, snapping his fingers against his hand. Out it all tumbled – how Hank Sheen (the second assistant director or the one with the cocaine habit?) was buying a house in Bel Air and his apartment was up for lease. And he was offering it to Jeff and Laura.

'It's absolutely gorgeous,' he told her excitedly. 'Modern, big, built-ins, a swimming pool. You'll love it.'

He sounds just like a real-estate salesman, she thought.

'And it's on Reeves, just south of Wilshire. Not a bad location. It'll really be a step up.'

'Sounds great,' Laura told him, stalling, smiling.

'Wait till you see it!' Jeff told her.

I wonder when he saw it? Laura thought. And why he didn't mention it before?

'It's got these great peg and groove floors, keristan carpets – '

Since when had Jeff started noticing floors and carpets?

' – and there's this terrific bar. We can really do some

entertaining now. Maybe even ask Lou Hinkle over. And the best part is, we can be in there by the first of next month.'

'What will this cost, Jeff?' she asked.

He shrugged, with a little guilty smile.

'Well, let's just say more than this place. But what the hell. This new apartment would be really good for my image, now that I've got the series. And besides,' he added, seeing her face, 'we're getting married. We need a honeymoon cottage.' He looked around their current apartment with a little laugh. 'And this sure ain't it.'

Laura felt, ridiculously, as though he had slighted their child. 'You always said you loved this place,' she reminded him a little tensely.

He laughed. 'I always said I loved eating at McDonald's, too. Baby, when you can't afford any better, you put a good face on what you've got. But let's face it – this place is a dump. And now we're moving up!'

She said nothing.

He went over to her, pulled her to her feet, and took her in his arms. 'You know what finally convinced me to take the apartment?' he asked. 'Off the living room, there's this cute little cubbyhole, and I thought, "Here's where Laura can do her writing." '

She stiffened in his arms. 'Do my writing? I thought you were going to say, "Here's where the baby's room could be." '

And he stiffened in *her* arms. 'The baby's room? Well, let's not rush things.'

And they continued to stand like two toy soldiers embracing.

It was taking a long time to pack up all those years.

'Can't you do it any faster?' Jeff asked, as every night

253

he came home to larger and larger piles of unsorted memorabilia.

But Laura couldn't seem to. The lethargy she had felt at the department stores was overwhelming her again. And everything she tried to throw away assailed her — with yeasty, subtle memories.

She came upon a pair of pink ballet slippers. Wearing them to the square dance, her third date with Jeff. The silly game — his boinging the elastic over the instep, making her guess the tune. Having them on when she heard the news about her cousin Matt.

Ticket stubs. A plastic comb. Jeff's old green sweater. The one he had worn the night they had gone to see *King of Hearts*. Laura unfolded the sweater, and put its arms around her neck, the way his arms had been. Moths had gotten to the material, and it was full of holes.

Finally, one morning Laura put everything in the trash bag and went down to the compactor in the basement. But she came back up a few moments later, without having thrown anything away.

It's damned superstition, she told herself disgustedly. Yet she couldn't get the idea out of her head. The idea that if anything were to happen to those relics of the old days with Jeff, that somehow the memory of the days themselves would be destroyed. But that as long as the sweater and the chemistry book and the grey sweatsock were around, it was proof that she and Jeff belonged together, that they had a history.

Laura couldn't believe how incredibly morbid she was being. A history! Was she crazy or something? They were getting married in April — they had a future!

But still the closet continued to bleed forth relics. Still the piles mounted and were not thrown away.

Laura had always dreamed of a wedding like Meg March's in *Little Women*. A tiny, intimate ceremony in the garden, a home-made wedding cake, the wedding dress hand-sewn by the bride, the service performed by her own father. But since Blake Alden was not a chaplain, she herself could not sew or bake, and the guest-list exceeded three hundred, this dream proved impractical. So things were otherwise arranged.

The wedding was to be at All Saints' Church, the reception at the Beverly Hills Hotel, and the catering was to be done by the group who had been entrusted with the Queen Mother's last visit to Los Angeles. The music was to be provided by several members of the Los Angeles Philharmonic Orchestra; Blake had, over the years, done the Music Center quite a few favors. And Laura's wedding dress was to be designed and made by Alex Tolken.

There was still uncertainty as to who was to be allowed to do the flowers.

Laura felt a little ridiculous, being the center of so much frenzied preparation. But she was touched that her father wanted all this for her, and even more so by the fact that he, usually so impatient of detail, was going to all this effort.

'I'll take care of everything,' was what he said to her every offer of help. 'Don't worry. It'll be fantastic.'

Laura sometimes found herself wondering what her mother would have thought of all this fuss and fury. True, Julia was famous in Hollywood for her fabulous parties, and yet, it had been she who had given Laura *Little Women* in the first place.

She was also unsure as to how Jeff would react. Jeff, who had been afraid even to wear a wedding ring, for fear of hurting his public image. But that mindset seemed to have totally changed in the last months.

Maybe the publicity department did some new research, and found that it's okay for him to be married, Laura thought a little grimly.

Whatever the reason, Jeff was taking all the wedding preparations in happy humor, especially the news that photographers from *Entertainment Tonight* would cover the reception. And of course there would be a special table for everyone connected with his new series.

'Lou Hinkle's doing something terrific,' Jeff told Laura one day. 'In fact, it's going to be his wedding present to us. He's hiring this little plane to fly over the party. It'll have a banner flying from it that says, "Congratulations, Laura and Jeff." Isn't that a cute idea?'

There were to be three bridesmaids, dressed in peach. One was Laura's cousin Mandy, one was Ginny, her best friend from High School who was flying in from Texas, and the other she could not decide upon. Finally, Blake let it be known that he would appreciate it if Mimi Craddock were asked.

'Mimi?' Laura asked blankly.

'Yes,' Blake said briskly. 'I think she's a little hurt that you haven't thought about it before. After all, she's gone to a lot of trouble to plan this wedding for you.'

'What does it matter who planned it?' Jeff said impatiently, when Laura came to him in tears. 'The only thing that matters is that it all goes well.'

So Mimi was asked to be a bridesmaid.

She tried on the peach dress. It looked exquisite.

Laura wasn't sure when the anxiety attacks had begun to come on. But soon they were coming every night. First, the dream that she couldn't breathe. Then waking and finding out it wasn't a dream. Then shooting upright, gasping. Her chest panicky, pounding.

256

She could never go right back to sleep after these attacks, but had to sit in the kitchen and drink tea until the terrors went away. Then she would sneak back to bed. And in an hour or so, she would be dreaming again that she couldn't breathe.

Laura saw Desiree on the street one day. Desiree saw her also. She stared a frozen moment, then walked on.

I know that woman, Laura thought in a daze. *That is Desiree Kaufman. The friend of Mama's. The one I have always been so terrified of. I think I will turn the corner very quickly.*

'Well, what do you think of it?' Jeff asked her excitedly.

Laura walked around the apartment carefully. She noted the fireplace, the closet space, the view.

It was the perfect apartment.

'It's the perfect apartment,' she told him.

He grinned. 'Told you.'

They signed the lease that afternoon. Jeff gave the landlady the first check from his new checkbook from his new account at City National Bank. The landlady shook their hands.

'An honour, Mr Kennerly,' she said.

On the drive home, Laura asked herself why she hated the new apartment so. Finally she realized. It was because Jeff had found it himself through his new friends from his new life – and that it had nothing whatsoever to do with her. *Oh, God, you're sick*, Laura told herself angrily. *Must you always be in control? Can't you ever be satisfied unless you're running the show? People like you are dangerous.*

That night's anxiety attack was the worst it had ever been.

One afternoon, Jeff called her from the set. Lou Hinkle had invited them to dinner that night at the Mandarin.

'The whole group will be there!' Jeff told her exuberantly. 'Look gorgeous.'

Then Laura could hear a voice calling, 'Jeff Kennerly!' over a megaphone, and he had to go. For a second, Laura pursued Jeff's end of the scene; his hanging up the phone, walking back to the hot lit set, the hairdressers fussing with his bright hair; everything light, color, action. And then it faded.

Laura spent most of the grey afternoon deciding what to wear to the Mandarin that night. She hated herself for both the worry she was lavishing on the decision, and for the fact that she was needing to lavish it. She should have known instantly what she should wear. The way Julia would have known.

Oh, Laura, you are so inept, she whispered to the ghostly girl in the mirror whose hair was unbrushed.

Finally she gave up and decided to work on her children's story. Philippe, the French hippo would comfort her.

She sat down, pulled out the manuscript and started to read through what she had written so far. She read at first quickly, confidently, then more and more haltingly. And finally, halfway through the story, in disbelief she stopped.

She put the pages down, chilled. No. She couldn't believe it.

She read through it again. And again, she dropped it.

No. There was no mistaking it. It was no good.

Laura stood up, shaking. *Maybe,* she thought quickly, *I'm just depressed. Maybe it's not really that bad. I mean, even at my worst, I'm better than most. Maybe it's the illustrations that need work. Maybe it's just a*

258

surface problem. Maybe another draft will solve it. But she knew she was just fooling herself.

There was a fatal phoniness about the plot, a coyness about the style. It was what she had always hated most; it was the work of an adult who was pretending, who was trying to grope the way back to childhood.

The real reason Laura writes such good children's books is because she's a child herself.

She lay back, trembling.

What a horrible way to find out that you've grown up.

And she knew, with a light-flash certainty, that she no longer had within her the magic. She balled her hands into fists, crushed her eyes and began to sob.

Jeff finished his take. He was making his way to his dressing room, when Janet, Lou Hinkle's young black-haired secretary walked up to him.

'Mr Kennerly, a message just came for you,' she said. 'It was from your girlfriend. She said she's sorry but she has this really bad migraine, and she can't join you at the Mandarin tonight.' Solicitously, she smiled at Jeff.

Damn, Jeff thought. *Just once, can't she make it easy for me?*

Then he realized Janet was still staring at him, and he gave her a big easy smile. 'So it looks like my better half's left me dateless,' he said lightly.

Delicately, Janet dropped her eyes. 'Spare ribs are my favorite,' she told him.

Tomorrow was moving day. The apartment was packed up at last, filled with boxes and bags like a giant under-the-tree on Christmas Day.

It was another night of not sleeping. *The last*, Laura promised herself ruefully. *This is absolutely the last*

*night that I will stare out this window at three in the
morning, and see that red Volkswagen parked under
that streetlight. In the new apartment, I shall sleep. The
new king-size bed will know me only as the girl who
is so calm, and sleeps so well.*

She thought doing a crossword might help. She found
her puzzle book and looked around for a pen. The
moving man had said to keep things in drawers whenever possible, so Laura had not emptied the contents of
her desk. She reached inside, searching for her black
marker.

She did not find it. Instead she came upon her parents'
old love-letters again. She pulled them out and, not
really wanting to, she read through them one more time.
Why am I doing this? she kept wondering. Every page
of every letter made her feel more and more depressed.
Each one seemed more remote than the last – further
and further from her own reality. No. She and Jeff would
never be like her parents. Even their getting engaged
hadn't changed that.

And then Laura remembered what Desiree had told
her about her father being unfaithful.

She guessed there was nothing that was safe.

Quickly, Laura pushed the letters back. Something
jammed against them as she shoved the envelope into
the drawer. When Laura saw what it was, she was still
a long moment. Then slowly she pulled out the marbled
notebook and held it in her hands.

It was her journal of the sessions with Christopher
Garland.

She sat with the book in her hands, remembering.
Then she read through it from beginning to end. Her
eyes were wet. Finally she closed the cover and sat back.

She felt she had lived a hundred years since she had
written those entries.

Who was that girl? she wondered. It seemed incredible to think that it had been herself. She guessed they had all been right – that she had been very, very close to the edge.

And yet, grudgingly, Laura found herself smiling.

She thought about those months with Christopher.

A bright green patch in a dying lawn.

She jerked with surprise. What a horrible image. She must be very tired. She had been stupid to read the journal again.

Christopher. Crazy, crazy Christopher.

She found she was near tears again.

I wonder if he ever thinks of me.

He had never even called back to see why she had cancelled the sessions.

I'll send him an invitation to my wedding, Laura decided. *It will be fun seeing him squirming in a church pew.* But even as she laughed at the thought, Laura knew she would never do it. She could not somehow bear the thought of Christopher there.

She snapped the journal shut. It was best thrown out. She laid it on top of the desk. She would destroy it first thing tomorrow morning in the basement compactor. No, wiser to do it tonight. But first she would have one more cup of tea.

She poured the tea and sat by the window.

The moon was very bright tonight – cats-eye secretive, magic. It looked just as it had that long-ago night – the night Laura had turned cold all over and known that she had fallen in love with Christopher Garland.

In spite of the tea, she felt parched. She squeezed her eyes tight. Then she sighed. It was moving day tomorrow. She had better get to sleep.

She put the teacup down and went into the bedroom.

261

She woke up early the next morning, alone in bed.

'Jeff?' she called, but there was no answer. She put on her robe and went into the living room. Jeff was sitting at her desk, staring at her. Her journal was open in his hands.

Chapter Fifteen

Reality slowed. Reality stopped. Laura stared at Jeff.

Then, she stared at the journal, stupidly, despairingly, as if, by the mere intensity of her gaze, she could excite the atoms to frenzy, and pulverize the notebook. *For if there were no journal*, she thought, *there wouldn't have to be this moment.*

But the journal remained.

'Jeff,' she said, going to him.

'Don't touch me,' he hissed.

He backed off and looked at her, loathing her. 'How could you do this to me?' he whispered.

Laura's mouth dropped. Opening lines were suggested and discarded like Kleenex.

Because I needed something so desperately . . . I was so lonely . . . All my life, it seems I've been . . . I was so afraid . . . After Mama died and you never . . .

There was a ring on the coffee table. She transferred her attention to it. She knew that the memory of that ring would be with her as long as she lived.

And Jeff kept staring at her. 'Look at you,' he said incredulously. 'You're not guilty. You're not sorry. Look at your face. You're as hard as a rock.'

'No!' she whispered. 'You don't understand!'

'Don't give me that!' he shouted. 'What's there to understand? I forbade you to see that goddam psychic, and I just find out you've been in love with him for the last eight months. The only doubt there seems to be,' he said with heavy sarcasm, 'is did you actually get around to screwing him or didn't you?'

'Please – ' she whispered.

'It doesn't matter whether you did or not,' he told her narrowly. 'Either way, you've betrayed me.'

'I didn't betray you,' she said desperately. 'It had nothing to do with you. It was a whole different thing. With Christopher, I felt – '

Jeff moved away. 'I don't give a fuck what you felt with Christopher,' he said. 'I thought you loved me. Me. I trusted you. I built my whole life around you. And this is what you've done.'

He began to cry.

'Jeff – ' she whispered.

'Get away. Just get away.'

She looked at him bleakly.

And this is what I've done.

They stared at each other in silence again.

'What's going to happen now, Laura?'

She licked dry lips. 'Why does anything have to happen?' she asked him. 'Couldn't we have a fresh start? Couldn't we just say I had some kind of breakdown – and forget it? Couldn't we?' Her voice was shaking. 'It's over, anyway. It's all over. I haven't seen Christopher for a long, long time.'

Jeff looked up. 'And does that make a difference?' he asked her quietly.

The question ricocheted through her whole body.

Then she covered her ears so she would not have to hear her own answer.

'I don't – know,' she said.

He sprang at her, pulled her hands away. 'Are you still in love with him?' he demanded.

'I don't know,' she whispered again.

'Well, are you in love with me?' He glared at her.

'We're supposed to be getting married in April. Do you at least know if you're in love with me?'

'No,' she screamed. 'I don't know! I don't know!'

Then the pounding in her head went mad. She ran from the apartment and down the stairs.

She hurried along the path. She could not breathe. He had to be in.

He opened the door at the second knock.

'Hello, Laura,' Christopher said.

He didn't seem surprised to see her.

'Come in.'

They went inside. The apartment seemed different to her, unwelcoming.

She could not read anything behind his eyes.

She was terrified to begin. With every polite syllable, the dread grew. With every polite syllable, the wall between them grew. And Laura charged back and forth in front of it, looking desperately, as brick mounted on brick, for her entrance in.

'Christopher,' she said raggedly, 'I have to talk to you.'

'Yes?' he asked her coolly.

She looked away. Her voice was ridiculous – shaky, stupid with fear. 'You turned out to be right about a lot of things,' she jerked out. 'Daddy. Desiree. And I guess you were right about Jeff and me, too.'

He still said nothing. She took a deep breath.

'And I came here to tell you something I guess I should have told you a long time ago. I'm – in love with you.'

There was a pause.

'Would you like some tea?' he asked calmly.

Laura burst into tears. 'Is that all you have to say?' she cried.

Christopher looked at her steadily for a long moment. 'What more do you want me to say, Laura? That I'd known about your feelings all along? That I'd known about them long before you did yourself?'

He forced a laugh. 'Actually, you were very cute about it all. It was fun trying to watch you manoeuvre me, week after week, month after month. All those poses, all those performances. The time you lied about your car being broken down was my favorite. I couldn't wait to see what you'd come up with next. You're really quite an actress,' he smiled. 'But I guess I'm an even better psychic.'

The humiliation was unbearable.

'Why didn't you tell me that you knew?' she whispered.

'I didn't want to embarrass you,' he answered simply. 'And I kept hoping that you'd understand. Understand it was impossible. Without having to be told.'

His calmness filled Laura with rage.

'Why is it impossible?' she demanded. 'Why is it so damned impossible? And don't you dare tell me it's because you're above these things. You're a man like any other. Don't deny it. I saw the way you looked at Mimi Craddock.' Her voice rose and rose. 'Why can't you look that way at me?' she cried. 'Am I so ugly? Am I so repulsive?'

'No,' he said flatly. 'As a matter of fact, I find you ten times more attractive than Mimi Craddock. And yes, I am a man like any other. But that's simply not what our relationship is meant to be. It never was and never will be.' He made a wry face. 'Someone like Mimi, sure. But if I were to get involved with you that way, it would destroy everything. I would be useless to you in the way that counts. My effectiveness as a counsellor would be ruined.'

Laura leapt on it eagerly. 'Who cares about your effectiveness as a counsellor? Couldn't we forget all that?'

266

she pleaded. 'Couldn't we have a fresh start – pretend we're just two people meeting for the first time – and see what happens naturally between us?'

Smiling, he shook his head.

Laura hid her face in her hands. 'I love you,' she wailed. 'Don't you understand? I'm in love with you.'

'Come here,' Christopher said.

She went to him. He held her. His body felt angular and cool not human.

'Laura,' he said. 'I'm so glad you came by today. Because it is so important that you understand what's going on here.'

He looked into her face.

'Listen,' he said. 'You're not in love with me. And you never really have been.'

She started to speak, but he stopped her.

'No,' he said. 'Be honest. How can you be in love with me? You hardly even know me.'

'I know enough,' she said stubbornly.

He laughed. 'You think you do. Just like you thought you knew enough to set up your father and Desiree as the romance of the century.'

She was silent.

'Oh, Laura, Laura,' he said. 'When will you let the universe alone? You get this idea in your head of what you want, and you're damned and determined to bring it about, in spite of the fact that it has nothing to do with reality.'

'But this *is* real,' she whispered. 'What I feel for you is real.'

'Yes,' he said. 'More real than you even know. But you don't understand what it is you're feeling.'

He took her hands. His own were icy.

'Remember what I told you happened to me, the first time I ever met my teacher Carmen? That my whole world turned upside down, and that from then on, nothing was the same? Well, it's the same with you and me. I was brought into your life to be a catalyst. I was brought into your life to set you on the right path.' He kept squeezing her hands in a strange rhythm that had nothing to do with the cadence of his words. 'The girl who first came to me last winter was suffocating. Losing herself more day by day. Dying. And something in you knew that,' he went on. 'Or you never would have kept on with the sessions. You thought it was Christopher you were coming for, but it was something else. Don't you see?' he asked her gently. 'It's not the teacher you're in love with, Laura. It's the teachings. What you love about me is the Light. I am in the Light. And it's the Light you are in love with.'

Only you, Laura thought, wanting to laugh, wanting to weep. *Only you, Christopher Garland, could say something like that and get away with it.*

'And if it's any comfort,' Christopher went on earnestly, 'I can't tell you how often this kind of thing happens. People thinking they've fallen in love with me. In my line of work, that's pretty much par for the course.'

Bitterly, she smiled. 'That's me,' she told him. 'Just another dime-a-dozen student who's fallen for your Light.'

Christopher laughed. 'Not quite. I told you once before, Laura. You are the one I've been waiting for. You are to me what I was to Carmen. As I was her Little Prince, so you are my Little Princess.'

She shook her head.

'I'm sorry, Christopher,' she said. 'I'm really sorry. But that just isn't what I want from you.'

He looked at her for a moment.

'No,' he said quietly. 'Of course it isn't. I'd forgotten for the moment who I was dealing with.' He turned from her and walked around the room. 'That kind of love would be a total waste for you, wouldn't it? You want things exactly the way you want them, or not at all – and if a man doesn't come with a wedding ring, then the love just doesn't count.'

He glared at her. His eyes were like dry ice.

'Forget growth. Forget destiny. What do they matter? All that counts with you is being secure. Having someone to hide behind. God forbid you ever have to be alone. Or have to evolve. Or have to face yourself. If Jeff doesn't work out, go on to Christopher. No mess, no fuss.' He hit the table with his fist. 'When will you learn?' he demanded. 'It's not Jeff you need to be in love with, Laura. And Lord knows it isn't me. Goddammit! It's yourself.'

She turned away. Then suddenly there was no more anger.

He looked at her and shrugged, gave a little smile. 'That's it, Laura,' he told her casually. 'That's the whole secret right there. Take it or leave it. Incidentally, it's what I've been trying to tell you from the first day you walked through my door.'

She was filled with such exhaustion and such unhappiness that she could barely keep on her feet.

'But it wasn't what you wanted to hear, was it?' he asked her. 'You were always so sure that the magic was inside Jeff. Or your mother. Or Desiree. Or me. And it's so much easier that way, isn't it? Flirting and falling in love and manipulating and being a doormat. Anything to fill the void. Anything to keep the delusion going. Anything to keep from facing yourself.'

He looked at her for a long moment.

'You know what's going to happen to you?' he asked her. 'You're just going to get lonelier and lonelier, more and more pathetic. And it doesn't really matter if you stay with Jeff or not. Either way, you'll end up miserable.'

He shook his head and his eyes filled with tears.

Laura tried to laugh. 'What are you crying about?' she asked him. 'I'm the one who should be crying. In the eight months that I've known you, you've taken everything away and you've left me with nothing.'

'Except yourself.'

She paused for a long time. 'You know that's never been good enough.'

He moved to the door and opened it for her.

'Then I guess we have nothing more to say to each other.'

'Goodbye, Christopher,' she told him. 'I'm going back to Jeff now, and we're going to be very happy.'

Laura did not remember getting into the car. She did not remember the drive. She did not remember stopping. But when she came to, she was sitting on a worn green bench in Brentwood Park. Beside her was a young black-haired woman, telling her little son he could not have another cookie. The child ran off at last to play, and the woman turned to Laura.

'You want to kill them sometimes,' she said with a smile.

'Yes,' Laura answered.

The woman nodded at a small blond girl running towards the nearby swings. 'Is that one yours?'

Laura looked dazedly at the lovely little thing. 'Why, yes,' she said.

'What's her name?'

Laura considered carefully. 'Laura,' she answered slowly.

'Do you live around here?' the woman asked.

'We live up Coldwater Canyon,' Laura told her. 'In a

Tudor house right off Cherokee. The one with the large garden and the jacaranda trees.'

'I drive by there on my way to work,' the woman said. 'Do you come to this park often? I don't remember seeing you here before.'

'We usually go to the park on Beverly Glen,' Laura told her. 'It's nearer my husband's studio.'

'What does your husband do?' the woman asked.

'He's a movie producer – his name's Blake Alden.'

'That name's very familiar. Hasn't he won a lot of awards?'

'Yes,' Laura told her.

'You must be very proud of him.'

'Oh, I am.'

'Are you in the entertainment industry, too?'

'Yes,' Laura said. 'I'm an actress. My stage name is Julia Foster.'

'What a fascinating life you must have,' the woman said enviously.

Laura smiled. 'It *is* pretty wonderful.'

Then suddenly the woman cried out and pointed. A tall lady was lifting the little blond girl off the swing, and carrying her rapidly away. The woman half-rose to rescue the child, but Laura stopped her.

'It's all right,' Laura said. 'It's probably her mother.'

'Her mother!' the woman gasped. 'But you told me that *you* were her mother.'

And she backed off from Laura, fear in her eyes.

An hour passed. The park was getting cold. But Laura still sat on the bench. It was time to go home now. But she did not move. The little blond girl she had named Laura was sitting beside her. She was coloring rainbows. Laura asked if she could borrow a piece of paper.

271

'My dear Jeff,' she wrote.

I am sitting in the park with all the children. I can't stop crying. I also can't believe I'm doing this. I think you know what I'm going to say. That I can't marry you.

I've tried and I've tried, but I keep coming back to the same thing. It wouldn't work out between us. I've just changed too much. Not into someone new, but into someone I guess I should have been all along.

It seems to me, from the day I met you, I've been pretending. Not about my feelings for you, but about myself. Pretending to be everything you wanted me to be; turning myself inside out, day by day, into something I wasn't. To please you. To keep you from leaving me. To make you love me. Not fair to you. And certainly not fair to me.

And I pretended a lot of other things, too. That your dreams were my dreams. That the life you wanted was the life I wanted. That I was happy, when I really wasn't.

I'm sorry I fooled us both for so long. And I'm even sorrier that I can't seem to do it anymore. But I'm just too tired. It's as simple as that.

I know you must think I've suddenly gone crazy. But I haven't. This craziness, if craziness it is, has been going on a long time. Don't blame Christopher. He was the catalyst but I somehow think it would have happened just the same without him. Maybe it really began when Mama died. Or the day you got the series. Or maybe it was just me needing to grow up.

I am thinking about our five years together, Jeff. And smiling. And crying. Thinking about how wonderful and safe you are. Thinking how I never had to struggle, with you there, how I never had to be alone. But I am also thinking about a young woman Christopher described to me this afternoon – one who has always tried so hard and so desperately to get love from everyone else, that she has never learned how to get it from herself.

Well, maybe it's high time I did learn.

A few practical matters. Go on and move into the new apartment. I'll stay in the old one. I'll shock you with my gaucheness, but I like it better anyway. And if Lou Hinkle and the rest ask what happened to me, tell them the truth. Tell them I'm under the influence.

I love you, Jeff, and I know you'll be happy. Tragedies don't happen to boys with golden hair.

There's a little girl by this bench, and she's reading *Stuart Little*. I always loved the last line of that book. Stuart doesn't quite know where he's going when he drives off in his car, but "the sun is warm, and he has the feeling he's headed in the right direction."

Let's hope that's also me.

Love,
Laura

She left the letter for him under the door.

He was gone by early afternoon.

Late that night, Laura came back to the apartment. It was in darkness, filled with piles of furniture waiting to be moved. She could not find the lamps, and the bed had been dismantled. She got down on the floor. She made herself a little Wendy-house of suitcases and packing boxes and she pulled it close around her. And she sat there through the night, looking out into the darkness.

Finally the sun rose, and she got up.

She was very cold and stiff.

The beginning of a poem, loved since childhood, came to her. 'Where am I going?' was the question. And the answer was 'I don't quite know.'

Laura looked around her. She got up and walked over to the sink. The glasses had been packed, so she filled her palms full of water.

She looked at the framed photograph of her mother that was on top of the packing pile. 'To new beginnings, Mama,' she whispered, and raised her hands and drank.

Then she lay down again, among the boxes.

The phone rang six times before she picked it up.

'Hello?'

'Hello,' a voice said. 'Is this my Little Princess?'

Laura smiled. She looked down at the receiver for a long moment. 'Yes,' she said slowly. 'I believe it is.'

Epilogue

The sun rose over Tenth Street, and came into the windows of the south-west facing sixth floor apartment.

The light first settled soothingly on the book-crammed, project-strewn floor, then it crept up the sides of the funky, antique furniture, investigated the art posters on the wall, illuminated the framed photographs, the hamster's cage, the potted plants. It gently faded the fine old Turkey carpet, awoke the old black cat, and moved onto the next apartment.

Laura dreamed on.

'Mama! Wake up!' came the sudden call. 'It's ten to eight!'

Ten to eight! Oh, God. Laura jerked out of bed. Get Jason dressed. Make his lunch. Write the note for the teacher. It couldn't possibly be done. The schoolbus was coming in five minutes. Oh, why, why, she moaned, had she stayed up so late watching *The Red Shoes*?

She threw on her robe, backwards and inside out, and lurched out of the bedroom. Six year old Jason was standing by the door, grinning at her. He had dressed himself, and made his own lunch. Laura knelt, and hugged him in a spasm of gratitude for being so grown-up and confident and capable.

The schoolbus pulled up outside the apartment building, and honked.

'Do you want me to come down with you?' she asked him.

'No, Mama, that's all right,' he said, looking at her tormented robe.

She laughed, kissed him, let him go.

She watched from the apartment window, saw him board the bus, heard the greetings of his friends. It was one of her favorite sights in life – Jason off to school, so complete, so successful.

Mark came up behind her. Another *Red Shoes* addict, he looked even more tired than she. They glanced at each other's bleary faces and laughed.

'I hope you have an easy day,' Laura said.

'Pretty easy – just some inventory coming in.' He looked at her hopefully. 'Want to meet me for lunch? I could sneak off.' Laura shook her head, loving, after seven years of marriage, the fact that he wanted to sneak off to her.

'Sorry, but I've got Amy Birch coming at eleven. She needs a reading – she's finally decided to move away from home.'

Mark nodded, surprised. 'Good for her.'

As a rule, Laura didn't talk about her clients – a metaphysical counsellor should be as discreet as a psychiatrist – but Amy, over the two years she had been counselling her, had become her favorite, her pet, a part. And she knew Amy wouldn't mind Mark knowing.

'Maybe you can get off early tonight instead,' she said hopefully.

He grinned at her. 'Maybe I can.'

She watched Mark as he dressed. It was another favorite sight – the big black-haired man with the beard, sitting on the antique brass bed and pulling on his turtleneck and jeans. Laura looked contentedly around at the messy, cozy room. She loved its craziness, its uniqueness, its Laura and Markness.

276

Mark hugged her goodbye, and he left for the bookstore.

After he was gone, Laura went back into the living room. It lay in bright primary pieces about her, like unjelled jello. The first step this morning would obviously be to tidy up. But somehow she just didn't feel like it. She sat on an easy chair, after having removed half a dozen books from the seat. *First the dining room gets made over into a library*, she thought bemusedly. *Now that's Jason's reading as well, we'll have to start suspending bookshelves from the ceiling.*

Next to the chair was a pile of newspapers, unread. *Genius!* Laura thought. *That's what I'll do with the morning. I'll sit quietly and read the papers till Amy comes.* She knew she had to be rested for that session. It would be an important one for the girl.

Laura picked up the top paper, and flipped to the Book Section. She found herself looking down at a half-page ad. 'Christopher Garland, author of *Real Magic* will be signing copies of his book at B. Dalton's on 5th Ave. and 52nd Street today from 11–12.'

She could not breathe for the cache of tears that were suddenly in her throat. She cried onto the ad for several minutes, cried onto the laughing picture of Christopher Garland.

Dimly, smiling, shaking, at last she pushed the ad away. Well, Amy would just have to understand. She could re-schedule her session for tomorrow, for any other day she pleased, but today Laura was going to be seeing Christopher. For the first time in nine years.

She leaned back, exhausted. The images from that year began to come, hot and thick. That year of Christopher; the year of Jeff and Desiree and Julia. Flowing back to her – the tide returning. She could barely contain those memories in her mind – they burned too brightly, too harshly, too beautifully. Christopher. She couldn't believe it. She almost couldn't bear it. She jumped from the chair. Tidy the apartment. Bathe. Dress. Get down to Dalton's.

As she straightened pillows and removed Jason's science experiment from the floor, she imagined excitedly how it would be.

She would get to the bookstore just at eleven. Christopher would be at the wooden desk, a line of people waiting to meet him. She would not make herself known to him right away. At first, she would just stand at the side, busying herself with other books, and watching him.

And then, at half-past eleven, she would buy a book to be signed, and join the line. When she reached him, he would be looking down.

'Would you please autograph this to "The Little Princess?"' she would say.

And he would look up.

Laura flushed madly, exultantly at the thought of how it would be.

After the book signing, she would take him to lunch. Then she would bring him home, introduce him to Mark and Jason. She would tell them, 'This is the man who made everything possible. This is the man who made me possible. This is the man who made you possible.'

And what would she say to Christopher? What would she say to him when they sat down to lunch and looked at each other for the first time in all these years?

It all came true, Christopher. Just as you said it would. The husband, the child, the counselling. I'm carrying on with what you taught me. With what Carmen taught you.

She would tell him about those first days in New York. Six months after Jeff had gone, four months after

278

her father and Mimi had married, she had moved. Everyone had told her not to – that New York was too tough,
that she would disintegrate anywhere but in Los
Angeles. Except for Christopher. It's time to leave, he
had said. You've learned all you can learn from me. It's
time for the next step.

It had been a horrible year. She had thought she would
try a job in children's publishing, but it hadn't worked
out. The winter had been very cold, and she had been
very much alone. She stayed by herself – meditating,
reading, doing the exercises Christopher had taught her.
A few times, late at night, she had tried to call him,
but the operator told her that the number had been
disconnected.

One Sunday, she had gone into Samuel Weizer's Metaphysical bookstore. She was ordering a book and the
manager came up to her – a tall man with a dark beard.

'Please, no nosebleeds today,' he said, smiling.

She stared at him, remembering the long-ago day in
the Bodhi Tree bookstore.

'You've changed coasts,' she said.

'So have you.'

They started talking, and she told him about all the
confusion in her life. He said it was simple – that she
should do what she really wanted to.

Laura figured it out that night – what it was that she
really wanted to do. And it was as Christopher had
always predicted.

Her first ad in the paper, announcing herself as a
psychic/metaphysical teacher, had not brought too
many students, but by the following spring, word of
mouth had established her in her career.

One Saturday, she went back to Samuel Weizer's. She
told the manager what wonderful fruit his suggestion to

her had borne. He asked her to dinner that night. A year later, they were married.

She had sent Christopher an invitation to the wedding, but it came back to her, marked 'Addressee Unknown.' Yet she saved an empty place for him in the church, and she imagined him there.

It was stunning to realize, as she often did, how different this new life was from her old one. Once, soon after they were engaged, she had taken Mark to Los Angeles to meet her father. It had been a funny trip, really — each had been so totally awed by the other. Mark unjudgingly, unenviously fascinated by Blake's preoccupations with worldly things, and Blake's fascination with Mark's total lack of preoccupation. One night, they had gone to a big Hollywood premiere. Mark enjoyed the evening, even though Blake made him get his hair cut and wouldn't let him wear thongs. And the following day, tit for tat, Mark took Blake to visit the Hindu Temple in Malibu, and made Blake do a punjab with the white-robed priests.

When Blake took them to the airport at the end of the visit, he had hugged Laura very hard.

'Stick with this guy,' he told her. 'He's crazy as all get out, but your mother would have loved him.'

When Jason was born, Laura took him out to California every year to visit his grandfather. They were magical visits. Jason was not very impressed with Mimi, but he adored Blake — the big, wonderful man with the big, wonderful house, who could serve raspberries anytime he wanted to. And Blake took Jason with him everywhere — to the studio, to a golf course, to a power lunch at the Beverly Hills Hotel.

It gave Laura a keen, sweet pleasure, seeing her father

280

through her son's eyes. It was like being allowed to grow up again herself. All the best things she remembered about Blake re-sprang to life. Only this time around, he was not too busy.

Blake died one Saturday afternoon in June. He died on the tennis court, instantly, after having just aced his opponent.

Laura flew out alone to the funeral. It seemed pointless for Mark and Jason to be there. After all, it was her father, her California, her past that must be said goodbye to. Going through her father's things, she came upon a little clay heart she had made for him in kindergarten. She asked that it be buried with him.

The funeral was monumental, extravagant, and everyone from Hollywood was there. From the young crowd of Hollywood, anyway – Blake had really been the last of the old regime.

Mimi, the disconsolate widow, wearing dark glasses and crying in hysterical gusts, had offered Laura the place next to her at the service, but Laura had not taken it. She noted, with bitter amusement, that the seat was soon filled by a young blond man – Mimi's golf pro.

After the service, a voice called her name. It was Desiree Kaufman.

It felt awkward, to see her.

'How are you, Desiree?' Laura asked her quietly.

'I'm moving to London,' Desiree said. 'My new play is being produced there.'

Laura took her hands. 'I'm so glad for you.'

Desiree looked at her searchingly. 'And you're happy?'

Laura thought with a sweet pang of Mark, Jason, her crazy, bohemian life, and she smiled at how horrible it would all seem to Desiree.

'Yes, very happy,' she said gently.

281

Then Desiree looked away. 'Laura,' she said. 'What I once told you about your father being unfaithful to your mother – it wasn't true, you know.'

'I know,' Laura said.

And then Desiree leaned over and gave Laura a hug.

Laura experienced the old warm shock. 'You still feel like my Mama,' she whispered in Desiree's ear.

'And you still feel like my daughter,' she was told.

Jeff was not at the funeral. But then Laura had not really expected him to be. Shooting had begun on his new television series, and rumors were that it was not going smoothly. Over the years, Laura had kept up regularly with Jeff through the *Inquirer*. She had felt a little pang, five years ago, when she saw the pictures of his wedding to the starlet. And a year later, she felt another pang when Jeff, Jr. was born. She had thought about sending the baby a set of her children's books, but decided not to. It was all just too long ago. Jeff was on his third marriage now – this one to an airline stewardess. And of course he still looked beautiful.

Laura looked at the clock. Nine-thirty. Time to call Amy and cancel the session. She tried the number, but it was busy. So she went ahead and took her bath, washed her hair, and started to get dressed. She tried on and rejected four different outfits. She didn't want to look Greenwich Village Bohemian today – she wanted to look legitimate, conservative, appropriate to B. Dalton's. Finally dressed in a suit and silk blouse, she was ready.

She went over to the large Victorian mirror that she and Mark had spent a summer refinishing, and looked searchingly into it. Her face looked a little tired, her hair was wild as ever. Long ago, Laura had given up trying to look beautiful. But now, she thought, she looked happy.

Unexpectedly, the phone rang. She picked it up.

'Hello?'

Amy was crying so hard that Laura could barely understand her.

'I feel so awful,' she wailed. 'I've got to see you. Please – please – can I come early today? Can I come right now?'

Laura swallowed, paused for a moment. 'Sure,' she said. 'Come on over.'

She hung up the phone, foolishly, terribly disappointed. So there would be no seeing Christopher, after all. No surprise in B. Dalton's. There was no way she could make it there in time.

She thought briefly of other routes – calling his publisher, finding out what hotel Christopher was staying in, leaving a message, making a formal date – but an odd lethargy came over her at the thought, and she gave up the idea.

And who knows? she wondered suddenly. Maybe it was better this way. Maybe it would be a mistake seeing Christopher again after all these years. He had fused, in her memory, into a pure white diamond. Maybe it was better to leave it like that.

But all the things she had wanted to tell him . . . For a moment, the disappointment was sharp again. And then Laura found herself smiling. For goodness sake, she thought, Christopher didn't have to be told anything. Anything at all. Christopher already knew. Christopher had always known.

So be it, she thought.

And, really, when you stopped to think about it, there was a certain sense of rightness about all this. For, in a way, her choosing to help Amy today instead of seeing

Christopher was the single greatest tribute she could give him.

She took her coat off, hung it slowly up. Then she made herself a cup of tea and sat down to wait for Amy.

The following day, Laura went down to B. Dalton's, and bought a copy of Christopher's book.

'You just missed seeing him,' the boy at the cash register told her pleasantly. 'He did a book-signing yesterday.'

'I know,' Laura said.

She opened Christopher's book and found that it was dedicated to her.

Daughters
Consuelo Saah Baehr

Daughters is an unforgettable story of courage, love and hope; of two worlds – one ancient, one modern – and of the extraordinary women who bridge them.

Miriam Mishwe is born into a Palestinian Christian family in the last years of the nineteenth century. She marries a man chosen by her family, but centuries-old traditions are on the verge of upheaval.

Nadia is Miriam's daughter. Sent to a local British school, she adopts many modern ideas but is not yet ready to renounce her heritage.

Nijmeh, Nadia's daughter, is the one who will call herself by her English name, Star, and go to live in America. There she will face problems of a new and unknown kind . . .

'A long, richly textured novel filled with wonderful characters and an extraordinary sense of historical detail. Consuelo Saah Baehr has written a blockbuster with a heart.'
Susan Isaacs, author of *Almost Paradise* and *Shining Through*

FONTANA PAPERBACKS

Hot Type
Kristy Daniels

When Tory Satterly starts at the second-rate afternoon paper, *The Sun*, she's just a lowly, overweight reporter, relegated to the women's pages and hopelessly in love with Russ Churchill, golden boy of the prestigious rival morning paper, *The Post*. But Tory is tenacious and she soon enters the hard news world of smouldering sex scandals and drug deals. As her career soars, Tory becomes a svelte and sexy woman equally at home at exclusive spas, Swiss resorts, and in the arms of multimillionaire Max Highsmith.

And when *The Post* and *The Sun* are merged, there's room for only one at the top. Russ Churchill becomes Tory's rival . . . as well as her lover. Which of them will get the plum job – the one they have both wanted all their lives?

FONTANA PAPERBACKS

Fontana Paperbacks: Fiction

Fontana is a leading paperback publisher of fiction.
Below are some recent titles.

- ☐ THE CONSUL GENERAL'S DAUGHTER Erin Pizzey £3.95
- ☐ THE HAWTHORNE HERITAGE Teresa Crane £3.99
- ☐ UNDER GEMINI Rosamunde Pilcher £2.99
- ☐ GLAMOROUS POWERS Susan Howatch £3.95
- ☐ BEST FRIENDS Imogen Winn £3.50
- ☐ NO HARP LIKE MY OWN Marjorie Quarton £2.99
- ☐ TEA AT GUNTER'S Pamela Haines £2.95

You can buy Fontana paperbacks at your local bookshop or
newsagent. Or you can order them from Fontana Paperbacks,
Cash Sales Department, Box 29, Douglas, Isle of Man. Please
send a cheque, postal or money order (not currency) worth the
purchase price plus 22p per book for postage (maximum postage
required is £3.00 for orders within the UK).

NAME (Block letters)_____

ADDRESS_____

_____